Her biggest fear had become human...

Then the lightning hit. It felt like ; into Samantha Ryan's head, driving her breath, her strength. Everything ...... white. It was as if she'd stepped beyond this world into a place of fierce brightness in which nothing else existed but that light, and the power within it—and within her. And it felt *good*. So very good.

She flung her arms wide, accepting the power burning around her, drawing it in even more. Flesh and bone seemed to burn away, until she was nothing more than a creature of energy, a being at one with the storm and the night and the intense heat of the lightning. And it called to her, that energy, wanted her. She raised her face to the skies she couldn't see, torn by the need to answer that call, and the growing knowledge that something was wrong, that this wasn't good, no matter how good it actually felt.

"Samantha!" The call ran around her—through her mind. But it wasn't one voice, but two.

Samantha! You must resist. You are not grounded and will be lost. You cannot do this yet.

The internal voice was one she recognized. *Joe.* Always there when she needed help the most.

But the storm called her name, and the thought fled. She closed her eyes, and enjoyed the caress of the power as she raised her arms a little more.

No! You cannot lose yourself to the storm. It would kill us both.

This book is dedicated to Debra, because a promise is a promise even if long overdue, and Diane, who has always wanted me to say "I owe it all to her."

Penumbra

***

Keri Arthur

Penumbra
Published by ImaJinn Books

ISBN: 1-933417-78-1

10 9 8 7 6 5 4 3 2 1

PUBLISHER'S NOTE:
This book is a work of fiction. Names, characters, places and incidents are products of the author's imagination or are used fictitiously. Any resemblance to actual events or locales or persons, living or dead, is entirely coincidental.

Books are available at quantity discounts when used to promote products or services. For information please write to: Marketing Division, ImaJinn Books, P.O. Box 545, Canon City, CO 81212, or call toll free 1-877-625-3592.

Cover design by Patricia Lazarus

ImaJinn Books
P.O. Box 545, Canon City, CO 81212
Toll Free: 1-877-625-3592
http://www.imajinnbooks.com

One

Samantha Ryan placed her hands on the front of her boss's desk and said, "I want a transfer, not more of your damn excuses."

She knew that speaking to your boss in such a manner generally wasn't a good idea, especially when he was the man in charge of both the Special Investigations Unit and the more secretive Federation. A man more inclined to kill first, and ask questions later.

Not that she thought he'd kill her. He had as much interest in finding out who and what she was as she did. But he certainly *could* make her life hell, which was precisely her current situation.

She leaned across and added, "*Sir,*" a touch sarcastically.

Stephan Stern, the boss in question, raised one blond eyebrow, as if mildly surprised by her outburst. An outburst he'd *known* was coming for months. "You know I don't want to do that."

"I don't honestly care what you want anymore. This is about what *I* want." She pushed away from the desk, unable to stand still any longer. Damn it, she'd spent more than half her life with her head basically in the sand, cruising through life rather than participating, and she'd had more than enough. The time had come to get greedy, to think about *her* wants, *her* desires, for a change. And what she wanted right now was not only a more active personal life, but a working life that involved more than a broom closet. "Transfer me back to State, let me resign, or find me another partner. As I said, I don't care. Just get me out of the current situation."

Her angry strides took in the length of the beige-colored office in no time. She turned to face Stephan. His expression was as remote as ever. But she'd learned very early on that Stephan was a master at hiding his emotions—and that *that* dead face was just as likely to mean fury as calm.

"I prefer to leave you with Gabriel. I still believe you two will make a formidable team."

She snorted softly. "That has never been an option, and I think you and I realize that now."

It wasn't as if she hadn't tried, for God's sake. But her damn partner was still going out of his way to exclude her from everything ranging from investigations to chit chat. Access to the SIU's vast computer system just wasn't worth all the frustration and unhappiness.

Especially since she was getting jack shit in the way of information about the past she couldn't remember. Hell, her dreams were providing more information than the SIU's system. Only trouble was, how much could she actually trust the dreams?

How much could she trust the man who constantly walked through them?

She didn't know. Nor did she have anyone she could talk to about it—and that was perhaps the most frustrating thing about this entire situation. She *needed* to get a life. Friends. People she could trust and talk to. Hell, even a pet would be better than going home alone to a soulless hotel room every night.

"I prefer to give the situation more time." He crossed his arms and leaned forward against the desk. "However, I do have another option that might suit us both."

She met his gaze. His blue eyes were sharp, full of cunning and intelligence. A shark by nature, and the reason he ruled the SIU and the Federation, rather than his twin, Gabriel.

Of course, that also meant she was beating her head against a brick wall where Gabriel was concerned, because Stephan was always going to look after his twin's interests first. Even if said twin didn't appreciate his efforts anymore than she did.

She came to a stop in front of his desk, and couldn't help feeling like a fish about to be hooked. "What might that be?"

"You remember Dan Wetherton?"

She nodded. Gabriel had found a clone of Wetherton in the trunk of a car after some goons had Gabriel beaten up and then kidnapped him. To what aim, no one knew. Nor did anyone know why the clone had been killed. The real Dan Wetherton— who was a minister with the current government—was still very much alive and well.

"Well, as it happens, it wasn't a clone Gabriel found that day. It *was* the original."

She snagged the nearest chair and sat down, interested despite her wariness. "I was under the impression no one could create a clone that exactly duplicates the mannerisms and thoughts of the original person. That they may be genetically identical, but are nevertheless different." She hesitated, frowning. "Besides, the newspapers reported the find *and* the subsequent tests. He was declared human in all scientific results."

"And a clone isn't?"

She grimaced. Clones were human, no doubt about that. But whether that fact actually gave them *humanity* was a point of contention between the scientists and the theologists. "Having only met one clone, who at the time was trying to kill me, I don't feel qualified to answer that particular question."

Amusement touched the corners of his thin lips. "The test results were altered by a party or parties unknown long before we got them. We just released them." He picked up a folder from his desk and offered it to her. "These are the originals. Have a look."

From past experience she knew it was pointless to ask how he'd gotten hold of the original papers. Stephan worked on a need to know basis—and generally, that meant the less every one knew, the better. She doubted even Gabriel was privy to all his secrets.

Not that Gabriel himself worked on a caring, sharing basis. Not with *her*, anyway.

She leafed through the information inside the folder. They included the genetic tests on both Wetherton and the clone, the coroner's report, and Wetherton's medical history.

"Wetherton had cancer," she said, looking up. "Incurable."

"Which the current version no longer has."

She threw the folder back on the desk. "If you know he's not the original, why release the press report saying he was? And why not simply kill him?" Which is what they'd planned to do originally, before he'd been declared human.

"Because we wanted to know why he was cloned. And where he was cloned."

"But not who had cloned him?" Did that mean they suspected that the ever-present, but never found, evil they called Sethanon was behind Wetherton?

"We find the where and we'll find the why. But there is only one suspect as to the whom."

"The military is experimenting with genetics. They might very well be playing in the cloning minefield, you know. There's no reason why Wetherton can't be their boy."

"No, there's not."

His voice made it sound doubtful, and yet she had a vague

notion she'd hit the nail on the head. That for some weird reason, he just didn't want to acknowledge it. "And what about the replacement parts industry? Have you checked to see if they have started developing fully-formed beings, or is that just too obvious?"

His expression became briefly annoyed. "We never overlook the obvious."

Of course not. She smiled slightly. Irritating Stephan might be akin to prodding a lion with a very short stick, but when she got even the slightest reaction, it was oddly satisfying.

"The black market trade in clones is booming," she said. Of course, it was fueled mainly by humanity's desperation to cheat death. An incredible number of people seemed willing to pay the exorbitant prices the marketers charged and take the risk of attempting a cloning miracle—a new body in which to live when their own was no longer of use.

But humanity was more than just a brain; it was also heart and soul. Medical science might be able to transfer flesh and brain matter, but how could anyone transfer a soul? Even if they could pin down what a soul actually was?

Not that rules ever stopped anyone, especially when there was huge money to be made.

And somewhere along the line, someone had succeeded in at least achieving part of the impossible—fully fleshed, viable clones who looked and acted like the original. Wetherton, and her ex-partner, Jack Kazdan, were proof of that.

"His source is not black market. We're sure of that."

She studied him for a moment, then changed tactics. "Wetherton's just been made minister for Science and Technology, hasn't he?"

He nodded. "Two years ago he was trying to shut down many of the science programs, stating the money could be better spent on the health care system. Now he's in charge of the whole lot."

"Why hasn't anyone questioned this sudden change of heart? Surely the press has noted it."

"Noted a political back flip?" Amusement touched his lips again. "You're kidding, right?"

Point made. Back flips by politicians were such an everyday fact of life that even the press had got tired of them. And the public at large simply ignored them, except when the flips directly affected their pockets.

"What advantage would having a clone in such a position be to someone like Sethanon? I would have thought it would be more advantageous for him to have the Science and Technology division's development hindered rather than increased."

"That question is not one we can answer."

Not until they caught Sethanon, anyway. And *he* had proven as elusive as a ghost.

"So, you've had Wetherton watched?"

"Had an agent in his office for the last two months. She can't get close enough. Wetherton plays his cards very close to his chest."

If the man was a clone, he'd have to. One mistake and the truth was out.

"What does all this have to do with my wanting a transfer?"

He smiled—all teeth, no sincerity. "The minister has recently received several death threats. He was given police protection, but the would-be killer has slipped past them on a number of occasions and left his notes. The minister now requests SIU's help."

She regarded him steadily. "So who did you use to drop the notes? A vampire? Or a shapeshifter?"

Amusement flickered briefly through his bright eyes. "The original threats were real enough."

Yeah, right. There was just a little too much sincerity in his voice to start believing that statement. "Am I the only agent being sent in?"

"No. You'll handle the night shift—it better suits your growing abilities. Jenna Morwood will do days."

Morwood wasn't someone she'd met. "What's her specialty?"

"Morwood's an empath and telekinetic."

So she'd be able to see an attack coming by simply reading the emotions swirling around her. A good choice for this sort of work. "We the only two going in?"

"Yes." He hesitated. "Wetherton has requested that the night watch stay at his apartment when he's there at night. Since the first two threats were hand delivered, I've agreed to his request. I want you to observe everyone he meets. Become his shadow and learn his secretes."

A big task. "I doubt whether I'll learn much. Surely most of his business will be conducted during the day?"

Stephan smiled grimly. "Wetherton has a surprising number of business meetings at night—and usually at nightclubs, where it's harder to get a bug in."

"He'll be suspicious of me. He's not likely to trust me with anything vital."

"Not for a while. It may take months."

Months out her life and her need to find her past. But also months away from the stone wall that was Gabriel. Would absence make his heart grow fonder? A smile touched her lips. Unlikely. "What about time off? You can't expect either of us to work seven days a week."

He nodded. "You get two days. Which two will depend on his schedule. Generally, it will be the days he spends home with his family. We have other arrangements in place there."

The man spends two days a week with his family? That didn't quite jell with the caring father image he'd painted of himself over recent years. "A real family man, isn't he?"

"Only since the original's death. Bought a nice apartment on Collins Street and now spends most of his nights there."

She frowned. "Will I be alone with the man? At night, I mean."

"Generally, yes."

Oh Joy. "I hope you're not expecting me to share the man's bed." *That* went way beyond the call of duty. Though maybe Stephan figured she'd be a shoe-in for under-the-cover work given her current lack of a sex life.

"No." He hesitated. "Though I should perhaps warn you that Wetherton has had an endless stream of beauties on his arm lately."

Great. She was protecting a lecher. Then she frowned. Wetherton was somewhat ordinary in the looks department, though that in itself didn't mean anything. Some of the ugliest spuds in the world had beauties far and wide eating out of their palms, simply because of the wealth these men had, or because of their sheer, magnetic power. But from what she remembered of Wetherton, the man possessed neither of those qualities.

So why the bevy of beauties? And how come it wasn't reported in the papers? Hell, any politician cheating on his wife was big news, let alone one doing the horizontal tango with a bevy of them.

"Will the press buy our sudden appearance in his life? This sort of protection is usually handled by the Federal Police, not the SIU."

"They won't question our appearance after tonight, believe me."

The dry coldness in his voice sent chills down her spine. "What have you planned for tonight?"

"A spectacular but ineffectual murder attempt. Wetherton may be injured, and will, of course, demand our help."

"Who's the patsy?"

Stephan shrugged. "A young vampire we captured several weeks ago. He'd been something of a political dissident in life, and afterlife has only sharpened his beliefs."

And Stephan had been feeding his madness, aiming it toward Wetherton. Meaning this plan had been burning in his mind for some time. And that the picture was bigger than what he was currently admitting.

Goose bumps ran up her arms, and she rubbed them lightly. Perhaps the vampire wasn't the only patsy in this situation.

"I gather the vamp will die?"

"He murdered seven people before we captured him. This death is merely a delayed sentence."

"What if he escapes?"

"He won't."

She shifted in her chair. "If Wetherton is up to anything nefarious, it's doubtful I'll be privy to it."

"No. There will be certain times you'll be sent from the room. This is unavoidable. To counter it, you'll bug the room."

"Most federal buildings have monitors. The minute a bug is activated an alarm will sound."

"They won't detect the ones we'll give you. The labs have specifically developed them for this sort of situation."

And no doubt developed a means of detecting them, too. "How long do you think I'll be guarding Wetherton?"

Stephan shrugged. "I can't honestly say. It could be a month, it could be a year. Parliament doesn't form again until the middle of next month. By then, the two of you will be such a fixture no one will comment."

By then, she hoped Wetherton would reveal his secrets and she could get on with her life. Spending months in Canberra, yawning her way through endless cabinet sessions, was not something to look forward to.

She crossed her arms and stared at Stephan. He returned her gaze calmly. The uneasy feeling that he wasn't telling her everything grew.

"You're doing this to get back at Gabriel, aren't you? You want him to care."

"I'm doing this because no other agents have your particular range of talents. Your ability to detect evil could be vital in this case."

No lies, but not the exact truth, either. She sat back, feeling more frustrated than when she'd first entered his office. Wetherton was not an option she really wanted, but what other choice did she have? It was this, or put up with endless hours of mind numbing paperwork in the shoebox.

"How do I keep in contact?"

"You'll be wearing a transmitter that will be monitored twenty-four hours a day." He reached into his desk and pulled out what looked like a gold ear-stud. "This is the current model. It records sound and pictures. You turn it on and off by simply touching the surface."

"I don't have to get my ears pierced, do I?" She'd rather face a dozen vampires than one doctor armed with a body piercing implement.

Stephan's smile held the first real hint of warmth she'd seen since she walked into his office. "No. The studs are designed to cling to human flesh. You actually won't be able to get them off without the help of the labs."

Just as well she could turn them off, then. She needed some privacy in her life, even if it *was* only to go to the bathroom.

"When do I start?"

"Tomorrow night." He picked up another folder and handed it across the desk. "In here you'll find detailed backgrounds on his friends, family and business acquaintances."

She dropped the folder onto her lap. There was plenty of time to look at it later. "You were pretty certain I'd take this job, weren't you?"

"Yes. What other choice have you actually got?"

Indeed. "And Gabriel?"

"Will be told you have been reassigned."

Which would no doubt please him. He'd finally gotten what he wanted—her out of his way. "And will I be? After this assignment is over, that is?"

Stephan considered her for several seconds. "That depends."

"On what?"

"On whether or not he has come to his senses by then."

A statement she didn't like one little bit. "You owe me, Stephan," she said softly. For ordering her shot when she'd been trying to stop the shifter who'd taken Gabriel's form. For the hour of questioning she'd faced afterwards when she should have been in the med center. For saving his twin's life. "All I want is permanent reassignment."

His gaze met hers, assessing, calculating. "All right," he said slowly. "As I said, this assignment could take more than a year to complete. If you still wish a new partner at the end of it, I shall comply."

She stared at him. His agreement had come too easily. She didn't trust him. Didn't trust that he meant what he said. But for the moment, there was little she could do.

"What happens if I need access to files or information?"

"You'll have a portable com-unit with you, coded to respond only to your voice and eye scan. You'll also have priority access to all files, though a copy of all requests and search results will be sent to me."

She raised an eyebrow. Priority access? Whatever it was Stephan thought Wetherton was involved in had to be big.

The intercom buzzed into the silence. Stephan leaned across and pressed the button. "Yes?"

"Assistant Director Stern to see you, as requested, sir."

"Send him in." He gave her a toothy smile that held absolutely no sincerity. "Thought you might like to say good-bye."

Gabriel was the last person she wanted to see. She was barely controlling her temper around him these days, and hitting him—a superior—would only get her into more trouble than Gabriel was worth. And Stephan damn well knew it. She thrust upright. "You're a bastard, you know that?"

"No, I'm a man faced with two people who won't acknowledge that, at the very least, they are meant to be partners at work."

The door opened, giving her no time to reply. She clenched the folder tight, but found her gaze drawn to the tall man entering the room. His hazel eyes narrowed when he saw her.

But just for an instant, something passed between them— an emotion she couldn't define and he would never verbally acknowledge. And that made her even angrier.

"Sam," he said, his voice as polite as the nod he gave her.

"Gabriel," she bit back, and glanced at Stephan. "Will that be all, sir?"

A smile quirked the corner of his mouth. He hadn't missed her reaction. "Yes. For now."

Gabriel stepped to one side as she approached. It was probably meant to be nothing more than a polite action—he was simply making way for her to get past—but it fanned the fires of her fury even higher. One way or another, this man was always avoiding her.

She met his gaze and saw only wariness in the green-flecked hazel depths . Ever since the factory shootout with Rose and Orrin six months ago, he'd regarded her that way. She wasn't entirely sure why. And in all honesty, it was time she stopped worrying about it. There were more important concerns these days.

Like finding out who she really was. *What* she really was. Getting a life beyond the force.

She stopped in front of him. His scent stirred around her, spicy and masculine, making her want things she could never have. Not with this man.

"You win, Gabriel. You have your wish. I'm out of your life." She held out her hand. "Wish I could say it's been pleasant, but you sure as hell made certain it wasn't."

His fingers closed round hers, his touch sending warmth through her soul. A promise that could never be.

"You've been reassigned then?" Relief edged his deep voice.

"Yeah."

He released her hand. Her fingers tingled with the memory of his touch. Part of her was tempted to clench her hand in an effort to retain that warmth just a bit longer. But what was the point of holding on to something that was little more than an illusion? A desire that probably came from loneliness more than any real connection?

"Who's the new partner?"

There was something a little more than polite interest in the question. With anyone else, she might have thought they cared. With Gabriel, who knew?

She shrugged. "It's really none of your business now, is it?" She glanced around at Stephan. "I'll talk to you later."

He nodded. She met Gabriel's gaze one final time, her gaze searching his, though what she was looking for she couldn't honestly say. After a few seconds, she turned and walked out.

Gabriel watched her go. The anger so visible in every step seared his mind, reaching into places he'd thought well shielded and far out of reach. Whatever this connection was between them, it was breaking down barriers not even his twin had been able to traverse, and raising emotions he'd long thought dead.

Which was just another reason to get her out of his working life. Whether or not she should appear in his social life was a point of contention between the two parts of his soul. The hawk half wanted no strings, no ties, nothing beyond those that already existed. But the human wanted to pursue what might lie between them. Wanted to discover if given the chance it could develop into something more than friendship.

Not that there ever *would* be a chance, if her anger was anything to go by. Which is precisely what he'd wanted, what he'd been aiming for over the nine months they'd been partners. So why did his victory feel hollow?

He shut the door and walked across to the chair. "So," he said, as he sat down. "Where has she been reassigned?"

Stephan leaned back in his chair, blue eyes assessing. "She's right. It's really none of your business now."

"Don't give me that crap. Just tell me."

Stephan smiled, though no warmth touched his cold expression. It was that, more than anything, which raised Gabriel's hackles. Stephan was up to something, something *he* wouldn't like.

"She's on special assignment as of tomorrow."

Gabriel regarded him steadily. His brother was enjoying this. He could almost feel the satisfaction oozing from his twin's pores. "Give, brother. What in hell have you done?"

Stephan steepled his fingers, and studied them with sudden interest. "I've assigned her the Wetherton case."

The Wetherton case. The *one* case she should have been kept well away from. "Get her off it, Stephan. Get her off it *now*."

His twin's gaze finally met his. In it was nothing more than steely determination. "She *is* the best person for the job, whatever the risks."

"You haven't even warned her, have you?" Gabriel scrubbed a hand across his jaw. Christ, she could be walking straight into a goddamn trap, and there was nothing he'd be able to do to save her.

"She knows we believe Sethanon could be involved," Stephan commented.

"Which is the *least* of our worries. Wetherton's and Kazdan's clones could have only one source, and we both know it. Neither the government labs nor the black marketers have succeeded with personality and memory transfers. Hopeworth has."

"So our spy tells us. It's not something we've been able to confirm."

"I think Hopeworth basically confirmed it when they maneuvered to get their clone in charge of the budget."

"If they wanted their clone in charge of the budget, they would have got him assigned the Defense portfolio."

Gabriel crossed his arms. Hopeworth had fingers in both pies, and Stephan knew it. "Did you even mention Hopeworth?"

"It was mentioned. But we don't know for sure if Hopeworth is, in fact, involved."

"Then did you at least tell her Sethanon is more than likely involved with Hopeworth?"

"No, because we have nothing more than a suspicion about his involvement. We have no picture of this man. We don't even know if he truly exists. He is currently nothing more than a name."

"*That* name has over thirty SIU and Federation deaths attributed to it. I don't particularly want her name added to that list." His voice was tight with the anger coursing through him. True, he'd wanted to lose her as a partner, but he certainly hadn't wanted to throw her to the lions, and that's basically what his brother had done. She would have been safer remaining his partner than taking this damn mission.

Stephan grimaced. "Nor do I, brother. Believe me. But we need to uncover the source of these clones. We need to draw out Sethanon, and we need to uncover whether or not he is involved as deeply with Hopeworth as we suspect. The truth is she's the best bait we have to achieve all those aims."

"What about our source in Hopeworth? Has he heard any whispers about Sethanon?"

Stephan shook his head. "It's not a code-name the military uses."

"Kazdan knew who he was. Others must. It's just a matter of uncovering the layers of his organization."

"Which is why Samantha has been assigned to Wetherton. We know he's a clone. We know his name was on that list she got from Kazdan. We need to know what that list was, and what Wetherton promised to do to get his new lease on life."

"But as I said, that puts her in too close a contact with Hopeworth. That could be extremely dangerous."

Stephan leaned back in his chair and regarded him steadily. "Only if, as you presume, she is a product of Hopeworth itself."

"You've seen the initial reports from O'Hearn. You've seen the coding. Whatever Sam is, it's definitely not a product of natural selection."

"Yet it was Sethanon who assigned Kazdan to monitor her every move. Sethanon who appears to know just who and what Samantha is. You noted that yourself. Couldn't that mean he's responsible for her creation?"

Possible, but not likely. Gabriel didn't doubt that Sethanon wanted to use her. But if the man had been responsible for her creation, why would he take the risk of releasing her?

"Sam had a military microchip in her side. The same sort that we found in both the Generation Eighteen rejects and in Allars." She was also afraid of Hopeworth. Though she had never said anything, he could feel it in her, feel her fear, as clear as if it were his own.

"And yet our source in Hopeworth can find no record of her, though he can find records on every other reject."

"Maybe because her project was destroyed by a fire years ago."

"A fire would never destroy every scrap of information. Nor could it erase every memory."

"Penumbra was destroyed *that* completely."

"People still remember the project, Gabriel. They just don't remember her."

The nurse who worked on the project apparently did. But she was just one mind of many, and a woman with a faulty memory at that. Partially thanks to Alzheimer's, and partially thanks to the military's habit of "readjusting" memories. Gabriel shifted restlessly in the seat. "What if she isn't a reject? What if she's something else entirely?"

Stephan raised an eyebrow. "What do you mean?"

He didn't really know. It was just a feeling. The extent of Sam's memory loss, the depth to which the truth appeared to be buried, and the fact that someone was willing to bomb the

SIU in order to destroy her test results—it all spoke of intent. It suggested that someone, somewhere, was protecting her from her past, whatever that might be.

He actually doubted that it was Hopeworth trying to conceal who she was, even if they were her creators. The military weren't that subtle. Besides, if Sam *was* one of their creations, they would never have let her go. Not with the potential she was now showing.

"Look," Gabriel said, somewhat impatiently. "All I'm saying is that if Sethanon feared her enough to place a watch on her, we should not risk using her as bait in an attempt to catch the man."

"We don't even know if, in fact, it is a man we are after."

Gabriel leaned forward and glared at his twin's altered features. It was in moments like this, moments when he almost wanted to punch the cold smile from his brother's face, that Stephan being a shapeshifter, who could take on the shape of any male he touched, became a real problem. It was harder to restrain the urge to hit him when he wasn't wearing his own face. "Damn it Stephan, don't play word games with me."

Something flickered through the blue of his eyes. Anger perhaps. Or regret. "Do you, or do you not, agree that we must learn more about Sethanon?"

"Yeah, but—"

"And do you, or do you not," Stephan continued, his voice soft but relentless, "Agree that Sethanon's interest in Sam might be the lever we need to draw him out of the shadows?"

Gabriel rubbed his forehead. This was one battle he wasn't going to win. Not that he ever won many against Stephan. "The first hint of danger, and I'm going in."

"Samantha can take care of herself. She's proven that time and again."

But this was different. This was leaving her roped, tied and blindfolded in front of an express train. "I won't see her harmed."

Stephan smiled. "And here I thought you didn't care for her."

"I've never said that. All I've ever said is that I don't want her as a partner. That I don't want to see her dead."

"Have you ever considered the fact that this fear of losing partners is irrational and maybe you should seek psychiatric help for it?"

"Considered it? Yes. Acknowledge it? Yes. Am I going to seek psychiatric help? No." He met his brother's stony gaze with one of his own. "If I wanted to talk to anyone I'd talk to our father."

"Because, of course, you couldn't talk to your brother." Stephan's voice was almost bitter.

Almost.

"My brother has a tendency to put the needs of the Federation and the SIU above the needs of everyone, including his brother."

Stephan didn't immediately comment, just leaned forward and picked up a folder from the desk. "Here's the file on your new partner."

Gabriel ignored the offered folder and stared at his twin through narrowed eyes. "What do you mean, new partner?"

"I've told you before. All field agents, whether SIU or Federation, now work in pairs. There's been too many murder attempts of late to risk solo flights."

"I don't want a partner." What was his brother trying to prove?

"Then you remain at your desk and leave the field work to the agents in your charge."

He was tempted, very tempted, to do just that. But both he and Stephan knew that being confined by four walls for any length of time would make him stir-crazy.

Besides, he was more valuable to the SIU and the Federation in the field.

"Who have you assigned?"

Stephan dropped the folder on the desk and leaned back in his chair. Though there was no emotion on his face, Gabriel could feel his twin's amusement.

"James Illie."

Who was the State police officer they'd recruited after he'd made a series of spectacular arrests—arrests that involved one of the biggest vampire crime-gangs in the city. He was good, no doubt about it.

Only trouble was, the man was a womanizer who was always on the lookout for his next conquest.

"It won't work." And Stephan knew it.

"Then make it work. And don't try dumping Illie in the dungeons. The man's a stickler on workplace conditions. He'll bring in the unions the minute you try."

Wonderful. Just what he needed in a partner. "Is this all you called me in here for?"

Stephan smiled. "No. There's been a break-in at the Pegasus Foundation we've been asked to investigate."

"The Pegasus Foundation?" Gabriel frowned, trying to recall what he knew of the organization. "They won a military contract recently, didn't they?"

"To develop a stealth device for military vehicles, yes. But whoever broke in wasn't concerned about stealth devices."

"Then what were they after?"

"That's something you'll have to find out. All I've been told is that the person or persons involved managed to get past several security stations, three laser alarms, and numerous cameras. Only the fact that a photosensitive alarm had recently been installed in the lab in question warned them there was an intruder."

"Why were we called in? The Pegasus Foundation has more military ties than we have agents. Why not ask them to investigate?"

"It was the military who asked us to investigate." Stephan hesitated. "Asked specifically for you and your partner."

"They mean Sam." But if the military didn't know anything about her, why had they specifically asked for her to be included in the investigation?

"Who signed the request?"

"General Frank Lloyd."

As Alice would say, curiouser and curiouser. "Sam met Lloyd at Han's." She'd been wary of the General and convinced they'd meet again. "You have to warn her about the military's interest."

"No, I won't." Stephan hesitated. "And neither will you."

Like hell he wouldn't. It was one thing to let her go. It was another to leave her blind. He crossed his arms. "What time is the Pegasus Foundation expecting us?"

Stephan glanced at his watch. "Four thirty."

It was nearly four now. Gabriel rose. "I'd better get moving."

Stephan nodded. "Illie's requisitioned a car and is waiting out front."

Then he could wait. Gabriel met his twin's gaze. "Thought I'd skip without him, huh?"

Stephan's smile touched his eyes for the first time. "I know you, brother. Know the way your mind works. Don't ever forget that."

Then he'd know Illie wasn't going to be a fixture in his life for very long. If he'd wanted a partner, he would have kept Sam.

"Then you'll know precisely what I'm thinking now."

Stephan's smile widened. "Yeah, and it's not polite to abuse a family member like that."

It was when your brother was being such a bastard.

Stephan's smile faded. "Keep away from her, Gabriel. She has a job to do. I don't want you getting in the way."

"What I do in my own time is my business, not yours," Gabriel said, voice flat. "I'm warning you, don't ever try to control my moves there."

Stephan raised an eyebrow. "You have an obligation to both the SIU and Federation, just as I have."

"Yeah, right." Gabriel turned and headed for the door. The Federation and the SIU could go hang if it meant letting Sam walk unwarned into a trap.

He may have succeeded in getting rid of her as a partner, but that didn't mean he wanted her dead.

"Gabriel, I'm warning you. Leave her alone."

He stopped with his hand on the doorknob and glanced over his shoulder, meeting his brother's gaze. "Or you'll what? Censure me? Bust me down to field agent again? Do it. I don't really give a damn."

"This could be our one chance to draw Sethanon out."

"That doesn't justify sending her out blind."

"I'm giving you a direct order. Do not go near her. Do not warn her."

"You'd better get my file out and add the black mark to it now, because that's one order I have no intention of obeying."

He slammed the door open and walked from the room.

Two

Sam glanced at her watch as she entered her office. It was just after four. She had an hour before she was due at the labs to have the studs attached and to be shown how the bugs worked.

All she really wanted was to go home. Not that she currently had a home to go *to*. Her Brighton apartment had sold almost as soon as she'd placed it on the market. The new owners had gushed over its size and closeness to the beach. That it had been bombed twice in recent months was a fact she and the real estate agents had failed to mention.

She slapped the folder on the desk and sat down. "Computer on."

A pink fluff ball with chicken legs appeared onscreen. "Afternoon sweetness."

"Afternoon, Iz. Any mail from that useless real estate agent of mine?"

"Not one."

Typical. He'd promised two days ago to get right back to her with the latest housing list. The man was either extremely forgetful or was tired of her nagging and trying to get rid of her.

Probably the latter, she thought ruefully. She leaned back in her chair and wearily rubbed her eyes. Maybe it would have been wiser to wait until she'd found somewhere else to live before she'd sold the apartment—as Gabriel had told her on the one occasion this week that he'd actually deigned to grace her broom closet with his presence.

And yet, she didn't really regret her actions, even if staying at hotels was costing a sheer fortune. The apartment had never truly felt right—maybe because it was something she had been given rather than earned. Maybe because the reasons for the gift had never really been clear.

Or perhaps it was the cop in her that couldn't get past the idea that, in the end, such gifts usually proved very costly.

She reached forward and picked up the folder Stephan had given her. Inside she found a series of photos—Wetherton's friends, family and immediate associates.

She shuffled through them until she found one of Wetherton. He was small, round and balding. Spud material, definitely.

And yet, there was something in his brown eyes that was not quite right. An odd sort of blankness that chilled her.

She threw the photo back down onto the desk. At least this assignment would save her some money, if nothing else. And she could still use the days to continue her search for a home.

Although, as her real estate had said—and more than once—if she wasn't so damn fussy, she'd have something by now.

Someone knocked on the door. It opened before she could answer, revealing Gabriel.

"AD Stern. Fancy seeing you again so soon." She couldn't help the sarcastic note in her voice. The only time he'd ever bothered crowding into her closet was when he'd had some inane task for her to complete. But he wasn't her partner now, wasn't her boss, so why was he here?

He crossed his arms, leaning a shoulder against the doorframe. His presence filled her small office in much the same manner as his frame did the doorway. With any other man, it might have felt threatening. With Gabriel, it felt cautious, almost aloof.

"Stephan told me about your new assignment."

There was a touch of concern in his rich voice. She raised an eyebrow. "And?"

"And he hasn't told you everything."

Like *that* was something she hadn't guessed. "That's because he works on a need to know basis. Like someone else I know."

Annoyance flickered through his warm hazel eyes. "I've never let you walk into an assignment blind."

She snorted softly. "Yeah, because you've never given me an assignment. Only desk work."

He at least had the grace to look guilty, if only for a second or two. "Look, I just came down here to warn you, not to argue."

"Then warn and leave." Before she asked him to stay, simply to warm the empty coldness in her office. In her life.

"Fair enough." He hesitated slightly, studying her with a slight frown. "He omitted two major facts. One, we believe the source of the clone to be Hopeworth, and two, we think Sethanon may be linked to both Wetherton and Hopeworth."

And Stephan was using her to draw them out, she concluded.

She'd been right. The vampire set up to attack Wetherton wasn't the only patsy in this situation. "Why does he think my presence will affect Sethanon's actions?"

"Sethanon placed Kazdan in your life to keep watch over you both professionally and personally. He had the birth certificate Kazdan gave you in his possession. He seems to know more about your history than you, or me, or anyone else. It implies long term interest."

Or long term responsibility. She rubbed her arms uneasily. "Sethanon is little more than a name. How the hell am I supposed to draw him out when no one even knows what he looks like?"

"Stephan's hoping he might make an attempt to snatch you."

If he'd intended that, why not do so before now? He'd had ample enough opportunities, especially when Jack was her partner. Few people would have missed her back then—only Jack, and he'd been Sethanon's right-hand man.

"I doubt the man would be fool enough to try it himself."

"No. But the transmitter you're getting also acts as a tracker signal. Stephan hopes to trace you to Sethanon's headquarters, at the very least."

And then what? A quick raid in the hope of flushing out the upper echelons of his organization? Stephan was a fool if he thought it would be so easy. They were talking about someone who had successfully covered his tracks for years.

"How deep are Wetherton's ties to Hopeworth?"

"Very, if Hopeworth is in fact responsible for his cloning."

"It doesn't make sense, you know. Why clone someone like Wetherton? From what I've read of the man, he's never been considered Prime Ministerial material."

"But David Flint was. Remember, Sethanon has already tried to replace him with a clone."

Which suggested that if the clones *were* coming from Hopeworth, then Sethanon was in control of the base. And yet, if that was true, why would Hopeworth be showing interest in her if Sethanon wanted her watched and knew what she was? There was too much conflicting information to believe things were *that* simple. "So this whole assignment is simply a setup to discover Wetherton's links?"

"Setup? No." Gabriel hesitated slightly. "But use, yes."

Either way, did it really matter? She'd been assigned the

case and, no matter what the dangers, it was sure as hell better than spending the rest of her life in this broom closet. "So I'll be careful. Anything else, Assistant Director?"

He hesitated again, then shook his head. "Keep in touch," he said softly.

A hint of regret ran through his eyes, and she steeled herself against it. She'd tried hard enough. Now it was his turn. "Why? I thought it was your life's ambition to get rid of me."

"I never said I wanted you out of my life."

He'd never said he wanted her in it, either. Had never truly thrust out the hand of friendship. Everything she knew about him she'd learned during the course of their work. He'd never attempted to extend the boundaries of their working relationship, despite the fact that there was obviously some sort of basic attraction between them.

Whether that attraction would have led to anything more than a night or two in the sack was anyone's guess. If she was the betting type, she would have said yes. But it takes two to undertake such an exploration, and Gabriel was having no part of it.

No part of her.

"Why do you think it's safer to have me as a friend than as a partner?" she asked.

He stared at her. His face held no emotion, and yet she could sense his unease as easily as if it were her own. He didn't want to examine his reasoning. Didn't want to look closely at his feelings. If he had shut himself off from his twin brother, what made her think she'd even have a hope of cracking his reserve?

She waved a hand before he could answer her question. "Forget it, Gabriel. Call me sometime and we'll go out for coffee or something."

"I will." He stared at her a moment longer, his gaze searching her face, as if memorizing her features. Then he turned and walked away.

She picked up the folder and shoved it into her bag. Then she opened her desk drawer, grabbing the few personal items she'd left in there: perfume, the pin Joe—the man she didn't actually know and yet had saved her life at least twice, and seemed to know so much about her—had given her, a hairbrush and several scrunchies.

She stood and grabbed the coat from the back of her chair.

But on the verge of leaving, she hesitated. As much as she'd hated what the broom closet had represented, at least it had been hers—somewhere she could escape to and be safe. A place few people knew existed or could be bothered finding. Whatever happened after the Wetherton assignment, she knew she wouldn't be coming back here. One way or another her life was about to change.

Whether it was for the good or the bad, she wasn't entirely sure. And right at this moment, she didn't really care. Any sort of change had to be better than stagnating, which is precisely what she'd spent the last few years of her life doing. She'd let Jack take over her life to the extent that she had no life beyond the force. In some ways, she'd started to make the same mistake again, with the SIU and with Gabriel.

"No more," she vowed to the emptiness. From now on, she would try to follow her own course, no matter what.

Grabbing her bag, she turned and headed down to the labs.

* * *

Gabriel climbed out of the car and slammed the door shut. The Pegasus Foundation's home was a huge strip of barren land out in the middle of goddamn nowhere. The main building was square-shaped, draped in black glass that oddly seemed to suck in the light and cast thick shadows over the parking lot and the nearby limp-looking garden.

He took off his sunglasses and looked upwards, squinting slightly against the bright sunlight. The building was six stories high, and even from where he stood he could see the radar dishes, antennas and various other bits of apparatus bristling from the rooftop. But he also caught sight of something else— security, armed with guns. And the uniforms those men were wearing looked a hell of a lot like military uniforms.

But if the military was involved with Pegasus on something deeper than research on stealth, why bring in the SIU? It didn't make sense.

The uneasy feeling that they were being played hit him. He rubbed the back of his neck and headed across the parking lot towards two black-glass front doors.

Behind him, a door slammed and footsteps echoed. Gabriel found himself clenching his fists, and he slowly flexed them in an effort to relax. An hour in Illie's company and he was ready to punch the man out. Not the best of beginnings.

The glass doors opened. He headed across to security and

flashed his badge. "We've an appointment with Director Douglas."

The security officer nodded. "Take the second elevator down to level five. You'll be met in the foyer and taken to the director's office."

"Thanks." Gabriel continued on. His new partner followed quietly. Maybe he'd finally caught on to the fact that silence was appreciated more than endless streams of chatter.

Gabriel punched the elevator call button. Illie stopped and cleared his throat. "Have you seen the recent photos of the director? The woman's quite a babe."

Then again, maybe Illie was silent only because he'd temporarily run out of inane things to say. "We're not here to access the director's babe rating."

Illie's responding grin could only be classed as cheesy. "Hell man, it doesn't hurt to look, does it?"

"I'd prefer it if you concentrated on the matter at hand, not adding another notch to your belt." He stepped into the elevator and pressed the button for sublevel five.

Illie's gray eyes narrowed slightly. "That would be easier if I knew why in the hell we were here."

Gabriel shrugged. "If you've read the file you know as much as me."

"Nothing like sending agents out blind," Illie muttered. "Though it's no wonder this mob got robbed. Security didn't even bother asking about our weapons."

Gabriel smiled. Despite his years in State Police, Illie had a lot to learn. "They didn't have to. Did you notice the black globe in the ceiling?"

Illie frowned. "Yeah. Camera, wasn't it?"

"No. It's a device that renders laser weapons ineffective. There were also metal detectors on either side of the entrance, so if we'd been carrying standard weapons, the guard would have known."

"I didn't see them."

"You wouldn't. They're built into the frame. The only giveaway is a faint red beam." Something human sight rarely picked up.

"Damn," Illie commented. "Must have missed that session of training."

According to his file, Illie hadn't missed any, which didn't mean he was actually paying attention. "O'Donnell was your instructor, wasn't she?"

A slow smile stretched Illie's mouth. "Yeah."

Which accounted for the lack of memory. O'Donnell was a pretty blonde in her mid-thirties and decidedly single.

The elevator doors slid open. The waiting guard motioned them to follow and led the way down a sterile white corridor.

They passed through two more security stations before the whiteness began to bleed away, replaced by muted greens and blues.

Kathryn Douglass turned from the window when they were ushered into her office. She was a tall, slender woman with silver flecked brown hair and alabaster skin. Her age was hard to guess—he thought mid-fifties, but wouldn't have been surprised if she was older. Either way, she was striking.

"Assistant Director Stern," she said, offering her hand. "Thank you for being so prompt."

Gabriel clasped her hand. Her touch was firm, almost challenging. More like a man's than a woman's. "This is my partner, James Illie."

She ignored Illie's outstretched hand and waved them toward two well-padded armchairs before sitting down herself. Her gaze was assessing, almost critical.

"I was under the impression your partner was a woman," she said.

The back of Gabriel's neck began to itch. The director's manner wasn't what he'd expected from a woman whose company had just suffered a major robbery. No concern, no tension, just an odd sort of watchfulness.

He met her cool, gray gaze. "Then your informant was wrong. Tell us about the break in."

The director leaned back in her chair, a slight frown marring her almost perfect features. "One of our research labs was breached last night at around two. We don't believe anything was taken, but the filing system had been broken into."

"Then you don't use computer filing?" Illie said, almost in disbelief.

The director's smile edged towards condescending. "No. Computers can be hacked too easily. Most of our top projects are paper only. This is a high security center. Until last night, we'd thought it perfectly safe."

No building or security system was impervious. There was always a weak spot somewhere. All you had to do was find it.

"What eventually raised the alarm?"

"We had a photosensitive alarm installed in the lab. It's a prototype we've been testing. It picks up any abnormal shifts in light reading, no matter how subtle. Whoever was in the lab last night was taking photos."

"Of what?"

She hesitated. "The lab is involved in the development of a matter transmitter for the military."

"Then why call us in? Wouldn't it have been more appropriate to call in the military?"

"We did. But whoever broke into the lab managed first to get past five security stations and three laser alarms, and they were never picked up by the cameras. *That* is more SIU territory than military."

Not if what they'd learned about Hopeworth over the last month was true. "Who recommended you call me?"

Illie gave him a sharp glance. Obviously he hadn't known they'd been requested.

"General Frank Lloyd. Said he'd had some dealings with your partner." She hesitated, her gaze shifting to Illie. "I'm sure he said your partner was female."

"Does it really matter what sex my partner is?" Gabriel said, unable to keep the slight edge of annoyance from his tone. This was looking more and more like a setup. But why?

The director raised an eyebrow. "No, I suppose it doesn't. Do you wish to see the lab?"

"If you wish us to actually solve this crime, then yes, that would be a good idea."

A small smile stretched her too-perfect lips, but there was little amusement in her cold gray eyes. She reached to her left and pressed a button on the intercom. "Security will escort you there. Please feel free to come back if you have any further questions."

Gabriel rose. "We will need to see the security tapes from last night."

"Of course. They'll be available by the time you finish in the lab."

"And we will need to question the guards who were on last night."

She nodded. "They're off duty, but a list of names and addresses will be provided."

This whole situation just wasn't sitting right. This was a

top-secret facility—one with severe military links. No matter how badly they wanted the crime solved, the director was being entirely *too* helpful.

"We'll see you afterward, then," he said, and followed Illie from the room.

As promised, a second security guard waited for them beyond her office doors. He led them back into the antiseptic white corridors and down a series of ramps.

Gabriel glanced at the ceiling. Camera's tracked their movements, but as far as he could tell, there were no voice recorders attached.

"Opinion?" he said softly. As an empath, Illie was able to read and define emotions to such a degree he could practically tell what a person was thinking.

Illie cast a wary look at the security officer in front of them, then met Gabriel's gaze. "That woman was lying through her back teeth," he muttered. "She has another agenda for having us here."

That much he'd already guessed. "Did any particular statement stand out?"

He frowned. "Yeah. The bit about it not being important whether your partner was male or female."

Because they wanted Sam, not Illie. But why? What had they intended to do once they'd gotten her here? Not even the military could think they could kidnap a SIU agent and get away with it.

"Just who was your partner before me?" Illie asked.

"She's not important right now." But even as he said the words, he knew the mistake. The only thing bigger than Illie's lust for women was his desire to know it all. By not telling him about Sam, he was all but giving the man permission to hunt her down.

And the mere thought of that happening had *his* temper rising. Sam might be a sensible woman, but she *was* a woman. From what he'd seen, there were few women who weren't seduced by Illie's charming ways.

Though what right did he have to object to anything she did in her life? None at all. He'd forced her from his professional life, and he'd ignored every attempt of friendship she'd made.

Which some in his family thought made him a fool. A fool who'd spent so long locking up his emotions he no longer knew how to accept something as simple as the offer of friendship.

Which was *not* what Sam was offering, and not at all what lay between them.

He could acknowledge all those comments, and in brief, black moments even agree with some of it.

But he'd been through hell once with the death of his childhood sweetheart, and that, more than anything, reset his resolve to remain alone whenever it started slipping.

He blew out a breath, and added, "Did you detect any lies when she spoke about the break-in?"

"No, that much was true." Illie studied him thoughtfully. "You have unresolved issues with your former partner, haven't you?"

"I told you, it's not important." And certainly it wasn't anything he intended to discuss with a man who'd been in his life for precisely an hour and a half.

Illie raised a skeptical eyebrow, but amusement danced in his eyes. "Maybe I'll have to get a second opinion on that."

Gabriel found himself clenching his fist again. "Let sleeping dogs lie, Illie."

The younger man studied him a minute longer then smiled slightly. Surprisingly, he made no further comment. Though as an empath, he would know when to push—and when to stop.

They continued on. The white corridor seemed to stretch on without end. The itch at the back of Gabriel's neck grew.

He tapped the security officer on the shoulder. "Where the hell is this lab? Siberia?"

The man shrugged. "It's one of the outer labs. We reach it via the underground tunnel system. Safer that way."

Gabriel shared a glance with Illie. The younger man looked as puzzled as he felt. "Why safer?"

"The ground above us is unstable."

As explanations went, it didn't help much. "Why would the ground be unstable?"

"It's the tests." The guard shrugged again. "They weakened the soil structure to a point where some sections are now almost liquid. Not deep, but dangerous all the same."

So they were testing weapons that could liquefy earth? Why anyone would want such a weapon was a question he didn't bother asking. Military minds did not work on the same rationale as the nonmilitary.

They finally approached another doorway. The guard swept his pass card through the slot, and the metal door slid aside to reveal a pale green corridor. Several doors led off it, though all were currently closed. Windows lined one wall, and through them they could see several white-coated technicians going about their daily business.

The guard continued on. Illie nudged Gabriel's arm and pointed toward the lab. "They seem okay to you?"

He watched a scientist measure some clear liquid into a vial. "I suppose so. Why?"

Illie's frown deepened. "Because I'm not getting any readings from them. It's as if they're emotionally nonexistent."

"Might distance be a factor? The walls look fairly deep here in the labs."

Illie shook his head. "Shouldn't matter when I'm this close."

"Maybe the labs are psi nullified."

"Then I wouldn't be able to read you, would I? Or the guard."

True. So what was going on? The guard stopped and punched several numbers on a keypad to the right of a doorway. The door slid open.

"This is the lab, gentlemen. I'll be out here if you need anything."

Illie stepped past the guard. Gabriel followed. The lab was narrow but long, all white walls and gleaming metal benches. The far end was lined with a map and upright cabinets, several of which had been forced open. Papers and folders were strewn over nearby tables.

"None of this makes sense." Illie walked down the aisle between the rows of tables, his footsteps echoing in the cold silence. "If our thieves could get into this lab unseen, why wouldn't they be able to break as easily into the cabinets? And if taking photos did set off the alarms, how the hell did they escape? I get the feeling there's only one entrance to this place."

"One entrance, but perhaps more than one exit." Gabriel bent to study the lock on one of the cabinets. Whoever had broken in certainly hadn't been subtle. They'd simply smashed the lock with something heavy. "If they're running equipment tests aboveground, they need some way to get up there."

"But it's not safe up there."

"Only for earthbound humans. Everything we've heard points to nonhuman involvement. You have the fingerprint scanner?"

Illie placed the device in Gabriel's outstretched hand.

Roughly palm size, the scanner had been devised to pick up and record surface variances. Skin was oily, and generally one touch was enough to leave a print behind, even if it wasn't visible to the eye. The only prints it generally couldn't pick up were a vampire's. There was very little moisture or oil in their skin.

Gabriel pressed the switch and ran the scanner across the lock. The unit beeped, indicating it had picked something up. Gabriel pressed the store button and then moved on to the next cabinet.

"I'll tell you one thing—the matter transmitter is not a recent project, if these plans are anything to go by."

Gabriel glanced up. Illie leaned against the table, studying the papers strewn there. "Why do you say that?"

"Simple. They're dated. These plans are over two years old."

"Check the other cabinets."

The scanner picked up several more prints. They wouldn't know until they got back to the labs whether any of them belonged to the felon who'd broken in. And they'd have to collect and eliminate the fingerprints of the scientists who worked here first.

"End cabinet has more recent projects," Illie said into the silence.

The end cabinet was one of the few that hadn't been ransacked. "Maybe our thief was working his way through the plans. Maybe he wanted the complete set of plans, past and present."

"Good theory, except there ain't no plans for matter transmitters in this lot."

"The thieves might have taken them."

"Why photograph them if they're going to take them? Makes no sense."

No, it didn't. Nothing about this case was making much sense. "Anything else of interest in the cabinets?"

"A lot of projects marked inviable." Illie slammed the cabinet door shut. "I'm getting a bad feeling about all this."

Gabriel had passed the bad feeling point minutes ago. Now it was more a sick certainty that something was about to happen. "Let's head back upstairs and view the tapes. Then we'll go interview the security personal from last night."

"I don't think we'll find much on the—"

A strident siren cut off the rest of Illie's sentence. A muffled explosion rumbled in the distance, and then the floor began to shake. Slowly at first, but growing in intensity.

"Quake," Illie said, calmly studying the ceiling, as if searching for any sign of collapse.

Gabriel did likewise. Spiderlike lines began to splinter across the concrete. Too quickly, he thought, and frowned. "I don't think so."

Another explosion vibrated the air around them. The siren cut off abruptly and the ensuring silence was almost eerie.

"I think we'd better get out of here, Stern."

Gabriel didn't reply. Wind stirred his hair, as if some unseen force was moving towards them. The back of his neck burned. Something was very, *very* wrong.

He lunged forward, grabbed Illie by the scruff of the neck and thrust him towards the nearest cabinet.

"Get in there, close the door, and do not come out until I say it's safe."

"Have you gone mad?"

"The cabinets are fireproof." The concrete bucked underneath him. Gabriel stumbled several steps backwards before he regained his balance.

"Holy shit." Illie's mutter was etched with fear. "The back wall is melting."

Gabriel glanced over his shoulder. Rivulets of concrete rushed towards them. A good third of the wall had melted, revealing a maelstrom of fire.

"Shut the door, damn you."

Another explosion ripped through the air, followed quickly by a sharp crack. He glanced up and saw the spiderlike cracks joining.

Chunks of ceiling began to rain down. Gabriel dove for the nearest cabinet, hoping like hell it would hold against the approaching firestorm.

Three

The locker shuddered as the force of the storm hit. The walls began to burn, becoming too hot, too quick. The air seethed with heat and every intake of breath burned Gabriel's throat and lungs.

He hunched in the middle of the locker and prayed that the fire-insulating properties would hold up long enough to ride out the storm. Sweat skated across his body, drying as fast as it appeared in the soul-sucking heat. He shifted his arm and licked several droplets before they could fully evaporate. It might not be much, but his mouth felt drier than the Sahara and he had to keep some moisture in his body or he wouldn't survive.

The viaphone vibrated against his side. It might have rung too, only he couldn't hear it against the whirlwind of noise battering the cabinet. He didn't answer it. Couldn't. He didn't dare move, lest he touch the sides of the locker. They glowed with heat and one touch could be deadly.

Two heartbeats later the noise began to bleed away. Silence reigned for several more heartbeats, and then a hissing began, softly at first but gaining in momentum. Water began to seep into the locker.

The sprinklers. Some of them must still be active, despite half the ceiling coming down. He waited several more minutes, and then cautiously touched the door. Hot, but not unbearable.

He turned the handle, but the door didn't budge. He shoved harder. A crack of light appeared along one edge. Through it, he could see chunks of concrete, scattered about like some giant's abandoned toys.

He shifted around until he could get his feet against the door, and then pushed with all his might. The door buckled under the force he applied, but eventually, the slabs of concrete moved enough so that he could climb out.

Water misted the air, quickly soaking through his clothes. He lifted his face and closed his eyes, allowing the moisture to cool his fevered skin.

Then he remembered his new partner. He quickly picked his way across the rubble to the locker that held Illie. The door moved slightly and relief swept through him. At least he hadn't managed to kill yet another partner.

"Hang on," he said. "There are several concrete blocks

piled up against the door."

He threw them to one side and forced open the locker door.

Illie scrambled out, his face red and suit stained black with sweat. "Now that was an experience I don't care to relive."

"Yeah, pretty awesome," Gabriel muttered

The viaphone rang into the silence, a shrill sound that made him jump. He dug it out of his pocket.

"Stern," he said, studying the mess that had once been a lab. What had probably saved them was the far wall—only a third of it had melted under the intense heat of the maelstrom. The rest had held, offering this lab some form of protection.

Sam's features appeared on the vidscreen, blue eyes clouded with worry. "Gabriel? Are you okay?"

Gabriel swore softly and rubbed a hand across his eyes. He'd hoped that by shattering their working relationship, he'd break the psi bond that was growing between them. That obviously wasn't going to happen—or maybe it was just too soon to have any real effect.

"Yeah, I'm fine, but I can't talk now."

It came out sharper than he'd intended, and the warm concern left her face, replaced by an iciness he'd seen all too often of late.

"Sure. Talk to you later."

She signed off before he could say anything else. Gabriel shoved the viaphone back into his pocket. Way to go, he thought sourly. Continue speaking to her like that and she'll definitely remain a part of your life.

"You know," Illie said casually, "you really could do with some tutorage in the art of speaking to a woman."

"Shove it up your ass," he muttered, and turned at the sound of footsteps.

Half a dozen white-suited men came into the lab, some carrying hoses and others medical equipment. Prepared for the worst, Gabriel thought.

"They're surprised," Illie muttered. "They didn't expect to see us alive."

"Relieved surprise, or annoyed surprised?" One pointed to a setup.

Illie hesitated, studying the approaching white suits. "Relieved."

So if this *was* a setup, these men didn't know about it.

One white suit separated from the pack, pulling off his breathing mask as he approached. "Assistant Director Stern? Glad to see you alive, sir."

Gabriel glanced at the man's nametag. "What the hell happened here, Rogers?"

"Near as we can figure, chemical spill in lab one resulted in an explosion. You're lucky to be alive, sir."

Wasn't that the truth. Though he had to wonder, if this *was* a trap, what had the military hoped to achieve? "Many casualties?"

Rogers nodded, his face bleak. "The security officer who escorted you both down here, and the five scientists working in lab one. If you don't mind, I'll have one of my men escort you down to the medical center, just to make sure you're both okay."

Gabriel nodded. "We'll need to talk to the director again."

"Once the doc's given a clearance."

"Let's get it over with, then."

Rogers motioned to one of his men and then moved away. Gabriel glanced at Illie, noting his frown. "What's wrong?"

"This is what they got us down here for," he muttered. "So they can do tests—on you and your partner."

Undoubtedly meaning his former partner, not his current one. "Who are you getting this from?"

"Small gent at the back. He was surprised when he first came in, then excited." Illie met Gabriel's gaze. "What's so special about your former partner that this mob is willing to kill five people just to run some tests?"

"We don't know." And that was becoming more and more of a problem.

Rogers's assistant approached. "If you'd like to follow me, gentlemen, we'll get this over with as quickly as possible."

No doubt they would. Without Sam, though, it was pretty much a pointless exercise—thankfully.

"They still want to test you, you know." Illie muttered. "Something you did during the firestorm has excited that scientist."

Gabriel frowned. "You sure you're reading him right?"

"Yeah. Positive."

They approached a set of doors marked with a red cross. Their escort swiped a card and the doors slid open. How many med-centers needed a security clearance to get into it? Why bother, unless the med-center did more than simply patch accident victims?

Whatever the military was up to, he'd just have to let it play out—for now. But the Pegasus Foundation and its director certainly needed closer scrutiny.

Their escort motioned them toward two well padded chairs. Gabriel sat down and watched the man disappear through a second set of doors. "When we get back to HQ, I want you to do a complete background check on Kathryn Douglas."

Illie nodded. "Including home security tapes?"

"If you can get them." It'd keep Illie off his back for a while, at least. In the meantime, he'd do a check of his own— on one General Frank Lloyd. There had to be information about the man somewhere.

His first priority, though, was Sam. Illie was right. If the military, via the Pegasus Fountain, was willing to kill five men just to get the chance to examine her, it could only mean they had a fair idea just who and what she might be.

And that, in turn, made her current assignment even more dangerous.

If Hopeworth *was* behind this bombing attempt, they wouldn't leave it at that. There would be more.

But he couldn't watch Sam's back twenty-four hours a day. Not without help. Gabriel frowned and dug out his viaphone. Time to arrange a meeting with his sister.

* * *

The shrill ringing of the telephone jerked Sam awake. She rubbed her eyes and glanced at the clock. It had just turned eight in the evening. She must have dozed off while reading the riveting account of Wetherton's life.

She blindly groped the coffee table behind the sofa arm and finally picked up the receiver. "Yeah?"

"Samantha? Doctor O'Hearn here."

O'Hearn was the nonhuman and rare species specialist she'd been sent to by Gabriel and Stephan. Apparently, if anyone could sort out precisely what she was, it would be this woman. A sliver of tension ran through her. Surely it was too soon to have reliable results back? She'd been told it could take months of checking and crosschecking. "Hi doc. What can I do for you?"

"I want your permission to discuss your case with Karl Morgan."

Karl? Gabriel's friend? "Sure, but why? Karl's an herbalist healer. How would he be able to help?"

"He also happens to be the Federation's resident expert when it comes to extinct races. I think he might be able to help make sense of some of these test results."

Obviously, O'Hearn had been unable to match the gene coding in the test samples with any known races if she was now considering extinct ones. "Was there any match to what's supposedly on my birth certificate?"

"Oh yes. There are traces of shifter and changer, as I mentioned earlier. We've also pinpointed the partial code of the were-people. But there's something else, something I've never seen before."

If she *had* come from Hopeworth, that wasn't altogether surprising. "I want to know the minute you come up with anything."

"Of course."

Sam hung up and yawned. What she needed was an early night. She shoved the folders to one side and got ready for bed.

Sleep came. So, too, did the dreams.

She was in a large, white room. Lights glared above her, their brightness as warm as the sun and almost as blinding. Sweat trickled down her face and her back. She was standing alone in that room, but she was being watched. Down the far end was another room. Men in white stared at her from behind the safety of shatterproof glass.

Joshua was with them, his small form dwarfed by the doctors. Silent but not afraid. Josh was never truly afraid.

"Feel the heat. Draw it in," the man with the dead gray eyes commanded.

Just hearing him speak made her shudder. Not because of the threat in his tone—though she knew from experience the threat all too often became reality—but because of what lay underneath his voice and his words. Evil soaked his very essence. Just being near him sickened her.

She looked at the fire, but she saw only flames, dancing brightly. She couldn't do what he wanted. He was asking the wrong person.

"I *can't.*"

The lights grew brighter, burning her skin as fiercely as the flames. She couldn't back away, couldn't move. They'd chained her down this time.

"Become one with the fire. Feel its power. Use its power," dead eyes said.

The urge to scream ran through her. It wouldn't matter to them if she did. It never did. Her gaze met Joshua's.

You have to do something, or they'll kill you, his voice whispered into her mind, calm despite the anger she could almost taste.

Fire is not my element.

No. They are fools who do not look beyond the obvious. You have other abilities. Use those instead.

They'll know. They'll see the difference.

They know nothing about us, despite all their tests. Trust me, Samantha.

She briefly closed her eyes and took a deep breath. Then she stared at the fire burning fiercely in the pit three feet away. The flames shivered, as if dancing away from an unseen wind. Sweat tracked down her face, stinging her eyes. She ignored it, concentrating, drawing power up from the depths of her soul. From the ground itself.

The fiery mass rose from the pit and hovered in midair for several seconds. She glanced at the control room and saw Joshua step back, well out of harm's way.

She smiled. It was a cold smile. A hateful smile. Aimed not at him, but at the men with him. The men who wouldn't let them be, wouldn't let them go.

The burning mass leapt across the arena and smashed through the control box's glass. White coats scattered like confetti. Then the lights went out and the screaming began.

Laughter filled the air, mingling with the screams. Her laughter; Joshua's laughter. Both old beyond their years and full of hate. The fire leapt from the men to the computers, and she realized he was feeding it, making it destroy the sensor readouts. Once again they would have no record of what happened here today. Nothing more than the words of those who survived.

Josh, I'm chipped. They'll kill me.

The flames died suddenly, sucked back into the void that had fed them. *I know. It is not our time to escape yet. But when it is, they will taste the fires more fully.*

The malevolence in his voice made even her shiver...

...She woke, a chill encasing her body. She ran a hand

through her sweaty hair and stared at the ceiling for several seconds. Were the dreams memories trying to break free? Or simply the imaginings of a fertile mind?

There was no way to be certain. But if *this* dream were to be believed, then she had not only killed, but she'd enjoyed it. Nor was it the first or the last time it had happened.

And she'd been no more than seven at the time.

"Lights on," she murmured, wanting to banish the shadows and the last remnants of the dream.

Brightness flooded through the hotel room. She sat up, drew her knees close to her chest, and hugged them tightly. If Joshua was in fact her brother, as the dreams insisted, why did he call her Samantha? According to Mary Elliot, the woman who'd supposedly looked after the two of them in Hopeworth, Joshua's sister had been called Josephine.

And why was she dreaming of a scientist with gray eyes when all the scientists who had dealt with the Penumbra project were dead?

Or were they?

They'd only had Allars word on that, and Allars was an old man whose memories might well have been altered by the military. No matter how reliable his information had seemed, no matter how much it had jelled with other sources, they had to take everything he said with a grain of salt.

She rubbed her arms and looked at the time. It was nearly eleven. Wetherton would be leaving the theater soon and heading home. According to the file, the vampire would attack just before Wetherton climbed into the car.

The theater was only four blocks down from her hotel. If she hurried, she just might make it there in time to see what happened. She had a horrible suspicion things would not go as Stephan planned.

And going was certainly better than sitting here in this hotel room, trying to stay awake in an effort to avoid the dreams that made no sense, and yet terrified her.

* * *

Gabriel swiped his credit card through the cab's debit slot, and climbed out. Illie had offered to drive him home, or even here, to his sister's, but he'd had more than enough of his brand new partner. At least Sam had been able to appreciate moments of silence—and she was a whole lot easier on the eye.

Not that he'd ever admit either to her.

He scrubbed a hand through his hair and wished he could just stop thinking of her. Damn it, he'd gotten what he wanted, what was best for them both.

So why did he feel so damn depressed about it?

Maybe it was just tiredness. He and Illie had spent an hour in the med-center at the Foundation being poked and prodded. Then they'd wasted another three hours viewing the security tapes and talking to the evasive Kathryn Douglas. Whatever secrets the woman hid, she wasn't giving them away easily. Even Illie had trouble deep-reading her.

Right now, he wanted nothing more than to go home, have a drink and go to bed. But he couldn't. Not until he'd looked after the woman he couldn't stop thinking about.

He climbed the front steps and reached out to press the doorbell, but the door opened before he could. His sister stood before him, brown eyes concerned despite her welcoming smile.

"A visit from my little brother at this hour of the night. Things *must* be bad." Her voice was soft as she rose on her toes to kiss his cheek.

Gabriel smiled and kissed her back. "I need help."

"I gathered that. Head on through to the kitchen. Alain's making coffee."

He made his way down the shadowed hall, his boots echoing loudly on the wooden floors. Alain, Jessie's brown-haired, large-limbed husband of six months, stood near the sink, pouring hot water into three mugs.

He glanced around as Gabriel entered, giving him a quick look over before his lips split into a wide grin. "Man, you look like shit."

Gabriel smiled and dragged out a chair. "That's pretty much an accurate description of what I feel like."

Alain placed a mug in front of him and sat on the opposite side of the table. The scent of coffee wafted up, teasing his nostrils.

"Things not going well?"

Though there was a sympathetic edge in Alain's voice, amusement crinkled the corners of his brown eyes. Gabriel had an odd feeling he wasn't actually referring to work problems. What had Jessie been telling him?

"Yeah, you could say that. Almost got blown up this

afternoon."

"Tough days at the office are the pits."

"But you're not here for sympathy, are you?" Jessie said, as she sat down and leaned her shoulder against Alain's.

Loneliness swirled through him. If only briefly, he found himself wanting what most of his siblings had—someone to lean on. To come home to. He rubbed a hand across his eyes. God, he *definitely* needed some sleep if he was thinking that. Besides, his chance at such a life had slipped away with Andrea's death "No. I want you to help me guard Sam's back."

Jessie shared a look with her husband, concern evident. Alain leaned forward, interlacing his long fingers. "Stephan's not going to like this."

"Stephan doesn't have to know."

Jessie smiled slightly. "You can't keep secrets from Stephan. None of us can. He has a nose for them."

Well, this was one secret he'd better keep his nose well away from or there would be hell to pay. "Look, Stephan's assigned her to the Wetherton case. He's hoping her presence will draw out Sethanon. I think it's more likely to draw out Hopeworth."

Alain's frown deepened. "Why would Hopeworth be interested in her?"

"Hopeworth's been playing in the genetic minefield for years, and Sam is more than likely one of their creations. Even if she's not, she's caught their interest."

Jessie picked up her coffee and regarded him steadily over the rim. "Why didn't you just keep her as a partner? You wouldn't have had this problem then."

"My partners have a bad habit of dying." He hesitated, and rubbed his eyes again. Andrea might have died by an assassin's bullet, but Mike's death had been *his* responsibility. He'd fired the killing shot. "I prefer to work alone. You know that."

A small smile touched her lips. "What I know, brother dearest, is that you're using your fear as an excuse."

He raised an eyebrow. "An excuse for what?"

"I remember a teenager holding his dying girlfriend in his arms and vowing to never let another woman come so close to his heart. A promise he has kept, until now." She hesitated, green eyes regarding him steadily. "Sam threatens that vow. You know, deep down, that she is the one. *That's* why you got rid of her."

Though an empath, his sister could sometimes be surprisingly off base. He frowned, and sipped his coffee. There was *some* truth in her words, though. He *did* have a connection with Sam, and he was definitely attracted to her. But as much as he might occasionally hunger for it, he really didn't want emotional complications of *any* kind in his life. That was part of the reason he continued to block Stephan's thoughts. Why he was so comfortable with Sandy, another SIU officer and his sometimes lover. She wanted no commitment, no emotion, beyond friendship.

As for Sam being the one... He put down his mug, and tried to ignore the ache in his heart.

"Andrea was my destiny, my lifemate. Not Sam. Whatever I feel for Sam, it could never evolve into something that lasts. My heart died with Andrea."

"Are you so sure, lad?" Alain said, deep voice holding a touch of compassion.

"Yes." At least Alain understood. Jess, and the rest of his family, probably never would. They weren't shapechangers. Weren't cursed with the knowledge that there could only be one permanent mate for them—ever.

Jessie sniffed softly. "You were so very young when Andrea died, Gabriel. Don't be so certain that what you felt then was life altering."

"Look, I came here to ask for help, not to be emotionally dissected."

Jessie placed a hand on his, squeezing gently. "I'm sorry." She hesitated, her face losing animation, and her brown eyes suddenly clouded, distant. "Sam is one half of a force—light to his shade. You are her anchor, her reality. Push her away and you force her into his circle of influence."

"Whose circle?" Gabriel said softly.

Jessie blinked. Warmth returned to her face and her eyes. She rubbed her arms and smiled ruefully. "I'm sorry. The vision's gone."

Gabriel cursed silently. Perhaps he shouldn't have spoken. Her visions were fragile at the best of times. "Will you help me?"

She glanced at Alain and nodded. "But I wouldn't hold much hope of keeping this from Stephan too long."

"Let me worry about Stephan." He gulped down the rest

of his coffee and rose. "I'll head to the office now and grab a copy of Wetherton's schedule. I'll email the roster once I work it out. Hopefully, between the three of us, we can keep her out of Hopeworth's hands."

* * *

Sam shoved her hands in the pockets of her jacket and leaned a shoulder against the bus-shelter wall. Across the road, people were beginning to file out of Her Majesty's Theatre and reporters jostled with spectators for the best position to view the exiting celebrities. Limos lined the curb, waiting for their passengers.

It was the perfect place to attempt an assassination. With the noise and the milling crowd, it was unlikely anyone would notice anything until it was too late. As yet, though, there was no sign of anything untoward.

The latest teen sensation came into sight, his blond head promptly disappearing amongst the crowd of waiting paparazzi and fans. Two seconds later Wetherton came into view and was greeted by resounding indifference.

He wasn't happy about it, either, if the look on his face was anything to go by. He hovered near the doors for several minutes, then roughly grabbed the woman by his side and guided her away. Three others followed in his wake—two men and another woman.

Sam pushed away from the bus shelter wall. Wetherton's chauffeur hadn't been quick enough to grab a front position and his car was parked half a block up.

She ran across Exhibition Street and fell into step several yards behind them. Though she kept an eye on the shadows surrounding the nearby buildings and shopfronts, and listened to the sigh of the wind, there just didn't seem to be anything out of place. No sign of the vampire. No sensation of evil humming through the night.

And yet, something *was* here—a presence that itched at the back of her mind. A memory waiting to surface.

She frowned and eyed the group ahead uneasily. The sensation was coming from their direction and she had no idea why.

Frown deepening, she tore her gaze from them and checked the night again. They were beginning to move well away from the theater and the crowd. Why hadn't the vampire attacked? If they went much further, there would be no witnesses, no press. No point.

A chauffeur climbed out of a white limousine when the group ahead approached it. As the chauffeur walked around to open the passenger door, Wetherton stopped and looked around. His gaze fell on her before she could avoid it, but it quickly moved on. Easily dismissed, she thought wryly, but stepped into the shadows of a nearby shop entrance anyway. She wasn't supposed to be here, so it was better if she kept out of sight as much as possible.

Once the chauffeur had opened the car door, Wetherton climbed in, followed quickly by the two women and one of the men. The last man hesitated, one hand on the roof, his gray hair gleaming silver under the wash of the streetlights as he turned to study the night in much the same manner as Wetherton had.

His blunt nose profile sent shock crashing through her.

He was the man from her dream.

The evil man with the dead gray eyes.

Four

Sam pressed the ear-stud, quickly activating it. "I want a search done on the man with the gray hair," she murmured. "All details, ASAP."

The man in question hesitated a bit longer, and then climbed into the car. The chauffeur walked back to the driver's side, and within seconds, the car purred to life and pulled away from the curb.

So much for Stephan's spectacular attack. What the hell was going to happen now? Without the attack, there was no reason for her to become one of Wetherton's bodyguards. No reason that wouldn't look suspicious, anyway.

And that, in turn, meant a return to the broom closet.

"There's never a vampire around when you bloody need one," she muttered, as she stepped from the shadows. "Someone had better contact me and tell me if this assignment is still a go."

She touched the transmitter and switched it off. Then she resolutely turned away. A return to her hotel was her only option now.

She'd barely taken three steps when an explosion ripped through the night. As her heart leapt to the vicinity of her throat, a wave of heat hit, sending her staggering. She swore loudly, but the words were lost to the sudden sound of screaming. She caught her balance and swung round.

What lay before her seemed more like a scene out of an action movie than something found on a Melbourne street.

Wetherton's car was up on two wheels, skidding forward under the force of the explosion. It crashed into a car parked on the right side of the road and thumped back down, the back wheels on fire and the flames spreading fast.

People were scattering, some running back inside the theater and others running down the street, most of them screaming and obviously terrified. The paparazzi were in a frenzy, cameras flashing as they jostled for the best picture position. Wetherton had finally gotten the attention he'd missed earlier.

Had he lived to bask in it?

The chauffeur scrambled from the car, blood pouring down

his face from a cut above his eye. A line of blue light bit through the night and hit him in the chest. He dropped like a stone out of her sight.

Laser fire.

He'd been hit with laser fire.

That certainly wasn't a part of Stephan's plans. She drew her weapon and ran forward, using the cars parked near the curb as cover as her gaze swept the surrounding rooftops. The laser shot had come from the top of a building down from the theater, but the light glaring from the many signs prevented her from seeing if the shooter was still up there.

But there was no reason to believe he wasn't.

She glanced at the limo. There were no movements from inside. Maybe the people had seen what had happened to the driver and were staying put, despite the dangerous fire. Or maybe they were unconscious.

Or dead.

The answers to those questions were something she had to find out—fast. But the closer she got to the car, the more the heat lashed at her skin. The smell of burning rubber damn near choked her, and thick smoke spun through the night. If Wetherton and his people *were* alive and didn't get out soon, the fumes and the heat would kill them. Not to mention the growing danger of the gas tank exploding.

From across the road, a familiar voice yelled at people to get back, that everything was under control. She smiled grimly. Briggs—someone she'd worked with and trusted.

But she hoped like hell Briggs wasn't the only one Stephan had sent in, because right now, she had a feeling they were going to need more than the two of them on the ground.

She hesitated at the nose of the last parked car before the burning limo. Twenty feet of free space now separated her from the wreck. She blew out a breath, glanced up at the rooftop, then sprinted forward.

Blue light nipped at her heels, sending jagged asphalt pieces exploding upwards. She swore and dove behind the burning car, ripping her jeans down to her skin. She swore again and rose on one knee, squinting against the smoke and the heat as she scanned the rooftops. She could see little through the thick, soupy haze.

Coughing as the smoke began to catch in her throat, she edged forward and felt for a pulse on the chauffeur. Nothing.

Though with a hole the size of her fist blown through his chest, that wasn't surprising.

She closed his eyes and shifted position. Flames were beginning to lick the underbelly of the limo, and this close, the heat was intense, almost suffocating. Every breath burned and the sweat sliding down her forehead seemed to sizzle. She had to get of here—had to get Wetherton and his people out— before they were either fried, suffocated or the gas tank exploded.

Sound whispered through the crackling of flames. Quick footsteps, approaching from the front of the limo. She swung and sighted her laser.

Only to recognize the blonde who approached. She lowered her weapon and said, "What the hell is going on, Briggs?"

Briggs stepped over the chauffeur's body and squatted near her. "I don't know. The vamp was supposed to hit as Wetherton was coming out of the theater. This wasn't in the works, believe me."

"You the only agent assigned?"

"Yeah. We're only talking about a vamp, and he's little more than a kid, at that. Shit, easy." Briggs hesitated, a grim smile touching her lips. "Or it should have been."

Should being the operative word. "Our first priority's getting Wetherton out."

"You check. I'll cover."

Sam nodded. Smoke and flames reached for almost every part of the car now. The paint had begun to peel, tearing away like sunburned skin. She pulled the sleeve of her jacket over her hand and opened the back door. Smoke boiled out, pungent and black. Inside the car, someone coughed. At least one of them was alive.

Another blue beam bit through the night. The rear window of the car shattered, spraying bright shards of glass everywhere. Briggs rose and fired several shots at the rooftop of a café just up from the theater.

Heat itched across Sam's skin, heat that whispered secrets and had nothing to do with the flames. It wasn't a vampire up there firing at them, but a shifter. Obviously, the vamp had done a runner, and other games were being played out here tonight. But if there was one thing she'd learned over her years as a cop it was that things rarely went the way they were planned. Mainly because all the various players were usually following a different script.

"SIU," she said, in between coughs, "Anyone seriously hurt inside the car?"

"Wetherton's unconscious. His wife has facial lacerations. The rest of us have minor cuts."

The voice was cold, efficient. Familiar. She knew without looking that it belonged to the man with the dead eyes.

"We're going to lay covering fire so everyone can get out. One of you will have to drag Wetherton clear." She hesitated, coughing again as the thick smoke and heat caught in her throat. "Make for the foyer of the theater."

At least there, Wetherton and his companions should be relatively safe from the laser fire. Unless, of course, the shooter moved.

Or there was more than one shooter.

"Say when," dead eyes said.

She checked the charge on the laser, then glanced at Briggs and nodded. As one, they rose and began firing.

"Go!" she said.

The twin lasers seared through the night, spraying the darkness with bright beams of light that danced across the metal rooftop with deadly force.

The car lurched. A woman scrambled out, followed quickly by a man who turned, reached back in and hauled Wetherton out of the vehicle. Gray eyes appeared, blood pouring down the left side of his face as he turned and dragged out a woman who looked more dead than alive.

"Go with them, Briggs."

She continued firing until Briggs and the others reached the doorway, even though the shadow on the roof had disappeared as soon as they'd returned fire.

If he moved too far, they'd lose him. And with him would go any chance of understanding what the hell was going on. She pressed the transmitter as she rose and ran back across the road.

"The attacker is a shifter, not a vampire. I'm in pursuit. Cleanup team and ambulance required."

Siren's were already screaming in the distance. People milled on the sidewalk, drawn like moths to the flame. Though the paparazzi feasted on it all, several of them ran in her wake, as if in anticipation of a scoop. She dug out her badge and flashed it in their direction.

"SIU, gentlemen. Get the hell back."

With reluctance, they obeyed. At least initially. She had no doubt they'd follow—just a lot less obviously. That was another thing she'd learned over the years—the press and a good story weren't easily separated.

And there was a hell was a good story here. One she wanted uncovered as badly as they did.

She ran into Little Bourke Street and headed for the alley behind the cafés. The nearby streetlight flickered off and on, causing brightness to sputter across the entrance of the small alley, briefly illuminating the broken asphalt and grimy puddles of water. She slowed. The perfume of rotting rubbish, urine and water long gone stale rose to greet her, and she wrinkled her nose. So much for the hope that she'd left places like this behind when she'd become a spook.

The alley ran behind half a dozen shops. Rubbish bins lined rear fences, most of them either overflowing or overturned. At the far end, huddled in the rear entrance of a building, was a sticklike mass of gray hair and stained clothing. He whispered obscenities to the wind, his voice harsh, strained, as he gestured wildly at the night.

A drunk, not the shifter who'd attacked Wetherton.

She hooked the laser onto the waist of her pants and climbed the old wooden fence. Once on the other side, she hesitated, listening. Lights glowed from the back windows of the café. People talked, a distant sound of confusion and concern that meshed perfectly with the sudden uneasiness of the night.

She looked up. The shifter was still up on the roof. His evil rode the air as easily as the wind stirred her hair.

Why hadn't he run? What was he waiting for?

Her.

A chill raced down her spine. It was ludicrous, it truly was, and yet the thought—or rather, the certainty that it was true—would not be shaken.

And yet, she was here by chance, by whim. How could anyone be so certain of her actions that they would know where she'd be at any given moment? It was impossible.

Though not, perhaps, for the man who shared her dreams and her thoughts.

And perhaps it wasn't even beyond the capacity of her makers, whoever they might be. Who really knew? Not her, that was for sure.

She rubbed her arms, but it did little to erase the cold sensation of dread running through her.

One problem at a time, she thought, and headed resolutely for the fire escape. Her footsteps echoed on the old metal stairs as she began to climb, a loud warning of her approach. Yet no sound greeted her appearance on the roof. No movement. She frowned, not liking the feel of it.

A billboard dominated the concrete expanse. Spotlights lined its base, their brightness aimed upward, leaving the rest of the rooftop a wasteland of shadows. A big old aircon unit rattled to her left. The awareness trembling across her skin suggested the shifter hid behind it.

She raised her laser. "SIU. Throw out your weapon and then come out with your hands up."

The man hiding in the shadows didn't respond. On the street below, the wailing sirens abruptly stopped. Flashes of red and blue light ran across the darkness, splashing color across the glass walled office building opposite. Almost normal sights and sounds in a night that felt anything but normal.

She forced her attention back to the aircon unit and the man who hid behind it. "I repeat, this is the SIU. I know you're standing behind the aircon unit. Lower your weapon and come out."

Still no response. She stepped onto the rooftop and edged forward. Underneath the sigh of the wind, she could hear the shifter. If the easy rhythm of his breathing was anything to go by, he wasn't worried by her presence.

She fired a warning shot. The blue beam flew across the darkness and hit the edge of the aircon unit. Metal flew into the air, tiny arrowheads that glowed with heat.

Still nothing. He didn't move. Didn't twitch. She frowned and moved closer. She'd almost reached the right edge of the unit when he exploded forward, his body little more than a shadowed blur as he sprinted across the roof.

He was too fast for a shifter—his speed was that of a vampire. He was across the roof almost before she could swear.

She was nowhere near *that* fast—a tortoise compared to the hare. But she ran after him anyway. If nothing else, she could track him with her senses until someone from the SIU got here to help her.

Speaking of which, where the fuck were they? This was Stephan's baby, his master plan, so why the hell didn't he have backup here already?

Or was this all part of a wider scheme—a scheme she knew nothing about?

Probably. But right now, she had no time to worry about it. The shifter leapt across to the next rooftop and ran on. His body faded in and out of existence as he moved, almost as if he were an image viewed through some badly focused lens. Weird.

She jumped the small dividing wall, then went down on one knee and sighted the laser. "Last warning. Stop or I'll shoot."

His only response was a fresh burst of speed. As he became little more than shadowed blur, she fired.

The blue beam arced across the night and hit him in the left shoulder. He flung his arms wide and went down with a thump. She waited, laser still raised and at the ready, for several seconds. When he didn't move, she rose and cautiously approached. Her shot might have caught him in the shoulder, might have torn through flesh as easily as it had his clothes, but that didn't mean he was down for the count. Far from it.

Her gaze went briefly to the wound. At least with lasers there was no bleeding and little chance of infection for those who weren't shot in kill points. The laser beam cauterized the wound in an instant—not that *that* made them any less painful.

The shifter himself was hooded and dressed in black from head to toe, his body solid but smudged around the edges, as if he were a drawing that wasn't quite complete. Odd, to say the least. There was still no movement, no sign of breathing. Warily, she nudged his foot. No response. She tried a little harder and got the same result. Or lack thereof. Maybe he was unconscious. He couldn't be dead. Not from a shoulder wound.

Cautiously, she knelt and reached for his wrist to feel for a pulse. In that instant, he came to life, twisting around to throw a punch. She dodged, but not fast enough. His fist hit her cheek, the force of the blow reverberating through her skull and throwing her backwards. Her head smacked back against the rooftop, sending a shockwave of pain through the rest of her body. For a moment, breath became scarce and stars crowded her vision.

Air stirred, accompanied by sound. The scrape of a heel against the roof. A grunt of effort.

She blinked back tears and tried to concentrate. She felt a

force of air coming from her left and rolled right. A booted foot landed inches away, the sheer power behind the kick seeming to shudder through the entire roof. If that blow had landed, he would have crushed her face.

He laughed. *Laughed*.

Then he tried stomping her with the other foot.

"Bastard," she muttered, firing the laser even as she dodged.

The bright beam of light speared into his chest. Skin and bone were seared into blackened bits that scattered on the wind, even as his body dropped lifelessly to the ground. The smell of burnt flesh was fiercer than before because of her proximity.

She closed her eyes and took several deep breaths. She hadn't meant to kill him, but her instincts had taken over and death was the end result. But worse than the knowledge that she'd killed was the sensation that something about all this felt *very* wrong.

With the speed that shifter had, he should have been able to dodge the laser. He didn't even try. Why not?

Why did he want to die?

She sniffed, and then winced as pain slithered across her face. A light probe with her fingers revealed a rapidly swelling cheek as well as a warm stickiness that could only be blood oozing towards her chin. The cut was a good inch long. The creep must have been wearing a ring of some kind when he'd hit her. The inside of her mouth was just as tender, and at least two teeth seemed horribly loose.

She spat out a mouthful of blood and slowly climbed to her feet. For an instant, the night swam and her stomach rose. She swallowed and rubbed the back of her head where an egg the size of a football was forming.

Great. Showing up looking like a boxer who'd taken one too many punches was just what she needed to impress Wetherton.

She grimaced and walked across to the body. Tendrils of smoke were rising from the wound. Maybe it was steam from his still warm body.

Or maybe it was something else entirely.

What that something else could be she didn't *want* to know. Though her imagination was certainly firing up some fantastical ideas—like maybe it was his soul rising.

As if *anyone* could see something like that.

Ignoring the goose bumps running rampant across her skin, she picked up his hand and studied the ring on his finger. It was a gold thick band with a square front. The symbol carved into it looked like a flame wrapped in barbed wire. Odd.

She let his hand drop, leaned forward and pulled off the mask covering his face. He had red-gold hair and green-gray eyes that were wide with shock. This wasn't any ordinary assassin, but a product of Hopeworth.

If Hopeworth was the birthplace of the Wetherton clone, why would it send an assassin after him?

Why send one after her, if they wanted to find out more about her?

It didn't make any sense.

But then, when had anything in her life ever made sense? It was frustrating, to say the least.

She rose to her feet and walked across to the edge of the building. The fire had been controlled and SIU officers were headed her way. She crossed her arms and waited for them. Right now, there was nothing else she could do.

* * *

The phone rang loudly. Gabriel reached out, making several empty grabs before he hit the vid-phone's receive button.

"This had better be good." He opened an eye and glared blearily at the time. Six in the damn morning. Couldn't he even have a day off without someone contacting him?

"You should try getting an early night for a change." Stephan's voice sounded altogether too cheerful.

Something *must* have happened. He rose on his elbows and looked at the vidscreen. His own image stared back at him. Stephan had to be at the Stern compound, not at his home or at the office. It was the only place he ever used his true form.

"You should try calling at a decent time." He yawned and dropped back down to the pillow. "What's up?"

"Hopeworth made an assassination attempt on Wetherton last night."

The last vestiges of sleep skittered away. Gabriel jerked upright again. "Is Sam okay?"

"Yeah, though she shouldn't have even been there. According to her report, the assassin was one of Hopeworth's creations. We can't ID him. Hopeworth is currently denying all knowledge, but I tend to agree with her."

Why would Hopeworth risk the life of one of their specialist killers on a man who was supposedly one of their own? It didn't make any sense.

He rubbed a hand across his eyes. "What about your vampire? He come through?"

Stephan frowned. "No sign of him. Looks like he may have taken the opportunity to run."

"You knew it was a possibility."

"A ten percent chance. Worth the risk, given what's at stake."

To draw out a man who was little more than a name, they'd let a killer back on the streets. Was it worth the risk? They wouldn't really know until Sethanon took the bait—if he took the bait.

"A warrant been issued?"

"Yeah. Francis and King are turning over his known haunts."

If the kid had any sense, known haunts would be the last places he'd go. But then, young vampires were inclined to think they were invincible and it generally tended to be their downfall. "Anything else? Or did you just call at this ungodly hour to piss me off?"

Stephan grinned. Gabriel wondered if his brother had been drinking. The last time he'd seen him like this was when they'd gone on a weeklong twenty-first bender. And *that* was years and years ago.

"Lyssa's gone into labor."

"Hey, congrats." At least that explained why he was at the compound. He must have taken Lys there so she'd have someone close while he was at work. It also explained why he was grinning like a drunken fool. "How's she doing?"

"Fine. I called O'Hearn down, just to check things out. She reckons it'll be a good five or six hours before anything major happens."

Changer births tended to be a lot longer than human births. He hoped Lyssa was strong enough. "You want me down there?"

"No point until something actually happens. Come down when he's born, and we'll get drunk together."

"Mom and dad hovering?"

Stephan snorted. "Half the bloody clan is hovering. The

rest are on their way."

"Well, your son *is* the first male grandchild to be born." He grinned. The Stern's didn't get together that often, but when they did, they made the most of it. There'd be a hell of party at the compound tonight. "Give me a call the minute anything happens."

"Will do."

The vidscreen went black. Gabriel scrubbed a hand across his eyes again. Though he couldn't have been happier for Stephan, this birth came at an awkward time for *him*. As much as he wanted to be with his brother, he also needed to ensure Sam was safe. Hopeworth was after her, of that he had no doubt, even though, as yet, there was no real evidence to back him up. He stared out the window for several seconds, listening to the starlings in the trees outside his window squabble, then reached for the vid-phone and quickly dialed Karl's number.

His friend answered on the second ring, looking as if he'd been up for several hours. His wild brown hair was tied back in its customary bandana, and dirt caked his weather-lined face.

Gabriel raised an eyebrow. "You eating mud for breakfast these days?"

Karl grinned. "You'd think so. It's been pissing down out here. Went out to check the greenhouses and lost my footing."

"You busy tonight?"

Karl hesitated. "Yeah. David's got the lead in a play at school. They're performing tonight. Why?"

David was Karl's youngest and Gabriel's godson. "Thought I'd ask you to do me a favor, but it really doesn't matter."

"I'm free after about eleven, if that's any help."

He hesitated. "No, it's okay." If Hopeworth *had* orchestrated the attack on Wetherton, surely they'd lay low for a day or two before moving again. He was probably worrying over nothing.

Karl scratched his chin, smearing mud further. "Are you aware that I'm seeing that pretty partner of yours later today?"

Gabriel smiled. He obviously didn't mean Illie. "Why? Something wrong?"

"Nah. O'Hearn called me in. Wants some help decoding the gene patterns."

"You had a chance to look at the test results I gave you?"

"Yeah." He hesitated. "Look, why don't you come down to the clinic today? I think we may need to talk to you both."

And wouldn't Sam be absolutely wrapped to see him there? He smiled grimly. He only had himself to blame. If he hadn't been such a bastard and so pointedly ignored her over the last few weeks, maybe she'd be a tad happier about seeing him outside of work.

"Why would I need to be there?"

Karl frowned. "I've been doing some research on Shadow Walkers. If O'Hearn's samples match what I've seen in the test results from Finley, she's definitely got Walker in her."

How could that be possible, when Walker's were little more than myths? "That still doesn't explain why my presence is needed."

"Her appointment's at five. Be there and I'll explain."

Obviously, he had no intention of explaining *anything* over the unsecured vid-phone. He blew out a breath. "Fine. I'll see you there, then."

The vidscreen went black again. Gabriel stared up at the ceiling, part of him wanting to get up and head for the gym, and the other half desperate to go back to sleep. The phone rang before he could decide between them. Didn't *anyone* sleep in these days?

Frowning, he shifted and checked out the caller ID. It was Sandy. He reached out to answer the call, then hesitated and pressed the auto-answer button instead.

"Morning, Gabe. Seeing we've both got the day off, thought we might get together."

Her voice was mellow, sultry, but for once it had little effect on him. Maybe he was more tired than he'd thought. Maybe he was simply getting old.

"Give me a call when you wake up," she continued. "Lunch is my treat."

Her words invoked memories of the last time she'd treated lunch. Eating hadn't exactly come into it, and damn if it hadn't been fun. Again he reached out. Again he hesitated.

If he went and saw Sandy, he'd have a hard time breaking away anytime before dinner. He couldn't go there simply for sex and then walk away. It wasn't fair to her, no matter how casual either of them were about their relationship.

Better for them both if he simply didn't respond. He rubbed a hand across his eyes and climbed out of bed. Seeing he had nothing else planned for today, he might as well grab the chance to exercise, then head down to Federation Headquarters.

Surely, somewhere in the vast archives there, he'd find something about Shadow Walkers.

* * *

Sam tucked a leg beneath her as she sat on the sofa. After placing her coffee on the table, she grabbed the portable com-unit and pressed her thumb into the lock.

"Voice identification required," the unit stated.

"Sam Ryan, SIU officer, badge number 1934."

Talking still hurt, but nowhere near as much as it had only hours before. Though her mouth felt tender, the swelling had at least gone down, and the bruise that stretched from her lip to her eye was already beginning to get that faded, yellow look. Even the cut had begun to heal.

At least she looked less like a boxer that had taken too many hits and more like something a cat had dragged in and toyed with for several hours. It was a definite improvement, but not yet enough of one.

"Voice scan correct. Eye confirmation required."

She looked into the small scanner fitted into the left-hand side of the unit. A red beam swept over her eye.

"Eye scan correct." The unit clicked open.

Izzy appeared onscreen. "Morning sweetness. Being portable is a new experience, I must say."

Sam grinned. Having her cyber character on the unit was an unexpected bonus. She'd thought Stephan would place voice-only response software on the portable unit—both he and Gabriel seemed to prefer it. Maybe he wasn't as insensitive as she'd thought.

"Morning Iz. Listen, I asked for a trace to be done on a gray haired man last night. The results back yet?"

Izzy twirled her purple boa for several seconds. "Yep. Got it right here. No ID match so far."

She frowned. How could there be no match? The man had to exist on a computer *somewhere*. "They checked the Motor Registration records?"

"No car registration, no driver's license or Medicare card match."

Every adult in Australia had a Medicare card. You couldn't go to the doctor without one these days. She picked up her coffee and sipped at it for several seconds.

"What about the shooter?"

"Again, no ID match. A formal request has been placed

with Hopeworth for ID."

Sam raised her eyebrows. That could cause a few waves. "Any response from Hopeworth?"

"Not a fig, sweetie."

Not surprising. What *was* surprising, however, was the fact that the SIU still had the body. She'd have thought Hopeworth would have tried a clandestine retrieval by now.

"They doing tests on the body?"

"Agent Finley is currently examining the body."

Then she'd have to remember to ask him what he discovered when she saw him at the meeting O'Hearn had arranged for later today.

"I have any mail from that real-estate cretin yet?"

The boa twirled. Response was slightly slower on the portable unit. "Yep. One came through last night."

"Put it onscreen, and thanks Iz."

Izzy disappeared, replaced by a three-page list. She smiled slightly as she scanned down it. He was obviously sending her every house he had that was near the sea, not just those within the metropolitan area. Some of them were as far away as Warrnambool, while others were over on Western Port Bay.

It wasn't until the very last page that one caught her interest. It was an old A-frame style house, surrounded by trees and close to the top of a hill, so it looked over the bay.

Kingston, she thought with a frown. Hell of a distance to travel to work every day, even with the recently completed Western-Port toll way. Still, she had nearly a whole day ahead of her and nothing to lose by looking. Leaning sideways, she grabbed the phone and quickly dialed the real-estate agent's number.

* * *

"You could fit six to eight villa units on a block this size, easy. Great investment for the future."

Sam ignored the agent's ramblings, and stared out the ceiling-high windows. Though classed as a part of Kingston, the house was actually several kilometers out of the resort township. Built on the side of a steep hill, the house had an almost unhindered view of Western Port Bay. Just across the dirt road, the cliffs plunged toward the ocean. With the wind blowing hard, as it was today, the waves reared high, as if trying to escape the bay's grasp, and foam sizzled across the black rocks lining the cliff top. The bay looked stormy—

dangerous—and yet it called to something deep within her. At night, she could lie in bed and watch the sea. Watch all the brightly-lit tankers glide by or the storms roll in.

She opened the sliding door and walked out onto the deck. The wind carried the rich tang of the ocean, and gum trees tossed and shivered. She leaned on the railing and looked at the ground.

The whole place was a rundown mess. Half the fence line had either fallen over or was in the process of doing so. The garden had long turned to weeds, and the driveway had ruts deep enough to lose a football in. The house itself was in little better shape. The kitchen was all orange and green, and it didn't even have an autocook. Apparently, the old couple who'd owned the house had preferred to do their own cooking and had installed an old-fashioned stove. Most of the walls were in desperate need of paint, the carpet covering the stairs leading to the upper floor was threadbare, and the banister wobbled worse than a drunk after a ten hour binge. Sections of both this deck, and the one on the side above the garage, were half-rotten and would need replacing.

It would cost a fortune to fix it up. A fortune she didn't really have. The money she'd got from the sale of her apartment would pay for this outright, and leave enough to buy a car. But that was it. There'd be nothing left for repairs.

It'd be madness to even consider buying it.

She raised her gaze and stared at the ocean for several minutes, watching the foamy fingers of ocean creep across the damp black rocks. She felt the power of the waves shiver through her, until her entire body seemed to tingle with its energy.

Common sense could go hang. There was something about the run-down, out-of-date old house that she just loved. And there was something about the raw closeness of the ocean that she needed.

She walked back into the bedroom. "I'll buy it."

The agent's face lit up. No doubt from the prospect of finally having her off his client list.

"I'll just run downstairs and get my com-unit. We'll get all the paperwork signed now, if you like."

He disappeared in a cloud of dust. Probably afraid she'd change her mind. Smiling slightly, she turned back to the window and its amazing view.

And noted the white Toyota parked down the road.

Under normal circumstances, she might not have taken notice. But the road was private, clearly marked as such, and didn't lead anywhere beyond the last house. The real estate agent had already told her the owners of the other nine properties were summer residents.

It might simply be someone enjoying the view. Or it might be someone casing his next hit.

She dug out her viaphone and contacted the local police station, asking them to investigate. Better safe than sorry, especially if her new acquisition was one of the houses being cased.

She turned and walked downstairs. The agent bustled back inside and motioned her toward the dilapidated kitchen bench. She'd contacted her solicitor earlier, getting him to do a quick check on the property. Everything was legit. Still, just to be safe, she scanned the countless forms with her viaphone and sent them on, refusing to sign anything until he'd given the all clear. Only then did she key in her bank details and transfer the funds. The house was hers.

"It'll take a day or so for this paperwork to go through and be fully registered," he said, and held out the keys. "I'll pass everything on to your solicitor to be double checked, of course."

She took the keys, an odd feeling of elation bubbling through her. "Thanks."

He nodded. "You going to hang around a while?"

She glanced at her watch and regretfully shook her head. "Can't. I'm working tonight."

He nodded again and held out his hand. "Pleasure doing business with you."

The relief in his voice made her grin. "They make you say that, don't they?"

His startled smile showed a hint of true warmth. "First lesson," he said cheerfully.

She checked the doors, ensuring everything was locked, and then followed him out. At her rental car, she stopped and breathed deep the heady aroma of eucalyptus and the salty hint of sea. Excitement pulsed through her. The scent of *home*. God, how she wished she didn't have to go back to the city and Wetherton.

Before the call to stay overwhelmed her common sense, she climbed into the car, and headed back to the city. She hadn't yet reached the toll way when she spotted the Toyota again.

It wasn't a thief and it wasn't a tourist. It was someone *tailing* her. She watched the car in the rear-view mirror for several minutes, then retrieved the viaphone from her pocket.

"Christine," she said, when the SIU's dusky-skinned electronic receptionist came on-line, "Agent Ryan here. Patch me through to someone in operations."

"One moment please."

The screen flickered. A thin looking black man replaced Christine. "Agent Donner here. What can I do for you, Agent Ryan?"

"I think I've picked up a tail. Four cars back from my current location. White Toyota."

"Hang-on while I do a trace."

He turned away. She glanced at the rear-view mirror. Whoever was driving the Toyota was damn good. She could barely see them behind the green four-wheel drive.

"Okay, got you. Fourth car back, you said?"

"Yep. I'd like a license plate and registration search done, if possible."

"I've gotta zoom in the satellite. Could take a few minutes."

"I'll wait."

Donner whistled tunelessly for a good five minutes, then gave a satisfied grunt. "Got him. Or her, as the case may be."

"Who's the registered owner?"

"One Jessie McMahon, from Eltham."

Sam swore softly. Jessie McMahon. Gabriel's sister.

The bastard was having her followed.

Five

"You want me to arrange an intercept?" Agent Donner asked.

Sam flexed her fingers in an effort to relax her grip on the steering wheel. "No, I think I'll handle it. Thanks, Donner."

He nodded. "Give me a call if you need help."

"Thanks. I will." She flicked off the viaphone and stared at the white Toyota through the rear-view mirror.

Why was Gabriel having her tailed? And why have his sister do it, when he practically had the entire SIU at his beck and call?

She doubted if he'd provide any answers if she confronted him on it, but Jessie might. The few times she'd met his sister, she'd seemed more upfront, more accessible, than her younger brother.

A green and gold sign came into view, indicating there was a side road half a kilometer ahead, on her left. Perfect.

She leaned forward, switched the computer from autodrive to manual, and moved into the left-hand lane. Leaving the indicator on, she slowed and glanced in the rear-view mirror. The Toyota had also switched lanes and was sitting behind a red Commodore.

She turned left. Not far ahead, the road did a sharp turn right and disappeared behind some trees. She put her foot down, accelerating round the corner. Once around it, she slued to a stop, the car shuddering as the tires struggled for purchase on the dirt road. As dust puffed around the car, she threw open the door and climbed out. A quick glance confirmed the beginning of the road was hidden by the trees. Jessie wouldn't know Sam had stopped until she rounded the corner.

She walked across to the gum trees and waited. Two minutes later the Toyota came around the corner, making an unintentional beeline straight for her car. She had a brief glimpse of Jessie's shocked face. Then Jessie braked and the Toyota slid sideways, coming to a halt inches away from Sam's rental car.

For several seconds, Jessie didn't move. She simply sat, her hands clenched around the steering wheel and her forehead resting on top of them. Wondering if she'd been hurt in the sudden stop, Sam hurried across and opened the door.

"You okay?"

"Yeah. Just a little shaken." Jessie glanced up, a wry smile touching her lips. "But Gabriel's going to kill me for being caught."

"That's if he's still alive after I get through with him." She hesitated, trying to control the swift jab of anger. "You want to explain why he ordered me followed?"

Jessie ran a slightly shaky hand through her dark curls. "There's a roadside diner about a kilometer up the road. Why don't we talk there? I need some coffee."

"I'll follow you there."

Sam slammed the door shut, walked over to the Ford and climbed in. After starting up the car, she followed Jessie back onto the main road.

Once they reached the diner and had their order taken by the gum-chewing waitress, she crossed her arms on the table and leaned forward. "So, why is he having me tailed?"

Jessie sighed. "He's worried about your safety."

"Yeah, so worried he wanted me dumped as a partner." She snorted softly. "Be honest, at least."

"I am." Jessie hesitated, gaze suddenly intent. "And you know why he didn't want you as a partner, don't you?"

"He thinks he's jinxed."

Jessie nodded. "His standard excuse for wanting to work alone."

She raised an eyebrow. "Do I detect a hint of sarcasm in that statement?"

"More than a hint." Jessie hesitated, glancing up with a smile as the waitress placed their coffee cups on the table. "Personally, I think he was desperate to get rid of you simply because you forced him to feel."

"Well, if I had that effect on him, I sure as hell couldn't tell it." He'd shown more emotion with Sandy, in the brief ten minutes she'd seen them together, than he ever had with her over the nine months they'd been partners.

Jessie's smile was a touch wry. "Gabriel's become very adept at controlling his emotions. But I think the fact that he's gone against Stephan's direct orders here proves he does indeed care."

"Or it could simply mean he wanted to ensure my safety until you've all discovered just how useful I might be to the Federation, his first and greatest love."

"The federation is not his greatest love. It's Stephan's."
Jessie tilted her head. There was a sharpness in her brown
eyes that made Sam uncomfortable. It almost felt like this woman
was capable of seeing far more than most. "How do you feel
about Gabriel?"

"He pisses me off more than any man I have ever known."

"You're not alone there." Amusement ran through her rich
but soothing voice. "But other than that, I mean."

She raised her eyebrows. "Why do you want to know?
And what does it matter anyway?"

"I want to know because I'm a busybody with the best
interests of my brother at heart. And it matters because I think
he's acting like a goddamn fool."

"Because he's having me followed?"

"No, because he's ignoring the blindingly obvious."

"Which is?"

Jessie smiled. "Answer the question first."

She sighed. "Okay, I'm attracted to him. Whether it's just
a physical thing, or whether it could be more, I'll probably never
find out."

"Why not? There is no law stating a woman can't ask a
man out. In fact, in this day and age, a woman is a fool if she
doesn't go after what she wants."

"I asked him out for coffee and he refused. I dressed sexily
and he didn't bat an eyelid. Whether he's attracted or not, he
obviously has no intention of pursuing it."

Jessie chuckled softly. "Yeah, well, it's going to take a
little more effort than that to land this particular fish."

Sam picked up her coffee, blowing lightly on the steaming
liquid as she studied Jessie over the rim. "That's his choice.
It's his life."

"In our family, no one flies solo." Jessie smiled, but Sam
had a feeling it wasn't meant to be amusing. That it was a
statement of fact and, perhaps, a warning. "If you want him,
you must take the lead. Be the hunter, even if it isn't in your
nature."

"You're telling me to go after your brother?"

"Yes. Until you nail him." She grinned. "Whether that be
sexually, emotionally or both, I don't care.

"Why?"

"Because he is going to end up a very lonely and bitter old
man if someone doesn't crack his reserve, and I don't want to

see that happen."

"So, why me, specifically? Especially when he apparently has a sexual relationship with another agent."

Jessie waved a hand. "That's just a mutual relieving of tension. You're the first person in a long time that he has shown any sort of emotion toward. Therefore, you're the logical choice."

"I can't believe you're discussing something as intimate as your brother's love life with someone you don't even know." And actually, she couldn't believe *she* was doing the same. But there was something very comforting *and* comfortable about this woman's presence.

"Ah, but I do know you. And we are going to be very good friends."

Sam raised her eyebrows. "So, basically, you're the crazy member of the family?"

"No. The clairvoyant. The future is my playground."

"I'm betting it isn't always a pleasant one."

Her bright eyes briefly shadowed. "No."

Sam sipped her coffee, then, in an effort to get onto a safer topic, said "So, he's actually having me tailed because...?"

"Because he believes Hopeworth is after you."

If last night was any indication, they were. And they didn't particularly care if she was dead or alive. Goose bumps skated beneath the small hairs along her arms.

"What makes him think that?"

Jessie shrugged. "I don't think he's got anything substantial. It's just a feeling."

Feelings were often more reliable than hard evidence— she'd learned that during her years as a cop. "And as the clairvoyant, what are your feelings?"

"That he could be right."

"Then he should have talked to me, not arranged all this behind my back."

"Would you have allowed him to arrange it?"

"No."

"Which is probably why he didn't bother asking."

No probably about it. She smiled wryly and glanced at her watch. If she didn't get moving soon she'd be horribly late for her appointment with O'Hearn. She sipped more of her coffee and said, "If I get you pulled, he'll simply replace you with people I don't know."

Jessie smiled, and tucked several dark curls behind her ear. "I dare say."

"Who else has he coerced into this?"

"My husband, Alain."

Sam raised her eyebrows. "Just the three of you? Doesn't he intend to sleep?"

"Obviously not. As I said, you mean more to him than he's willing to admit."

She'd try to remember that the next time he was giving her hell over something stupid. "Next time you're on watch, why not give me a call? If I'm off-duty, we might as well be bored together."

Jessie nodded. "Are you going to confront him over this?"

"Maybe. Maybe not." If Gabriel had the feeling Hopeworth was after her, she wasn't about to knock back any protection he offered, however covertly. Not when her instincts suggested she'd need all the help she could get.

"Good." Jessie paused, brown eyes suddenly intense. "Give me your hand."

Sam frowned and didn't move. "Why?"

"Because I have an urge to do a reading." She arched a dark eyebrow. "It doesn't hurt, unless, of course, you fear what might be revealed."

Which, of course, she did. What sane rational person wouldn't? God, she had no past to speak of. Why on Earth would she take the chance on knowing that there was no future, either?

How depressing would *that* realization be?

Though if she knew the future, then maybe she could change it. Surely such things weren't set in concrete, but fluid, shifting according to the decisions she made?

She gulped down more coffee, then, after a slight hesitation, held out her hand. Jessie's fingers wrapped around hers, her touch warm.

Almost too warm.

She resisted the temptation to pull away and watched the other woman carefully. Though she'd often seen clairvoyants work the Brighton market near her old apartment, she'd never been tempted to get a reading done herself.

Jessie's face lost animation, and her eyes were suddenly distant. "Do not trust the dream man. He tells no lies and yet speaks no truths."

Dream man? She raised her eyebrows. Did she mean Joshua, or Joe? Both haunted her nights and her thoughts. But she held the question back, knowing if she spoke, she might break Jessie's concentration.

"Fight not the storm bond. It will save you when nothing else can."

Again, a statement that only raised more questions. Jessie knew about her ability to siphon the power of the storms. She'd been at the warehouse when the storm's energy had helped her defeat Orrin and Rose, and save Gabriel's life. And yet, she had an odd feeling it was not *that* storm bond Jessie was referring to.

"When Hopeworth tests, remember the dreams. Channel, as you did back then."

Not *if* but *when*. Gabriel's feeling about Hopeworth would obviously reach fruition. Trepidation danced a chill across her skin.

"Watch the man with the dead eyes. He is more than his makers believe. He beds the devil and walks the path of treason. He is our enemy, but not yours."

And yet he'd seemed very much an enemy in all of her dreams. So, who was right? The dreams or Jessie's sight?

Jessie suddenly shuddered, and she squeezed Sam's fingers lightly before releasing them.

"Not what I'd expected, to say the least," Jessie said, wiping a hand across her brow.

Sam smiled at the wry edge in her voice. "You were trying to get a reading on me and Gabriel, weren't you?"

"Yes." Worry clouded the amusement in her eyes. "My visions merely show a possible outcome. They don't always come true, you know. Life has a way of taking its own path."

She had a bad feeling this was one set of visions that would come true.

"Then I'll try not to panic just yet." She glanced at her watch again. "Look, I really have to go, or I'll be late for my appointment with O'Hearn."

Jessie smiled again. "At least if I lose you on the way back, I'll know where you're heading."

Sam grabbed the bill and stood up. "You won't tell Gabriel about the house, will you?" He'd no doubt tell her she was a fool to spend so much money on a run-down house on the edge nowhere.

Jessie raised her eyebrows in surprise. "If you don't want me to. But be warned, he's almost as adept as Stephan when it comes to sniffing out secrets."

"He doesn't see me enough to know whether or not I'm keeping secrets." He barely even saw her enough to say hello.

"That will change, believe me."

"Oh yeah? Saw that in your visions, did you?"

Jessie's sudden smile was almost blinding. "No. Just a sister's instinct. You'd better get moving. My next shift to watch you is Monday. I'll give you a call then, okay?"

Sam nodded. As she paid the bill and headed for her car, she couldn't help feeling oddly buoyed. Maybe she'd not only gained a house today, but the beginnings of a lasting friendship.

* * *

Gabriel drummed his fingers against the steering wheel. If the traffic didn't start moving soon, he was going to abandon the damn car right here and take to the sky. It was four-forty already. Twenty minutes to get through the center of the city to O'Hearn's office was cutting it fine.

Why the doctor had decided to move her practice out to South Bank was beyond him. It wasn't as if she'd gained any space, and he knew for a fact the rent wasn't any cheaper because the Federation was still picking up half the bill.

Of course, he *should* have left the archives earlier. But if had, he wouldn't have found the journal. It had been written by a Vietnam vet back in the mid-twentieth century, at a time when the human race was still in semi-denial about the existence of 'nonhuman' races. Amongst its catalog of death and destruction, there was a brief description of a man who walked from the shadows and saved the soldier's life.

From the brief description given, it might have been easy to think the soldier had encountered a vampire, except for two facts. It happened at midday, and the stranger had walked into the flames surrounding the soldier and consumed them.

Vampires might not be killed by fire, but they certainly *were* killed by sunlight. Particularly midday sunlight.

So was the journal nothing more than the ramblings of a crazy man? Maybe. But he'd heard more than once that walkers *had* been used in the race wars. The fact he could find no hard evidence of it didn't mean it wasn't true. If the Government had used them in that war, why not in earlier wars? Later wars?

And what did the ability to consume fire say about the walkers? Fire-starters were one thing, but fire-eaters?

The sharp ring of the viaphone broke the silence and made him jump slightly. Which, he thought irritably, was just plain stupid. He leaned forward and pressed the receive button.

Illie's cheery features came on-line. "Hey boss, how's the day off going?"

"Great." He'd choose a day spent hunched over a com-screen over several hours of hot sex anytime. *Not.* Still, he could hardly complain when the decision had been his own. "What do you want, Illie?"

"Ran a background check on Kathryn Douglas. Nothing out of the ordinary, though it struck me as odd that a woman on her salary has so damn little in the bank."

"How little is little?"

"Just over fifty thou. Not much, when you consider what she makes in a year."

Gabriel frowned. "What about other assets? Stocks and such?"

"According to her broker, she's been selling steadily over the past year, though always at huge profits. The money's obviously going somewhere other than the bank."

"Boyfriend? Husband?"

"Currently, neither. Several of each in the past, but no alimony being paid."

Given her position, Douglas's earnings had to be in the high six figures. So what the hell was she doing with all her money? "I'll put a request through for full banking records. Did you get her home security tapes?"

"Yeah. She had one visitor last week who was not on the list of known associates. A bloke by the name of Les Mohern. Small time crim, petty theft, arson, that sort of stuff."

"So why is he associating with the likes of Douglas?"

"A question I thought I'd ask when I caught up with him."

"Good. Have you had any luck with the security guards who were on duty last night?"

"Contacted one so far. Wouldn't let us see him till tomorrow."

Until after he'd been briefed, perhaps? "What time?"

"Nine."

Great. He needed an early start after standing watch all damn night. "See you then."

Illie's grin was almost cheesy. "Sure will, boss."

Gabriel punched the off button and stared at the snail-paced traffic ahead. Les Mohern? He'd heard that name before. But where?

"Computer on," he said.

"ID required," the metallic voice intoned.

"AD Stern. Badge number 5019."

"Voice patterns correct. Please proceed."

"I want a search done on Les Mohern. All details."

"Search proceeding."

He glanced at his watch, and then resumed his steering wheel tapping. He was going to be late, no doubt about it.

"Details onscreen," the computer intoned after several minutes.

He studied the rap sheet. As Illie had said, Mohern had a long history of minor crimes. But it wasn't *him*, specifically, that he remembered, but his brother Frank. Like Les, Frank was a small time crim, but he'd also been listed as a source for Jack Kazdan, Sam's former partner.

That's where he'd seen the name before. Sam had purloined Jack's phone records and diary the day she'd been suspended from State under the suspicion of murdering him. Of course, it had been a clone she'd killed, a clone sent to test her, and it had been deemed self defense in the end. And Jack had still ended up dead—killed in the process of trying to kidnap the prime minister and replace him with a clone.

Frank Mohern was one of two phone calls Jack had made just before he'd disappeared.

Of course, Frank was now dead.

But why would someone like Les visit someone like Kathryn Douglas? Hell, she was more likely to be his target than his friend or even business associate.

He'd have to have a closer look at both the diary and the transcripts to not only find out why the Mohern brothers had been involved with Kazdan, but why Les might be involved with Douglass. He had an itchy feeling it just might provide some much needed clues as to what Douglass was *really* involved with at the Pegasus Foundation.

O'Hearn's green-glass office building came into sight. He took the car off autodrive, sped into a side street, and parked illegally. He flipped his ID onto the dash, just to ensure the car wasn't towed away, and ran the rest of the way to O'Hearn's office.

Karl was already seated on one of the waiting room sofas when Gabriel arrived. His bear-like frame dwarfed the seat. His blue Hawaiian shirt and the red and gold bandana restraining his brown hair looked totally out of place in the muted, soothing colors of the waiting room.

Sam wasn't in the room, but Finley, the SIU's resident research doctor, was.

"Didn't realize you were involved in this, Finley," he said, as he sat next to Karl.

"O'Hearn called me in." The young doctor pushed his thick glasses up the bridge of his nose. "Thought I might be able to sort out some of the test results."

"And did you?"

"Some." Finley cleared his throat. "Karl here proved to be of more use than me."

Gabriel raised an eyebrow and glanced at his friend. Karl merely smiled and patted Gabriel's knee.

"Wait until your pretty partner comes, then I will explain it all."

"You'd better." Gabriel stretched out his legs. "And she's not my partner."

"More the fool you, then," Karl said. When Gabriel glanced at him, he grinned and added, "Well, she's pretty and she's single, and you haven't exactly got a social life."

A mix of amusement and annoyance ran through him. He got this sort of lecture from his brother, his mom and his sister. He didn't need it from his friends as well. "And this is important to you because?"

"Because you're my friend, and I care about your emotional well being."

"I'd almost believe that if it wasn't for the insincerity in your voice."

Karl chuckled. "Well, let's just say that a man your age needs a good woman to look after him."

Gabriel raised his eyebrows. "A man my age? You make it sound like I'm an old man."

"Well, you are rolling rapidly toward the big four-o."

"Which is barely a baby in shapechanger terms, and you know it."

"I know it, but *you* try explaining it to my good wife."

Gabriel groaned. "Don't tell me she's plotting another

matchmaking session?"

"Well, it seems she has this second cousin who would be perfect—"

"Tell her I have a girlfriend I'm perfectly happy with."

Karl raised his eyebrows. "Really? You with a girlfriend? I'm just not seeing that."

"Depends on how you define the term 'girlfriend.'"

"Ah. A bed buddy." Karl nodded. "Not as good as the real thing, but a suitable decoy for determined matchmakers. She won't be put off for long, though. You know that, don't you?"

He opened his mouth to reply, but it was lost to a sudden buzz of awareness. Though perhaps buzz was the wrong word to use—it was more a flash fire that ran across his senses and then slid deep inside, seeming to warm his very soul. He glanced at the door as it opened. Sam stepped in, nodding a brief acknowledgment Finley's way before her gaze met his.

The awareness that burned his mind was more than one way now. He could see the flame of it in her eyes.

She stopped in the doorway and said, "What the hell are you doing here?"

He shrugged. "Karl asked me to come."

Her angry gaze switched to Karl. "Why?"

"Because you both need to hear what I have to say." He hesitated. "And I don't think either of you will like it."

Gabriel met Karl's gaze again and saw the compassion mingled with excitement in the brown depths. Something clenched in his gut. Whatever Karl had to say, it boded no good for *his* future.

"Fine. But that doesn't mean he comes into that room with me." She thrust a finger in the direction of O'Hearn's office. "My business is *not* his business."

"I'm afraid," Karl said heavily, "that in this case, it is."

Karl's comment left her looking more disgruntled than before. If *that* was possible.

Not that Gabriel could really blame her. Hell, the last few months hadn't exactly been easy for her, and here he was, the creator of many of those problems, sitting in on her medical reports.

It was a wonder she wasn't ranting and raving about the injustice of it all. He would have been doing so.

The door leading to the office opened and O'Hearn's matronly figure appeared. "We all here? Good. Why don't you come in and get yourselves something to drink?"

Sam walked straight to the autobar and ordered a double scotch. Gabriel did likewise. She raised her glass in a brief salute, and then downed half its contents before sitting on the chair nearest the window. Her hair gleamed like fire against the darkness gathering outside, but the rest of her seemed cloaked in shadows.

He sat on a chair opposite her. Not that he really needed to see her reaction to anything said here this evening, simply because he could feel them. The link that had sprung to life the minute she walked in the door had become a freeway of emotion. If it wasn't for the fact that he was so used to blocking his brother, the assault might have overloaded him.

Karl and Finley helped themselves to coffee and sat down on either side of him. O'Hearn leaned against the edge of her desk.

"Okay, I'll start this off," O'Hearn said. "I've managed to isolate code sequences from four other races—shifter, changer, vampire and were. But there was one I couldn't identify. I called in Finley, but he's been unable to define the sequences, either. Then there was the problem of the unknown chromosome."

"How can there be an extra chromosome?" Sam asked, her voice terse. "From what I understand of genetics, humans have forty-six chromosomes, and they work in pairs. So how can there be just one unknown chromosome?"

O'Hearn raised an eyebrow, as if surprised by the question. "Human's do have forty-six. Vampire's who were once human have forty-eight. Shifters have fifty, changers and were's fifty-two. If any of those become vamp, then they gain an extra pair of chromosomes. You, my dear, have fifty-five."

"Meaning what?" Sam crossed her arms. The gray ring around the blue of her eyes gleamed ice-bright in the quickly fading light. "You said you detected partial shifter-coding, but even with the extra chromosome that still only gives me a max of fifty-three."

Finley cleared his throat. "The two extra come from the vamp coding we found."

Gabriel frowned. "I thought you had to undergo the change to gain the extra chromosomes?"

"So did I." O'Hearn's voice was dry.

"Normally, yes," Finley said. "But in recent government

tests, vamp chromosomes have been successfully introduced into both pig and rat embryos."

Sam's face echoed the horror Gabriel felt. Government meddling with the very beginnings of life could never be a good thing.

"What the hell is the government doing that for?"

Finley shrugged. "Vampires have what humanity has long searched for. Life everlasting."

Sam snorted. "Yeah, but at what cost?"

"To some, the cost doesn't matter." Finley hesitated, frowning slightly. "Anyway, while we were trying to decode the unknown strands, I remembered my father once saying he worked with a man who could melt into shadows. Handy, when you were a member of covert operations. At the time, I thought my father meant a vampire, but since A.D. Stern here questioned me about the existence of Shadow Walkers, I began to wonder."

"So you questioned him?" Gabriel interrupted tersely. Finley had a tendency to ramble if left unchecked.

The young doctor nodded. "He confirmed the man was a walker. One of six the Australian military had on the payroll."

If they were on the payroll, why was there no record of them now? "What happened to them?"

Finley shrugged. "Dad wasn't sure. Seemed they disappeared after the race wars."

Sent to Hopeworth, perhaps? It was certainly a possibility, especially if Sam proved to have walker blood in her.

"Could he point you to anyone who might know more?"

"He did—to two men, actually. Robin Deleware and Frank Lloyd. Deleware died some three years ago, and Lloyd—"

"—is a General stationed at Hopeworth," Sam muttered. Her gaze met Gabriel's. "That man's name keeps reappearing."

And the reason behind Lloyd's interest in Sam was becoming clearer. "Lloyd's not likely to help us."

"No," Finley agreed. "But Deleware still might. It appears he was Karl's uncle."

"On my mother's side," Karl explained with a grin. "I inherited all his books when he died, you see. Among them were his journals."

Gabriel raised an eyebrow. "I thought personal journals were banned in covert operations?"

Karl's grin widened. "Rules are made to be broken, as you

should know."

Ignoring the jibe, he asked, "So what did the books reveal?"

"The answers, at least to some extent. It appears both Lloyd and my uncle were involved in the research side of operations. Walkers are mentioned extensively in three of his journals, and then they abruptly disappear."

Because the walkers themselves disappeared? Or was there a more sinister reason?

Sam shifted slightly on her chair, and her tension was a darkness that crawled through his mind. Her thoughts flashed like fire behind that darkness. He only had to reach out and he could be there, sharing them.

He didn't reach out. Didn't dare. He had a feeling that once breached, he would never again be able to raise the barriers that had protected him for so long against the psychic bond of his twin—and the more recent one he'd developed with Sam. "What did the journals say?"

"For a start, they noted that walkers had an extra chromosome, one that resembled an S. While it had no pair, it seemed able to fuse itself onto the X and Y pairings. To what purpose, we have no idea, but it's exactly what we've seen in Samantha."

"All of which means diddly-squat to me." She hesitated, drinking the remainder of her scotch in one quick gulp. "Nor does it really tell us what the hell walkers were."

Karl smiled. "I suppose it's hard to get excited if you're not a scientist. From what the journals say, walkers were not, in fact, human. Not even in the sense that changers and shifters are human. They are, in fact, an entirely new species, rather than a human offshoot."

Other than a slight leeching of color from her face, there was no immediate reaction from Sam. But her shock clubbed his mind, almost numbing in its intensity.

"Not human in what way?" she said, her voice soft and tightly controlled.

"They were elementals—the essence of nature itself. There were apparently four types—sun, earth, wind, and water."

"Then a sun elemental could, say, control a fire, even appear to swallow it?" Gabriel said, remembering the story he'd read in the archives. And a water elemental could control a storm, using the lightning as a weapon, as Sam had done.

Karl nodded. "Each walker was the master of his element.

Their ability to disappear into shadows came from the fact they were more energy beings rather than flesh. Vampires disappear into shadows by exerting psychic pressure on the human sense of sight, making it appear the shadows wrap around them. A walker merely lost his human shape, reverting to energy form."

Sam scrubbed a hand across her eyes. "So basically, what you're saying here is that *I'm* not human? That I never was?" She hesitated, swallowing heavily. "How is that even conceivable? I'm flesh and blood. I'm not made of energy, for Christ's sake."

"Sam, you have human elements in your coding, the same as a changer, a shifter, or even were." O'Hearn's voice was gentle, almost soothing. "But the dominant sector in your DNA seems to be what we presume is walker coding."

"If the walkers were all powerful, why even bother patching in changer or were coding? It's not as if I can shift or change." She scrubbed a hand through her hair, eyes a little wild.

She didn't want to be anything more than human, Gabriel realized. She might want to discover her past, but in many respects, she feared it. Or, rather, feared discovering just what she might be—and what she could do.

While that fear was totally understandable, if what O'Hearn was suggesting was true—and he had no doubt that it was—then it was more important than ever that they press forward on the quest to discover who had made her, and why.

Because not only was the military now interested in her, but someone far worse also held an interest. Sethanon.

"But you *can* channel the power of the storms," O'Hearn continued softly. "Which suggests, perhaps, that the walker strands *are* dominant in you."

"Meaning I'm likely to dissolve into darkness at any given minute?"

The silence seemed filled with sudden tension, and Gabriel wondered why.

Finley cleared his throat. "As a matter of fact, you have already begun to fade."

"What the hell are you on, Finley?" Gabriel snapped. Sam was sitting there, as plain as day, despite the darkness that had gathered in the office. He could see the fear in her blue-grey eyes, the whiteness of her knuckles as she clasped her hands in her lap.

O'Hearn and Karl shared a look. Karl waved a hand in Sam's direction. "You can see her?"

Stupid question—wasn't it? "Yeah." He frowned. "You honestly can't?"

"No," Karl said, and glanced at O'Hearn again. "It's as we thought."

"Yes." O'Hearn sighed.

Gabriel took a deep breath to calm a surge of anger. "Would you three kindly explain what the hell is going on?"

"Sorry, my friend. We just had to be sure." Karl held up a hand as Gabriel opened his mouth to make a retort. "My uncle's journal's had one very interesting side note about walkers. They came as a pair. Had to, apparently. If a walker does not have a base—someone to call them back, if you like—there is a huge risk of them becoming lost in the powers they seek to control."

Something cold washed through him. *You are her anchor, her reality,* Jes had warned. "I'm not a walker."

"No," O'Hearn agreed. "But I've talked to your father, and I checked your genetic background. It's highly possible that there is walker blood in your line."

"Meaning what?" The question came out harsh and was, in some ways, inane. He understood the implications clearly enough. He just didn't want to face them.

"Meaning," Karl said softly. "That's it's possible that you and Sam are destined to be a pair and there's not one damn thing either of you can do about it."

Six

Sam met Gabriel's gaze. Though there was absolutely no emotion on his face or in his hazel eyes, his horror washed through her mind like lava.

He'd spent half his life fighting a similar bond with his twin, and he was not likely to accept it with her.

Not that *she* wanted to be tied to anyone right now, either. Her social life might suck, but being alone was far better than being forced into the company of a man who didn't want to be there.

Damn it, why was *nothing* ever simple in her life?

Right now, she wasn't sure whether she should laugh or cry or rant at the heavens and fate itself for throwing so many spanners her way.

She glanced back to Karl. "What exactly did your uncle say about the walker pairing?"

Karl sipped his coffee, as if considering the question. Though it was more likely he was considering how to phrase his reply without upsetting anyone, she decided.

"He said it was destiny. That, in much the same manner as a shapechanger, they pair for life. They share thoughts, and to a lesser extent, powers, and even when apart, they know what the other is feeling or doing."

"Two halves of a whole," Gabriel murmured. But he wasn't looking at her, wasn't looking at anyone. His gaze was withdrawn, internal. He was seeing—remembering—things none of them were privy to.

And yet his words sent a chill through her. Joe had said that exact same thing more than once. And he certainly *hadn't* been referring to Gabriel and her.

"So, simply because Gabriel can see me when I fade into shadow, you're presuming he's my...What did you call it? Base?"

Karl nodded. "That, plus the fact you've formed a connection, despite Gabriel's efforts to stop it."

"A connection that is entirely one-sided, I assure you." Which was not exactly true, but damn it, she couldn't help fighting the finality of Karl's words. Life had thrown some pretty shitty things at her lately, but being stuck with a man who really didn't want her in his life had to be one of the worst.

And it didn't matter a damn just how much she was attracted to him. Being forced together would destroy any chance she had of changing his mind.

"Since your abilities are still in their growth stage, perhaps that is to be expected," O'Hearn said.

"Or it could be taken as a sign that you are way off course," Sam said.

"Maybe. But when you add the fact that Gabriel shares your pain when you've been injured, I think it's pretty conclusive." O'Hearn hesitated, her gray gaze eagle-sharp. "You might be interested to know that now that we've noted your fading, you've become solid."

"Subconscious reaction rather than conscious," Finley murmured. "Interesting."

She glanced down. Not that the lower half of her body looked any different now than it had a few minutes ago, when she'd apparently become one with the darkness. She met O'Hearn's gaze again. "If I do have walker genes that are beginning to assert themselves, then there's another possibility. Base wise, I mean."

O'Hearn frowned. "Who?"

She glanced at Gabriel. There was sudden stillness about him that spoke of...not shock, not anger, but a weird mix that was both, and yet not. Suddenly she wished she'd never spoken. Hell, she didn't even *know* who Joe was. He could be a mortal enemy of everyone in this room. *She* could be, for all she knew. She swallowed to ease the sudden dryness in her throat.

"I mean that I'm in telepathic contact with another man. Have been for months." Years. "He seems to know an awful lot about me, and he's said more than once that we're two halves of a whole."

Gabriel didn't move, didn't physically react. But his gaze burned into hers, and his tension washed through her mind. Tension, and something else, something she couldn't define.

"Who is this man?" His voice was soft, as devoid of emotion as his face.

It was a shame she couldn't say the same about the link they seemed to have developed. She rubbed her arms. "I don't know. He tells me his name is Joe Black, but it's an alias. There's no information on record for a Joe Black matching his description."

"Then you've met him?"

She hesitated. "Had coffee with him, in fact. He's a shapechanger. His other form is a crow."

"I see."

She had a horrible feeling crows had just made his hit list, which made no sense. Surely he should be happy that there was the possibility he wasn't her base. That there was someone else who might fill that roll. He didn't want ties of any kind. Not with his twin and certainly not with her.

O'Hearn cleared her throat softly. "You've never mentioned this before."

She shrugged. "Never thought it was important before."

The doctor glanced at Karl. "This puts an interesting spin on things. Did the journals mention anything else about the pairings?"

Karl shook his head. "Regretfully, no. As I said, the mention of the pairing was little more than a side note."

"Well, we certainly need to find out more about Mr. Black."

"Leave that to me," Gabriel said, his voice a monotone.

O'Hearn raised an eyebrow but didn't comment. "I'd also like to perform some tests with you both. See just how strong the connection is between you."

"We also need to perform tests," Finley added, "to define your psychic talents and strengths."

She frowned as his words bought back memories of the dream. Memories of being chained to a chair while the flames licked her face and the trauma and anger it had caused. The deaths *she'd* caused as a result.

If the dream was to be believed, that is.

But even if it wasn't, there'd been too many tests in her life already. She really didn't want to do any more. Yet, if she wanted answers, what other choice did she have? Still, that didn't mean she had to be an overly willing guinea pig, either.

"That might be difficult, given my current assignment."

Especially since whatever spare time she *did* have she wanted to spend down in Kingston fixing up her house, not hanging around either SIU's or O'Hearn's labs. As much as she wanted to discover who and what she was, she also longed to get on with her life. She'd already been in a holding pattern for far too long. For the first time, she actually had something she was *excited* about.

Besides, what was the point of discovering how strong the

connection between her and Gabriel was when he had every intention of fighting it?

"Surely you can spare an hour or so a day." Finley's tone suggested she was a fool if she didn't. But then, he was the poker, not the pokee.

"Maybe." She glanced at her watch. She was due to meet Wetherton at his office by six-thirty. If she left now, she'd not only make it there with time to spare, but she'd beat the storm brewing outside. And how she knew *that* without even turning around to look was something she didn't want to think about now. "Look, can we wrap this up soon? I really have to get going."

O'Hearn nodded. "Shall we book you both in for Friday then? After lunch, perhaps?"

She sighed. "Try three. That'll give me time to catch up on sleep after my shift."

The doctor nodded, her gaze on Sam's. Not meeting it, just *looking* at it. She raised an eyebrow and said, "What?"

"The blue in your eyes is receding as the night falls. The silver is growing brighter."

"There's a storm gathering outside," Karl commented. "If storms are her element, then that could be an indicator of power."

"Or maybe just a sign that it's easier to see the silver in my eyes at night." And yet, even though her back was to the window, the electricity of the oncoming storm danced across her skin, filling her with power, energy.

And *that* was simply scary.

She rose. "Let's continue this Friday, then."

"Gabriel, perhaps you'd better escort—"

She held up her hand, halting Karl before he could finish. "I'm a big girl now. I don't need a nanny."

"But the storm—"

"Is just a storm, like a thousand other storms I've walked through before without harm." Something clunked at her feet, and she looked down to see her phone had somehow fallen out of her pocket. As she reached down to pick it up, she noted the tiny sparks leaping from finger to finger. As if the storm's energy had filled her to overflowing.

She wrapped her hand around the phone, hiding her fingertips in the process. Maybe it was a stupid reaction since she was here to discover answers, but right now, she just wanted out. Wanted time to contemplate everything she'd been told—the worst of which was not the fact that she was something other than human, but rather, that she could be eternally tied to a man who wanted nothing to do with her.

She straightened and gave the watching scientists a tight smile. "I'll see you all Friday."

"Be careful," Karl said. "If you *are* a walker and the storm is your element, you could find yourself lost in its power without even realizing it was happening."

"The walker gene might appear dominant, Karl, but it is only one part," O'Hearn said. "Don't you think the nonhuman mix might mute its force?"

Karl shrugged. "Until we do more tests, we don't know."

"So, I'll be careful." She glanced at Gabriel. He didn't say anything, just looked at her, an annoyed light in the green-tipped hazel depths. Yeah, he was *really* pleased with the turn of events. She turned and walked out the door.

It wasn't until she stood outside the building that she stopped and took a long, shuddering breath. God, that was *so* not the result she'd been expecting. Hoping for.

It was finally confirmed. She *wasn't* human. She was something else. Something created in a lab somewhere and bought up in clinical surroundings. To what end? That was the question she had to seek an answer to, though her last dream was perhaps an indicator. Hopeworth had been playing in the genetic and psychic minefield for some time, trying to create the perfect soldier—the perfect weapon. Her dreams indicated that she'd begun training to control her abilities at a very young age.

But if the walker genes were strongest in her, did that mean she wasn't a product of Hopeworth? Her birth certificate—her *real* one, not the fake one that had been placed into the system the day she'd appeared on the steps of the State Care center for orphaned kids—gave the name of the eight people who were her "parents." None of them were walkers, but shifters and psychics.

So if she was a product of the Penumbra project, as they were all presuming, where in hell did the walker strain come from?

The "real" certificate could be a fake, of course. But she had confirmation of both the project and the people involved from a man and a woman who were at Hopeworth at the time of Penumbra. She even had confirmation—albeit from a woman with memory problems, about her presence there. But that same project had been totally—and perhaps a little conveniently—destroyed by fire, so there were no records available to confirm anything they were told.

The one person who might be able to shed some light on her confusion was the mysterious Joe. Every discussion she'd ever had with him had taken her just a little bit farther along her path of remembering. But how much could she really trust him? She knew even less about him than she did herself.

As she stood there, contemplating whether she should try and contact him, the heavens opened up. Big, fat, heavy drops of rain began to splatter across the pavement, quickly darkening the concrete inches away from her feet. Thunder rumbled, the sound so loud it seemed to rattle the air itself. Two seconds later, lightning split the sky, briefly turning the night as bright as day. The energy of that flash burned across her senses, as warm as the sun and as sharp as glass.

A tremor ran through her, but it wasn't fear. It was something far worse.

Excitement.

Pleasure.

As if part of her soul rejoiced in the storm's energy.

She rubbed her arms and warily stared at the skies. Maybe Karl was right. Maybe she should have an escort to Wetherton's...

Damn it, *no*. She'd been touched by the power of the storms before, had drawn it deep into her body. This storm was no fiercer than the one she'd used to help find Gabriel, and she'd walked away from that with nothing more than a brief bout of shakiness and exhaustion. If it hadn't affected her then, why was she acting like a Nervous Nelly now?

She wasn't sure. Maybe it was just Karl's warning. Or maybe it was the growing sensation—or rather, the expectation—that something was about to happen.

Something that *needed* to happen. Which made no sense at all.

She stared into the storm-held night for a few seconds longer, and then she resolutely dashed out into the thickness of it. The wind tore at her as she ran, making her stagger like a drunkard, and the rain fell so heavily that visibility was almost impossible. Her pants became plastered to her legs in an instant and her shirt clung like a second skin. Only in Melbourne could a day whose weather had started off so nicely do a complete one-eighty and become a bitch.

And, of course, the closest parking spot she'd been able to find near O'Hearn's office was a block and a half down the street. Wetherton's office wasn't that much farther beyond that. She might as well run all the way, because by the time she got to her car, she'd be soaked anyway. Besides, she wasn't likely to find parking any closer to Wetherton's office at this hour. There was too much traffic.

She ran down the street, jumping over puddles and barely avoiding other madly dashing pedestrians. Another flash of lightning ran across the stormy evening, and the power within it skipped across her skin, crackling like slivers of fire between her fingertips. Every breath she took sucked that energy inside her, until it felt as if it were surging through every pore, every fiber. Her whole body seemed more alive than it ever had been before.

It scared her. Terrified her.

And the fact that it felt so *right* made her fear even more.

Overhead, thunder rumbled again. The power of it echoed through her, a force that filled her to breaking, completing her in a way she couldn't even begin to understand.

Then the lightning hit.

It felt like a gigantic hammer, smashing into her head, driving through her body, snatching her breath, her strength, even as it knocked her down to the pavement. Her knees hit the concrete with a sickening crunch, but she felt no pain, had no awareness of anything going on around her, because everything had become white. It was as if she'd stepped beyond this world into a place of fierce brightness, in which nothing else existed but that light, and the power within it—and within her. The air itself burned with the intensity of that light, but not half as much as her skin.

And it felt *good*.

So very good.

Without thinking, she flung her arms wide, accepting the power burning around her, drawing it in even more. Flesh and bone seemed to burn away, until she was nothing more than a creature of energy, a being at one with the storm and the night and the intense heat of the lightning. And it called to her, that energy, wanted her, reaching for her like a lover might welcome a much missed partner.

She raised her face to the skies she couldn't see, torn by the need to answer that call, and the growing knowledge that something was wrong, that this wasn't good, no matter how good it actually felt.

"Samantha!"

The call ran around her—through her mind and past her ears. But it wasn't one voice, but two.

Samantha! You must resist. You are not grounded and will be lost. You cannot do this yet.

The internal voice was one she recognized. *Joe.* Always there when she needed help the most.

But the storm called her name, and the thought fled. She closed her eyes, and enjoyed the caress of the power as she raised her arms a little more.

No! You cannot lose yourself to the storm. It would kill us both.

His fear vibrated through her, briefly stalling the flow of energy swirling around her. But it was a voice, a *real* voice, hard and loud, that shook her more.

"Sam!" Hands appeared through the maelstrom of energy, their flesh almost black compared to the brightness of the lightning-fed power. They grabbed her arm, her hand, and a shock more explosive than the storm ran through her. Suddenly she could feel the chill of the wind, the splatter of rain across her face, the throbbing in her knees, and the ache in her mind.

And with that, the energy leapt away and returned to the heavens. The feeling of oneness was gone, the light was gone, and all that was left was weakness. Complete and utter weakness.

She fell forward into arms that were warm and solid and real, and she knew without looking that it was Gabriel. She didn't ask how he was there, or why he was there, and didn't particularly care. She simply rested in the security of his touch as her body trembled and she gasped for breath.

His grip tightened slightly, as if he'd felt her need for closeness. His warmth began to seep into her, heating her skin, leeching away the last vestiges of energy and making her feel "real" again rather than a creature of the storm. She closed her eyes, listening to the steady beat of his heart, feeling her own begin to echo its rhythm.

"Are you all right?" he asked, after awhile. His breath

caressed warmth across the top of her head and a tremor of desire ran through her.

Not a feeling she needed right now.

She nodded in answer to his question and pulled back. His grip moved to her shoulders, holding her steady and preventing her from totally drawing away. His gaze searched hers, the green in those hazel depths glowing like emerald fire, as if the storm had somehow empowered him, too.

"What the hell just happened?" he asked

She gave a shaky laugh and wiped a hand across her wet face. A useless gesture given the rain. "I now understand what Karl meant with his warning. And he was right."

He raised a hand and gently brushed bedraggled strands of hair from her cheek. She didn't see the point since the wind and the rain just flung them back, but she wasn't about to object, either. Call her weak, but his touch was too comforting. Too good.

"Then you called the storm to you?"

She shook her head. "It called me." She hesitated. "It felt so right, so damn pleasurable, like I was coming home to the arms of a lover long missed. It would have been very easy to get lost in that feeling, as Karl warned."

He frowned. "So what bought you back?"

"You did." She paused. "And Joe."

She'd half expected her answer to annoy or anger him, but he merely raised his eyes. "Both of us?"

"Yes. Joe contacted me, briefly halting the call of the storm. And then you touched me, loosening the storm's grip and bringing me back."

He studied her for a moment, and then said, "That would suggest that this mysterious Joe and I might both play a part as the position of base. And yet, according to what Karl has learned, there is only one base for a walker."

She blew out a breath, her gaze searching his. "You know, I thought you'd be pissed off about that—about possibly being my base, that is."

"I am, but there's no use raging against something I can do nothing about." He hesitated. "Besides, we still know very little about walkers as a race. Karl's journal may have proven useful so far, but it isn't as in-depth as we need it to be. Even *if* the dominant genes in you are walker, we will still be uncovering information and truths as we run through trials and experiments. And it is by no means certain that I *or* this Joe are your base. Nor is it certain that actually you need one."

If what had just happened was *any* indication, she did. But he knew that as much as she did. "But if it *is* true, you could end up tied to me. We both know you don't want that."

"I don't *need* that, true." He brushed his thumb down her cheek, lightly touching the corner of her mouth. Another tremor ran through her and, like before, it had nothing to do with the night or the rain or the fact she was drenched. He half smiled and added, "But if I have to be stuck with someone on a working level, then I guess I could do worse."

"Well, gee," she said dryly, glad the tremor running though her limbs wasn't evident in her voice, "that is such an overwhelmingly sentimental statement that I might just cry."

He chuckled softly and dropped his hand to her shoulder again. "Look, I've been a bastard the last few months, and I will undoubtedly be a bastard again in the future. I don't want a partner, be it you or the idiot they've now assigned me. I play solo. I *have* to. It's not personal."

"None of which is answering my original concern."

"I know." His touch left her shoulders as he sat back on his heels, and the night suddenly felt colder. "It's not that I don't want any sort of connection with you—"

"It's just that you're afraid of it," she finished for him.

A wry smile touched his lips. "Not afraid. Just wary. The more people in my life that I care about, the more targets I give my enemies."

"That doesn't mean we can't be friends." Nor did it mean he cared about her. Damn it, she wasn't even sure if he was physically attracted. His touch here tonight may have been nothing more than concern for a workmate. And she couldn't take the word of his sister to heart. After all, most families weren't above a bit of matchmaking if they felt the mix was right.

Not that she had firsthand experience of families and their habits, having never had a family herself. But she'd seen it often enough in her years as a cop, observing from the sidelines the interplay between her workmates and their families.

He rose to his feet in one smooth, almost elegant, gesture and held out his hand. "I think we'd better get out of this storm."

Which was a neat way of avoiding her question and not committing himself one way or another.

"We're drowned rats anyway, so it doesn't much matter whether we stay here or not." But she gasped his warm fingers and let him help her up.

Pain slithered up her legs as she rose. She glanced down, and saw the rents in her pants and the scrapes on her knees. She must have hit the concrete harder than she'd thought. "Oh great. This is going to make such a wonderful first impression."

"As far as first impressions go, you can't get much better than saving the man's ass last night. Even if you weren't supposed to be there."

"If I hadn't been, all of Stephan's carefully laid plans would have gone to hell." She plucked material from the wound on her left knee. Though the worst of the two, the wound wasn't deep, just nasty looking. "And besides, Wetherton was out of it when his ass was hauled out of that car. He probably remembers zip about my involvement. Especially since Brigg's handled all the follow up interviews with the man." Mainly because *she'd* been getting raked over the coals by Stephan for shooting their suspect.

"What time were you supposed to be at Wetherton's?" he asked.

She grimaced and glanced at her watch. "I start at six-thirty, but I'd like to get there just after six and look around."

"Which leaves time enough to buy a change of clothes, if you want."

"Could be a good idea. Wetherton doesn't seem the type to be impressed by drowned rats."

He grinned as he took her arm and began guiding her down the street. "Wetherton is the type to be impressed with anything that has breasts and a figure. Even drowned, I think you'd qualify."

She raised an eyebrow and looked up at him. "Have you had a personality transplant or something?"

His grin faded into a grimace. "No. But I saw that lightning hit you, and I guess I'm just relieved to see you're unharmed."

"Oh, I bet it hurt admitting that."

"I'm not an ogre, despite what my behavior may have made you believe."

"So you're saying the ogre actually does have feelings?"

"Very occasionally." He gave her a half smile, but there was a seriousness in his eyes that suggested his words were more a warning. "It doesn't mean that you—or anyone else—

will see the other side all that often. I will never again get more than casually involved with someone."

"Sounds like you're setting yourself up for a very lonely old age, Assistant Director."

"If I make it to old age, I'll worry about it then." He paused. "What can you tell me about this Joe?"

Meaning the subjects of his emotions and his life were officially closed—for now, at least. She shrugged. "He's been around for a while. He mostly used to talk to me in dreams, but lately we've been in contact through direct telepathic thought. He seems to know a lot about my past."

"And have you questioned him about his identity?"

"Of course. He's more than a little cagey." She shrugged. "There is a connection between us, a bond that goes beyond telepathy. I just don't know what that is as yet."

"Could he be another of Hopeworth's rejects?"

She glanced at him. "We're not actually sure that I'm a reject yet."

"No." He paused. "Is he military?"

She remembered the time they'd had coffee. Remembered the way he walked, the military-like alertness. "If he isn't now, I'd say he has been."

"Could you do a sketch of him? That way, we could search military records and see if we find a match."

"Hopeworth is not likely to allow a search of their personnel—past or present."

He raised a dark eyebrow. "You think he's Hopeworth?"

"Yeah. Everything else seems to be tied back to that place. I can't see why he wouldn't be."

"If that's the case, he might be a means of keeping an eye on you."

"And yet Hopeworth seemed to have no interest—no idea that I even existed—until I contacted them over the Generation Eighteen murders."

They reached the department store. As the front doors swished open, he ushered her through. The air in the store was so warm it felt like they'd stepped into a sauna. She resisted the urge to strip off her soaked sweater and dripped water all over their shiny floors as she made her way towards the women's section.

"That could be because all evidence of the Penumbra project was destroyed," he said, watching as she sorted through the racks of clothing.

"Or it could mean that I was never a part of that place, and came from somewhere else."

He raised an eyebrow again. "Do you believe that?"

"No." They might not have gotten a whole lot of concrete information about the project or her part in it, but the little they *did* have was convincing enough. Plus, there was now the fact that—according to O'Hearn and all the tests done so far— she wasn't human. And not only wasn't she human, she wasn't a creation of nature, either. Which invariably led to the conclusion that she *had* to be lab-created.

Fact was, there weren't many labs around capable of a supporting such a long-term commitment like developing a being. Timewise *or* moneywise.

Only the military. And perhaps other covert government departments they didn't know about.

Her search through the racks eventually turned up suitable pants, a warm sweater, shoes and a hooded, waterproof jacket. Once she'd paid for them, she went into the dressing room, stripped off her soaked clothes and redressed. After brushing her hair, she almost felt human again. Although *that* term was apparently relative when it came to her.

"The drowned rat has disappeared," Gabriel noted, his gaze sweeping her as she came back out. "Though I bet Wetherton would have preferred the wet—and therefore see through— blouse to the bulky sweater."

"If that old lecher comes near me, I'm going to punch him out." She held out the plastic bags of wet clothes for him to hold while she donned her jacket. Now that she was beginning to warm up, she didn't want to step outside and get drowned again.

"And wouldn't that get the two of you off on the right foot."

"Well, at least he'd know the boundaries."

His smile faded. "Be careful with Wetherton. He might be a Hopeworth plant, or he might be one of Sethanon's, but either way, he's going to be dangerous."

She zipped her coat, pulled up the hood and grabbed her bags back. "Is that why you've placed a twenty-four hour watch on me?"

He had the grace to look guilty. But only briefly. "How did you find out?"

She snorted softly. "I've been a cop for more years than I care to remember. Why on Earth would you think I *wouldn't* notice a tail?"

She pushed the door open and stepped back into the storm-held night. The wind seemed even stronger than before, buffeting her sideways until Gabriel touched her arm and steadied her. But unlike before, the power in the storm seemed muted. She could feel it, but it was distant, no more than an electric murmur in the background.

But one that could sharpen instantly given the slightest provocation.

"I had very experienced people following you," he said, as the doors swished shut behind them. "I just didn't think you'd spot them so quickly."

"Those experienced people were your sister, her husband and sometime in the next twenty-four hours would have been you." She squinted up at him. "Did you actually plan to sleep anytime?"

His hazel eyes met hers, the green-tipped depths showing little in the way of emotion. The caring, sharing version of Gabriel Stern she'd enjoyed for the last few minutes had all but disappeared. This version she knew all too well.

"I'm a changer. We can survive on very few hours of rest," he said.

"Not over a long-term period."

"I was hoping it wasn't going to be long-term."

"Ah." She glanced ahead, noting with a little annoyance that Wetherton's office building was less than half a block away. "And if it was?"

"I would have dealt with the problem when it arose."

Which was not every practical. Though surely it was a sign he cared far more than he was admitting? Or was it simply that he had no intention of losing her until he knew what she was capable of and how they might use her growing abilities for the benefit of the SIU and the Federation?

And why did she even care? Hadn't she just made a resolution to stop centering her life around her work and her partners?

Trouble was he'd touched her. Brushed the hair from her face and ran his fingers down her cheek to her lips. And those two actions had her long-ignored hormones dancing.

From the very beginning she'd been attracted to him, and

while they might not have shared anything more intimate than a brief hug, that attraction still flared up at the slightest provocation.

No matter how annoyed or how angry she might be with him, it appeared that the attraction wasn't going to go away. Ignoring it might work in the long run, but only if she wasn't seeing him regularly. As long as he was still in her life, she was stuck with it.

And since *he* obviously wasn't going to pursue it, maybe she should just bite the bullet and do as Jessie suggested. Become the hunter.

Could she do it?

She didn't know. She'd never actually pursued *any* man, whether it was for sexual or emotional pleasure. Which wasn't to say she hadn't indulged in either—she had, and had enjoyed herself immensely. But in the past, she'd always allowed men to do the pursuing, and she always knew going in that neither the man nor the relationship—however good or emotional it felt at the time—would last.

Why she'd always been sure of that she couldn't honestly say. Nor could she say why she was so sure that her attraction to Gabriel was more than just the natural attraction of a female to a sexy male.

Maybe it had something to do with the walker gene and the bond that might be between them. Maybe it didn't.

Maybe it was nothing more than wishful thinking on her part.

Either way, perhaps asking herself if she *could* pursue him wasn't the right question in the first place. Maybe what she *should* be asking was, what did she actually want from him? What did she expect? Just another good time? Just another emotionally satisfying month or two in her life?

No.

Whatever this thing was between them, it definitely felt bigger than that. Which in turn meant she was expecting something more than a month or two of mutual pleasure. Something deeper that just caring.

But given his stance against any emotional commitment in his life, wasn't she just setting herself up for heartache? If he could keep his twin—his own flesh and blood—at arm's length, what made her think she'd be any different?

So maybe that was the *real* question she needed to ask

herself. Was she ready to face that heartache if it went belly-up? And could she live with it, face being around him day in and day out if it was proven that he was, in fact, her base?

Probably not.

But maybe she had to try, anyway. Because surely it was better to attempt a relationship on her own terms, in her own time, than to be forced into it by genes and fate.

At the very least, if she seriously tried now to start something happening between them that went beyond civil friendship and duty, she'd know whether the attraction went both ways. Which was far better than realizing sometime down the road that he was only with her because he had no other choice.

Freedom of choice was important, no matter what fate and the future planned for them both.

"Earth to Sam. Are you still with me?"

She blinked and looked up at him. "What?"

"I've been talking to you for the last few minutes. Did you hear anything I've said?"

"Ummm...no. Did you say anything important?"

He rolled his eyes. Amusement touched his lips, yet his concern whipped around her, as chill as the wind, and his grip on her arm tightened a little. "The storm calling again?"

"Not really." She shrugged. "Just thinking about Wetherton and how little I actually want this assignment."

"Then why accept it? You have the choice to refuse, you know."

She stopped and turned to face him. "How could I *not* accept it? At least it got me out of the broom closet and let me do some real police work. You're not the only damn one who hates being confined indoors, Assistant Director."

He grimaced. "You know why I was doing that—"

"Yeah, you're an ass who would rather force an unwanted situation to go away than being upfront and talking about it. Cowardice is not something I would have associated with you, but I guess I was wrong."

Anger flicked through his eyes. "I had no choice in taking you on as a partner. And the only way the situation could be changed is if you requested a transfer."

"So why not come out and say that straight off the bat? Between the two of us I'm sure we could have come up with a strategy that would have changed Stephan's mind. But oh no, you found it easier just to stick me down in the dungeons and ignore me."

He thrust a hand through his wet hair. "Damn it, I was doing what I thought was right—"

"What was easier for you," she corrected. "You knew it wasn't right, or you wouldn't have apologized for being a bastard. Or didn't you mean that apology?"

"I did—"

"Prove it."

He raised his eyebrows. "How?"

"Take me out to dinner. To a nice, expensive restaurant."

"And how, exactly, will that prove I meant my apology?"

He looked a little confused, which was good. Because she had a feeling confusion was a state she'd have to keep him in if she was going to get anywhere with her plan of seduction.

Not that she specifically had a plan. Right now, she was just jumping at an opportunity which had presented itself.

"Well, in the brief time I've known you, you haven't exactly been free and easy when it comes to money. And word around the office is that you're a first class tight-ass—"

"It is?" he asked, his surprise evident in his voice.

"Yes. So, if you go to the trouble of buying me dinner at an expensive—and I do stress the word *expensive*—restaurant, then you're putting your money where your mouth is. And that, in turn, means you really are sorry." She couldn't help the smile playing around her lips. "In that case, your apology will be graciously accepted."

"This sounds to me like a sneaky method of getting a high class meal without having to pay for it."

"Are you saying I don't deserve it? Even after your harsh treatment over the last few months?"

"No. I'm just saying that this will be a one-time apology. Don't be expecting future apologies." He paused. "Or dates."

"I'm not after a date, Assistant Director, not now *or* in the future. I don't date men I work with." Which was true, up to a point. She'd certainly never dated Jack, her partner in the State Police, though she *had* dated coppers in other divisions over the years. Just not those in the areas where she worked. She raised an eyebrow, silently challenging him to answer honestly. "Why would you think I'm after a date with you? Especially after the way you've treated me over the last few months."

He didn't take up the challenge. No surprise there. "I have

no idea." He motioned her to move on. As she did, he added, "So, dinner at an expensive restaurant. When?"

She shrugged. "I'm on the night shift, so it'll have to be during the day."

"Lunch? How about tomorrow, then?"

"Get the ordeal over with as quickly as possible, huh?"

He smiled but didn't deny it. Boy, was she ever going to have some fun attempting to shock this man's starched sensibilities. She might end up in tears, but at least the journey would be interesting.

"Give me a call when you finish your shift tonight," he said. "We can make arrangements then."

She glanced ahead and saw that Wetherton's office was only two doors away. Damn. She looked back to Gabriel. "Who's watching me tonight?"

He hesitated, and then said, "Alaine."

"After which?"

"Jessie takes over. Though since we now might be having lunch, I'll probably step in and let her rest."

"You're expecting a bit much of your sister and her hubby, aren't you? They have their own lives to live, too."

"No one in my family has their own life. Everything revolves around the Federation."

The edge of bitterness is his voice surprised her, but she didn't question him about it. He wouldn't tell her anything. When it came to family, he was tighter than a clam. "But I'm not involved in this Federation of yours."

Hell, even though she knew the historical facts about the Federation's origins—that it was formed to protect the political and legal interests of nonhumans after the war of the races— she had no idea what it truly did these days. Though the few things he had said about it suggested that not only were they still very much involved in protecting the interests of nonhumans, but they were also some kind of undercover, independent "spy" agency.

His gaze met hers briefly. "No, but who you are, and what you are, might very well affect the Federation and its operations in the future. So, in that respect, you come under Federation interest."

"So why hasn't Stephan assigned other—" She paused, remembering what Jessie had told her. The urge to grin was almost overwhelming, but she somehow kept a straight face.

Which didn't mean she could resist the temptation to pull his chain a little. "He doesn't know you've assigned me guards, does he?"

"No."

"So, you're having me guarded twenty-four hours a day against your brother's direct orders, but you refuse to admit there might be anything more than professional interest in that?"

He glanced at her. "That's about it."

Anger rose so fast she could barely restrain it. He *knew* there was something between them, something that needed to be sorted out. Something that was more than just a possible connection due to DNA. Why couldn't he give her at least *that* tiny crumb of admission, even if he never intended to chase it?

"You're so full of shit, Assistant Director, that it's almost scary." She stopped as they reached the front of Wetherton's office building. "Call off your guards or I'll call Stephan and let him know what you're up to."

Annoyance flashed through his eyes. "But Hopeworth—"

"You know what?" she cut in, "I don't care if either Hopeworth or this mythical Sethanon *are* after me. Let them come, and we can finally sort out all this mess."

"But if they grab you, we may not be able to find you let alone rescue you. The whole Wetherton operation last night went to hell. It's possible this will too."

"Your brother isn't a complete fool. I have trackers inserted, so they can find me no matter where I'm taken." She paused and thrust her hands on her hips. "I want it all over with as soon as possible. I just want to get on with my life."

"But the danger—"

"Walking across the street during rush hour is dangerous, but I do that every damn day to get to work. Back off, Assistant Director. If you wanted to be involved in this operation—and my life—you shouldn't have pushed me away."

"That is beside the point in this situation."

"No, it's not," she said quietly. "I have no desire—and no need—to be baby-sat. Especially when that person isn't courageous enough to get over the past and get on with his life."

With that, she turned around and walked into the building.

Seven

Gabriel swore softly as Sam walked away. No one looking at her slender figure right now would guess at the steel and determination hidden within her slight frame.

Or the depth of sheer, damn foolhardiness.

There was a *huge* difference between acting as bait and walking into a situation seriously underprepared. No matter what she or Stephan thought, she *couldn't* handle this sort of job alone. There were just too many angles they could neither guess at nor cover.

As for her last jibe, where the hell did she get off telling him he's cruising through life when she was basically doing the same thing? God, at least he had a family...

He stopped the thought. That was hardly fair. And she couldn't be blamed for her reluctance to have backup when her past was a blur. She'd been abandoned as a teenager and, for all intents and purposes, had grown into adulthood alone. She'd spent half her life having few friends and depending on no one but herself. It wasn't entirely surprising that she was rejecting his offer of help now.

What was surprising was the fact that she still wanted to see him socially, even after all he'd done to her.

He blew out a breath, and then he spun on his heel and hitched the collar of his jacket up in an attempt to stop the rain dripping down his neck as he walked across the road. He'd spotted Alain as he'd followed Sam from O'Hearn's office earlier, and the big man had been their distant shadow ever since. He was glad Sam hadn't spotted Alain. Undoubtedly, that would have made the situation worse.

Lightning split the wet darkness, a blinding, ragged streak whose power seemed to echo right through him. He frowned. When he'd stepped out into the storm earlier, he'd felt the energy in the night. It was a sensation similar to walking underneath high-voltage power lines—the crackle of electricity was very audible, and static had caressed his hair and skin. If he *had* been standing under high-voltage lines, and if he *were* stupid enough to climb the pylons, he could have touched all that power, feel it running through him. And die in the process.

The storm had felt like that. Power that was enticing and dangerous. Power he could reach out and touch if he wanted to. Power that would kill him if he tried.

He glanced at his hands. There were no burn marks, despite the fact he'd shoved them into the middle of the lightning strike. Neither he nor Sam had been hurt, and that in itself was a miracle.

Or maybe it wasn't. Maybe it was just another sign that Karl was on the right track. She'd used the storms before, and she was certainly no stranger to the power of them running through her. Maybe touching her had somehow protected *him*.

Or maybe, as Karl had stated, she and he had a bond in which the storms were a major component—one they couldn't yet understand, and maybe never would.

For someone who didn't want bonds of any kind, he seemed to be gaining more than his fair share. And there wasn't much he could do to stop it. Ignoring the bond—and trying to push her away—certainly hadn't worked so far.

Actually, he pretty much suspected that despite her words to the contrary, he'd only made her more determined to explore what might lie between them.

And he wasn't actually sure how he felt about that.

He didn't *want* bonds of any kind. He'd been telling himself that for half his life. Yet, part of him now hungered for it. Hungered for the closeness his brother and sisters had.

Maybe the lightning *had* affected him. Short circuited a brain wire or two.

He hurried inside the small café where Alain had propped. His brother-in-law sat at a table to the left of the entrance, out of immediate sight but with a full view of the road and Wetherton's building. Gabriel took off his coat and shook it out as he walked over. Droplets of moisture scattered over the nearby chairs and tables, but since the café was almost empty, it didn't really matter.

"Ordered you a coffee," Alain said, sliding one of two steaming cups across the table.

"Thanks." Gabriel slung the coat over the spare chair and sat down. "You saw what happened?"

Alain nodded. "It was pretty damn scary, too." He glanced down, his gaze skimming Gabriel's hands. "You don't appear to be suffering any side effects from the strike. How did Sam fair?"

"Much the same." He shrugged, not wanting to get into explanations when he really didn't have them. "We have a bigger problem."

"What?"

Alain picked up his coffee and sipped it, but there was the faintest touch of amusement in his brown eyes. Which, knowing the man as well as he did, suggested to Gabriel that his next comment would come as no surprise. "Sam knows we're following her. She wants you both called off or she'll call in Stephan."

"So what are you planning to do?"

"Nothing. I want you and Jes to keep watching as planned. Except for tomorrow. I'll take over the day shift."

"Will she go through with her threat if she sees us?"

"Most likely, so you need to be careful."

Alain raised a bushy eyebrow. "Stephan will not be happy if he discovers what we're doing."

"Undoubtedly." Gabriel picked up his coffee and gulped down some of the steaming liquid. "But I don't care."

"So, basically, you're saying the only thing you *do* care about is Sam's safety." Alain paused, a grin stretching his lips. "One could take that as an indication of emotional interest."

"Or professional interest. Especially if she proves to be our link to Sethanon."

Alain put down his cup and crossed his arms. "And do you believe that she is the link? After all these years of successfully avoiding us, do you seriously think Sethanon will come out of hiding for one scrap of a woman?"

"Seriously? Yes."

"Why?"

"Because I don't believe he would have placed a watch on her if she was of no use to him."

"True." Alain paused. "But he might have intended to cultivate her, as he had her partner."

"No. Kazdan's orders where to watch her, keep her safe. That implies interest, not cultivation."

"And yet Kazdan was trying to recruit her."

"For himself, for his own takeover bid. Not for Sethanon."

"You can't be sure of that."

Yes, they could, because that's exactly what Kazdan had told Sam. She believed it, and so did he. Still... "We can't be sure of anything until we know for sure who she is and where she came from."

"Is that why you won't admit to feeling anything for her?"

Gabriel snorted softly. "No. I'm not admitting anything because there is nothing to admit." And even if *that* wasn't the entire truth, even if there *was* destined to be a bond between them, he'd successfully contained the link with his twin and he had every intention of doing the same with Sam. No matter how much a part of him might wish it otherwise.

Truth was, while he couldn't deny his attraction—at least to himself—he would *not* break his long ago vow to never get involved. He wouldn't do that to someone ever again. And if, as Jessie predicted, he became a sad and lonely old man, so what? He could at least rejoice in the fact he'd actually lived long enough to become sad and lonely. That another human being hadn't been killed simply because being involved with him made them a target.

"So," Alain said thoughtfully, "that look of horror and panic on your face when she was hit by lightning had absolutely no emotional basis whatsoever?"

"None at all." He couldn't actually remember much about that moment, because when the lightning hit her, it had echoed through him, burning away all thought and emotion. He'd reacted instinctively, without really knowing what he was doing or saying until his hands had touched her.

But before he could actually reply further, his viaphone rang. He said a silent prayer of thanks for the timely intervention. No matter how he'd answered Alain, his brother-in-law would have twisted his words.

He retrieved his phone from his coat pocket, and hit the receive button. "Agent Stern."

"Hey Boss." Illie's usually cheerful expression looked subdued. "We've got a problem."

"Just one? That would be a minor miracle." Gabriel rubbed his eyes wearily. "What's up?"

"You remember Kathryn Douglass?"

"It was only yesterday that we visited the Foundation, Illie. I may be older than you, but I am not senile."

His would-be partner snorted. "Yeah, well, the SIU just received a call from the State boys. It appears Kathryn Douglass has been murdered."

"What?"

"Yeah. Happened last night, at her home. State boys called us because there was no entry or exit point to the scene. They're saying there's obviously nonhuman involvement."

"I'll meet you there—" He glanced at his watch. "—in fifteen minutes. Did you manage to interview the foundation's security guards?"

"Still no dice. But I did find out some more interesting

information about Douglass's bank accounts."

"Fill me in at the scene."

"Be there in fifteen." Illie hung up.

Gabriel looked at Alain. "I've been called to a murder scene. Make sure you keep out of Sam's sight."

Alain gave him a grin that held very little humor. "I've been doing this for more years than she's been alive."

"Yeah, but she's a whole lot cleverer than most of our usual targets." He drained his coffee and stood. "If anything happens, call me immediately."

"Don't worry. I won't let anything happen to your lady."

Gabriel didn't dignify the comment with an answer. Just turned around and headed back out into the weather.

* * *

Sam leaned against the elevator wall and watched the numbers roll by. Wetherton, despite his supposed fear of heights, had moved his office from the third floor to the twenty-fifth floor, claiming a good third of the top floor's expensive floor space for his board room, office and waiting area. If anyone in the government or press thought this was outrageous, they weren't saying anything. Maybe they were just so used to the excesses of government ministers they simply didn't bother questioning it anymore.

Or maybe Wetherton was simply paying off the right people. It certainly wouldn't be the first time something like that had happened.

The elevator stopped and she walked out. The standard blue carpet in the lobby area gave way to a plusher, more luxurious plum once she'd pushed through the doors leading into the minister's office.

A buxom blonde looked up and gave her a practiced but totally false smile. "Good afternoon. How may I help you?"

Sam dug out her badge and showed it to the woman. "Samantha Ryan, SIU. I have an appointment to see the Minister."

"Ah, yes. If you'll just have a seat, I'll let him know you're here."

The blonde picked up the phone. Sam sat on the nearest pale lemon couch and let her gaze roam. The first thing she noticed was the security camera in the corner to the left of the reception desk. It was pointed at her rather than the doorway, meaning someone was probably watching her.

Or maybe *all* visitors were watched this intently. Paranoia surely had to become a fixture in the life of a man who was a clone rather than the real thing.

Or did the clone actually *think* he was original? Certainly Jack's clone had thought and acted like the real Jack—though she didn't know how that was possible. Even if they were genetically identical, surely the way they'd been raised—in a lab rather than in a loving environment—would cause basic differences in thought and behavioral patterns.

How could a clone ever think the same way as the original when their life experiences were so drastically different? They couldn't, surely. Unless, of course, someone had succeeded in transferring memory and personality. Or, even more unlikely, whole brain matter. Though the original Wetherton *had* been intact when it came to brain matter—it said so in the report.

So, how could *this* Wetherton survive so long without someone close to him realizing something was drastically wrong? Or, at least, realizing he was drastically *different?*

It was certainly a line they needed to explore. Particularly since it was obvious that whoever was making these clones had successfully traded one of his creations for an original, and had tried to do the same with the prime minister himself. If Sethanon was involved with Hopeworth, as Gabriel and the Federation presumed, then these clones and the attempts to replace government ministers wasn't going to end here.

She let her gaze move on, studying the two other doors leading off this main room. One was a standard door, the other a double set with plusher handles. Wetherton's office, obviously.

But as her gaze rested on those doors, the feeling hit. A wash of heat, followed by the certainty that there was a shifter inside—a shifter whose very essence felt malevolent.

A tremor ran through her. Not so much because of the thick sensation of evil, but because she'd felt this particular baseness before.

In her dreams of Joshua and fire.

The man with the gray eyes was in that room with Wetherton.

Her heart accelerated at the thought and her stomach began to churn. She licked her lips and tried to get a grip. Damn it, she'd seen gray eyes last night, had even interacted with him, and she hadn't felt anything *close* to this.

So why now, and not then?

It didn't make sense. Maybe her psychic wiring had been short circuited by the lightning strike. Or maybe there'd been too much other shit happening last night and she simply hadn't had the time to notice psychic sensations.

"The minister won't be too long," the blonde secretary said into the silence.

She jumped, just a little, but managed to fake a smile of thanks. God, this was ridiculous. Anyone would think she was a green trainee, not a cop with years of experience behind her. She crossed her legs, tapping her foot impatiently as she waited.

After another five minutes or so, the doors opened and two men walked out, both of them wearing that happy-to-have-met-you smile that was obviously as fake as the secretary's.

Gray eyes was dressed in military blue that made his silver hair stand out all the more. Just watching him, watching the calm, assured way he moved had the sensation of evil sharpening, until it felt as if her entire body burned with his wrongness. Looking at him was making her physically ill, but she wasn't entirely sure whether it was a result of psychic distaste or a reaction leftover from her dreams.

Wetherton stuck his hand out to gray eyes and said, "I'll certainly mention your concerns when the matter comes up in parliament, General Blaine. Thank you for speaking with me today."

General Blaine? It wasn't a name she'd heard mentioned in relation to Hopeworth *or* her, but then, given the security surrounding the military base and its projects—old or new—that wasn't really surprising.

So was Blaine one of the scientists involved in the Penumbra project, as her dreams seemed to indicate? If so, how had he escaped the fire that had killed nearly everyone else?

And why was there no sign of a cut or burn marks on the left side of his blunt features? Last night, when he'd climbed out of the car with the woman, the wound on his head had appeared nasty—and if the amount of blood that had been pouring down his face was anything to go by, it had been deep. Wounds like that didn't disappear overnight. Not without a trace, anyway. Shapeshifters and shapechangers *did* have the ability to heal wounds fast—it came as a side benefit of what they were—but even they were usually left with scars.

Her gaze flicked to Wetherton. His spud-like face bore several nasty scrapes, and he had an egg-sized lump near his right temple. No anomalies there, at least.

Gray eyes nodded and shook Wetherton's offered hand. "I

appreciate that, Minister. The military cannot afford to have our funds cut for the third year in a row. Several projects vital for national security could be in jeopardy if they are."

"I'll put your case forward, General. I can't promise more than that at this time."

Blaine nodded and turned for the exit doors. His gaze met hers as he was walking out and he paused. Deep in those gray, soulless depths, she saw surprise. Maybe even shock.

The sort of shock that came when you suddenly and unexpectedly met someone you knew but hadn't seen for a very long time.

Which again, didn't make sense, given the events of last night. If he *did* recognize her, did know her from the projects, why hadn't he reacted last night?

"Do we know each other?" he asked, eyes narrowing slightly.

Yeah, she wanted to say. *I helped save your ass last night.* But something inside stopped her from uttering the words. Instead, she simply said, "I don't believe we do."

He stepped closer. She resisted the urge to sink back into the sofa. This close, the feel of his evil was so strong her insides felt like they were trying to claw their way out and her stomach just about jumped up her throat.

"Are you military? Ex-military?"

Energy crawled around her body, her mind, a sensation wholly different to the evil of his soul but just as sickening. That pressure seemed to build around her, as if the energy was trying to crawl into her mind. Telepathy, she realized. He was trying to read her thoughts.

And while the fact that she couldn't actually feel him *in* her mind suggested he wasn't having any immediate luck, she wasn't about to give him the time to succeed, either.

"No, I've never been in the military, General." She rose, retrieved her badge from her pocket, and flipped it out for him to see. "Samantha Ryan, SIU. If you have questions, please ask them. I do not appreciate your mind reading efforts."

"Mind reading?" Wetherton said, voice all bluster despite the quick flick of concern he cast the general's way. "This office is fully shielded against such events, so I think you must be mistaken, Agent Ryan."

"No," she said, her gaze not leaving Blaine's. "And shielding is not always one hundred percent effective."

Wetherton's expression didn't give much away, but she

had the distinct feeling, just from the way he was looking at the general, that the news the general could mind read horrified him. Which meant that maybe Wetherton *did* have secrets he had no wish for the military to uncover. It also meant that there was a whole lot more going on here than what Stephan and the SIU presumed.

The general's smile was slow and cold. "No, psi shields are never one hundred percent effective. But you are wrong, Agent Ryan. I was not trying to read your thoughts."

So what the hell *had* he been trying to do? She shoved her badge back into her pocket, and decided to tackle Blaine head on. "So, General, do you work in the same division as General Frank Lloyd?"

He raised his eyebrows. "You know General Lloyd?"

"Yeah. Had a very brief conversation with him about some former military employees that were getting murdered."

"Ah yes, the retired scientists."

"And the retired specimen donors. Don't suppose you know anything more about the projects they were involved in, do you?"

"No. I was never involved in that side of operations."

"Then what were you involved in?"

"Why do you wish to know?" he countered. "You caught and killed the people involved in those murders. The case is now closed."

"Actually, no, it's not, because one murderer is still loose. The kite." It was risky mentioning it, because few people had any idea they existed. The SIU hadn't yet released an all-points about their existence.

"Kite? What the hell is a kite?" Irritation was very evident in Wetherton's voice. He had no idea what was going on, and he didn't like it one bit. But if he was the military's puppet, shouldn't he have had at least some clue? "Beyond something flown on a string, that is."

Blaine didn't react to the mention of the kite. Didn't do anything more than stare at her in that flat, calculating way. Either he knew about the kite and wasn't about to give her any information about it, or he didn't know anything and wasn't going to admit it.

She ignored the minister and added, "The kite might yet come after you and Lloyd and anyone else involved in those projects. We'd like to prevent that and would appreciate the military's cooperation."

"The military takes care of its own, Agent Ryan." He tilted his head a little, his gaze intensifying, as if he was trying to see into her head and her memories without actually using his psi skills. Or maybe he was simply recalling the past and juxtaposing his memories of a flame haired child against the woman who now stood in front of him. Comparing the two and drawing God knows what conclusions. "And my involvement in those projects was in the area of training, as I'm sure you're already aware."

A chill prickled across her skin. His words were an indication that his comparison had drawn the obvious conclusion. But for now, it was one she had to let ride.

"General, getting information out of the military is harder than getting blood out of the proverbial stone. So no, I have no awareness of either yours or General Lloyd's position in Hopeworth."

"And I would be surprised if that was the truth, Agent Ryan." He glanced at Wetherton. "If you wish to discuss the funding matter any further, please call."

Wetherton nodded. His expression was still a mix of confusion, irritation and concern. And she had every intention of finding out why.

Blaine met her gaze again, gave her a remote smile that sent another bout of chills down her spine, then turned and walked out the door.

She didn't relax, and didn't move. Not until she heard the soft ding of the elevator button, and then the electronic hum of machinery as the elevator moved down.

"Would you care to explain what the hell was going on between you and General Blaine, Agent Ryan?"

"I'm afraid that would involve revealing details of an ongoing case, Minister, so no, I can't discuss it."

He grunted, his expression suggesting he was far from happy. She was tempted to tell him tough, but since she'd probably have to work with this man for several months, she'd better play nice. At least for a little while.

"Well, come into my office and I'll give you my schedule for the next few weeks."

He spun on his heel and stalked back into the office. She followed him in. It was a huge expanse, filled with the latest chrome and glass furniture and plush leather sofas. The minister was a man with expensive tastes, obviously. His office was situated in one corner of the building, so two of the walls were

all glass. The view over the city and the bay was truly amazing—
a vista of fading sunlight, sparking lights and blue-gray ocean.

Wetherton stalked over to his desk and picked up a folder.
"My schedule. You'll notice I have several important meetings
at various restaurants in the evenings. During these events,
you will keep an eye on proceedings from a distance."

Which was standard procedure, but she wasn't about to
point that out. What it did mean was that she might need to
place a bug on Wetherton himself. He obviously had secrets
he didn't want her to overhear. She stopped in front of the
desk and accepted the folder. "Why was the General here?"

"As you probably heard, he was here to discuss the military
funding. The budget is to be discussed in parliament soon."

"Did he ask anything else? Mention anything else?"

Wetherton sat down on his plush chair and frowned. "What
he and I discuss is really of no importance to you. You're my
bodyguard, nothing more."

Despite his arrogant tone, she gave him her politest smile.
Even if all she wanted to do was smack his dumb ass. "And as
your bodyguard, I have the right to question the motives of
certain people. General Blaine was with you last night, and yet
he shows no obvious sign of injury. I think that's a little odd,
don't you?"

His frown deepened. "Not really. All it means is that he
wasn't injured in the attack."

She picked up the newspaper lying on his desk and threw
it across to him. "So you're telling me that photo, the one that
shows blood pouring from a wound on his head as he's carrying
a woman away from the car, is fake?"

He picked up the paper and studied it. "Might not be his
blood."

"Minister, I was there last night. I was one of the two
people who helped save your ass. I know for a fact that the
general was injured. So, I ask you again, what was the general
doing here and what did you talk about?"

"I told you—just the military budget."

He threw down the paper. Despite the calm assurance in
his voice, the hint of concern in his eyes was stronger. Which
meant that maybe he recognized something *had* happened here
this afternoon, even if he didn't know what it was.

And did he not know because his memory had been erased?
Blaine had been able to use his powers, despite the deadeners,
so that was more than likely.

"What time did he arrive this afternoon?"

"He had a five o'clock appointment."

She glanced at her watch. "So, you discussed the military budget for just over an hour?"

"Yes."

"And is that usual?"

He shrugged. "It depends."

On what? On how much information the general needed to siphon from him? Why could he not see something was very wrong? Or could he see it, and just wasn't about to admit it to her? And if that was the case, why not admit it when she was the person being paid to protect him?

Nothing about this situation was making any sense. Including her two vastly different reactions to a man she could remember seeing in her dreams but not in real life. Until now, that is.

She frowned and tried a slightly different tact. "Why was Blaine in the car with you last night, anyway? Are you friends?"

Wetherton hesitated. "Not really. But my wife knows his wife, so we occasionally see each other during social events."

"And his wife's name?"

"Andrea Blaine."

"I mean before she married him."

He paused. "I think her surname was Grantham. Or something like that. I'd have to ask my wife to be certain."

She nodded. "Was his wife in the car last night?"

"No." He hesitated, and she had a sudden feeling he was searching for the "right" answer. Odd, to say the least, especially since she'd sensed no outright lies so far. Just avoidances. "He said she was ill, but they had the tickets and he didn't want to waste them. He'd come by taxi, so I said we'd take him home. He doesn't live that far from us."

"You mean not far from your wife's house and not your Collin's Street apartment?"

"Yes. I'm afraid my ministerial duties often mean I work late. It's easier to have an apartment close by than going home and waking my family at ungodly hours."

And wasn't that a well rehearsed excuse. "Which is commendable, Minister." No sense in totally annoying him, as much as she might want to. "So, getting back to my original question—why was the general here, talking to you about the military budget, when you're the Minister for Science and Technology, not the Minister for Defense?"

"Easy. Certain military research allowances come out of

the Science and Technology budget."

"But why? Isn't that why there's a Defense portfolio? To assign and control the military budget?"

"It's the *Defense* portfolio," he said patiently, as if he'd answered this question a million times. Or as if he were talking to a simple child. "Therefore, it concentrates on defense items. Personal, big hardware items, small hardware items, etcetera. The research section of the military is lumped in with my portfolio."

Well, there you go—she'd learned something new. "Just one more thing, Minister, and I'll let you get on with your work."

"Good."

"I need to do a sweep of your office. Just to make sure there're no bugs or anything."

"I can assure you, this office is swept regularly, and nothing has ever been found."

"I'm sure it hasn't, but it's still part of my job to check."

He muttered under his breath, and then ungraciously stood up. "I'll go get a cup of coffee." He paused. "And the door shall remain open."

"Minister, if I wished to snoop through your paperwork or filing cabinets, I'd simply pick up the phone and get a court order to do so."

He grunted and walked out. Knowing she was in full view of the secretary, she began her check, searching quickly and efficiently. She didn't find any bugs, but she did manage to place her own.

All she had to do now was sit back and hope it picked up some clue as to what the hell was going on with Wetherton— and what his true connection was to Blaine.

Eight

Gabriel showed his ID to the black-clad police officer keeping watch and ducked under the yellow crime-scene tapes. The rotating red and blue lights of the nearby police vehicles washed across the night, splashing color across the white walled, ten story apartment block directly ahead. He looked up. The building had million dollar views over Albert Park Lake, which became part of the Grand Prix racing track when the Formula One party was in town, and yet the design of the building, with its small windows spaced far apart, was such that the views almost seemed unimportant. It was almost as if privacy and darkness had been the ultimate concerns.

Odd, to say the least.

"There're three apartments on each floor. Douglass lives in ten-o-three, which is the one with the lake view." Illie was looking at his notebook more than where he was going, and Gabriel rather churlishly hoped he'd run into something. But the man seemed to have a six sense when it came to objects in his path and sidestepped each one at the last moment. All without actually looking up. "The building has keypad number and thumbprint code security in place, and the system records details of all visitors."

"You've checked the records for her apartment?" He flashed his badge at the officer standing at the heavily-barred front door, and nodded a thanks when the officer keyed open the door for them.

"Yes. No visitors recorded for the last forty-eight hours," Illie said. "She left her apartment at five-forty five this morning, and returned at two thirty this afternoon. She was alone both times."

Another state police officer stood at the elevator. Gabriel again showed his badge, and asked, "Who's the officer in charge up there?"

"Captain Marsdan."

Who was the head of Sam's squad when she'd been a state police officer, and a man who had no real liking for SIU interference. But he was an excellent cop and, despite his adverse opinion of the SIU, he was probably the reason they'd been called in so fast.

They made their way up in the elevator. Illie shoved his

notebook back in his pocket and clicked the record button on his viaphone.

Gabriel watched with mild amusement. It was always easy to tell raw recruits from those who had been with the bureau for years, simply because the newbies followed the rules to the letter. Those who had been around for a while only recorded information when there was actually something to record. And in cases like this one, there'd be a crimecorder in place, anyway, so there was really no point in doubling up.

Black uniforms dominated the fifth floor, several interviewing neighbors and others guarding Douglass's door. Gabriel flashed his badge yet again and stepped inside the apartment.

A spherical-shaped crimecorder hovered in the middle of the living room, red light flashing to indicate it was recording. It swung around as he entered. "ID please."

"Assistant Director Gabriel Stern, SIU, and Agent James Illie, SIU," he said almost absently as he looked around.

Douglass might have made a ton of money, but aside from the location of her apartment, there was little else to indicate wealth of *any* kind. There was only a small TV, a coffee table and a brown leather sofa that had seen better years in the living room. The pale gray walls were bare, and the claret colored, heavily brocaded curtains had that aged, dusty look that only came after years and years of neglect.

"A woman of minimalist taste, isn't she?" Illie commented. "Hard to imagine, given the image she'd presented at the Foundation."

"Yeah, it is. You want to check out the rest of the apartment, see what you can find?"

Illie nodded. Gabriel looked around as a balding man in his mid-forties came out of a doorway to his right. The captain himself. Surprise flickered briefly through Marsdan's small brown eyes. "Didn't think this case was big enough to bring out an assistant director."

"It is when the case has links to an investigation already underway." He walked across to the doorway Marsdan had exited. It led into a bedroom—the place where Kathryn Douglass had met her death.

And it hadn't been an easy one, if the evidence indicator tags were anything to go by. There were at least ten of them, but only five of those caught immediate attention. They were spread through the room, each one joined by a trail of blood that was already beginning to dry and darken. They were an indication of where the body lay. Kathryn Douglass had been torn apart.

His gaze rose. A warning had been painted—in what looked like blood—on the wall.

Do not revisit Penumbra.

Something inside him went cold. Penumbra. The project that seemed the one most likely to have produced Sam.

What the hell did Kathryn Douglass have to do with *that* project? She was far too old to be one of the children raised from those projects. According to her records, she'd never been a part of the military, even if the foundation she controlled had deep military links.

So who was the warning aimed at? The military? The SIU? Or someone else entirely?

Someone like the mysterious, ever elusive, Sethanon? But what did he have to do with someone like Kathryn Douglass?

"Who reported the murder?" He walked over to the wall, carefully avoiding the outlines, blood trails and evidence markers.

"Neighbor. Apparently she heard screams and strange thumps."

"Did she hear any voices? See anyone enter or leave?" He stopped and looked a little closer at the writing. It smelled like dried blood to his hawk-sharpened senses, and given the almost "scraped" effect of each letter, it appeared something other than fingers had been used as a writing tool. He'd guess rolled-up paper, or something like that. It certainly wasn't the type of effect achieved with cloth, though there'd obviously been plenty of blood soaked material lying about.

"The neighbor didn't hear the elevator or other voices, but these apartments have good soundproofing," Marsden said. "The screams would have to have been extremely loud for the woman to have heard them."

"How many minutes passed between the report and a squad car arriving?" He stepped back to take another overall look at the writing. The letters sloped to the left more than the right, which was usually a good indication that the murderer was left-handed. Not that that meant anything in itself. A good percentage of the population was left-handed these days.

"The report came in at three-fifteen. The squad car was

here by three-twenty one."

Gabriel looked around. "That's fast work by your men, Captain."

"There was a car in the area." He shrugged. "They saw no one coming out of the building, and after gaining access to the apartment via the building's super and finding the woman's naked pieces, they immediately secured the main door."

Gabriel raised an eyebrow. "Naked?"

Marsden nodded. "The bedding was rumpled. We've sent it to the lab to test for body fluids and DNA."

Meaning Douglass might have known her attacker *extremely* well. "Is there a fire exit?"

"Yes, but it's alarmed. No one has come in or out of it."

"No broken windows or anything like that to indicate entry from the rooftop?"

"No, sir."

Then how had the murderer gotten in or out? There had to be *something* here. Some access point Marsden and his men had missed. "What about air conditioning ducts or vents? Does the building share the one system, or does each apartment have separate air conditioning units to look after its own needs?"

"The second option, I'm afraid." Marsden paused. "So far, the only prints we've picked up are the victims."

"Not surprising. Whoever did this obviously had it well planned." He looked past Marsden as Illie came to the door. "Yes?"

"Found something you might want to look at."

"What, exactly?" Gabriel asked, as he and Marsden followed Illie through the living room.

"This apartment has a guest bathroom as well as a regular bathroom. It's little more than a toilet and washbasin, but it's situated on an outside wall and has a small, wind out window which I presume is meant to give ventilation." Illie glanced over his shoulder. "The window was open."

"Big enough for someone to get in?"

"Someone? No. Something? Yes."

Illie stopped in the doorway. Gabriel stepped past him. As his partner had stated, the room had nothing more than a toilet and a basin. The soap sitting on the edge of the small metal basin was old and cracked, suggesting this room hadn't been used in quite a while, though the toilet itself was spotless. The window above it was roughly two foot in diameter, which was certainly big enough for someone to crawl through if they weren't so high up. With the winder in place, though, the amount the window could open was severely restricted. Windows and winders could be broken, of course, but this one was still intact. And right now, it was only open a couple of inches.

"Seems your people missed this," he commented, without glancing at Marsden.

"The open window was noted, but we are duty bound to assume human intervention first. Our searches are for more conventional clues and entry points." He hesitated, expression annoyed. "You were called as soon as other options were eliminated."

Gabriel squatted and looked behind the bowl. "I would have thought the fact that she was torn apart precluded human involvement."

"She was ripped apart?" Illie said, surprise evident in his voice.

"Yeah. Poor bitch."

"There're not many folk in the paranormal community who have the strength to do that," Illie said. "I mean, bear changers would, but a bear changer wouldn't get through that window."

"Nor would any of the big cat changers, though they certainly could tear someone apart. But there would be teeth marks and I presume if something like that was evident, our good captain would have mentioned it."

"He would," Marsden confirmed. "But it wasn't teeth and the separation wasn't clean enough to suggest a blade had been used."

Gabriel shifted to get a better view of the s-bend area, and saw something odd—a feather. A black feather.

"Though of course," Marsden said, "the coroner still has to make her report."

"Found something." Gabriel leaned a shoulder against the wall, and said, "Crimecorder, record image and location of feather for evidence."

The black sphere responded immediately, zipping into the room to hover inches from his head. "Image recorded," a metallic voice stated.

"Resume original position."

Gabriel put on a glove, then reached in and grabbed the dark feather. "It would appear our murderer is a raven."

"A raven shifter wouldn't have the strength to tear someone

apart."

"This one obviously did—unless Douglass herself is a changer."

"She's not listed as one." Illie frowned as he handed Gabriel an evidence bag. "A raven is a fairly large bird. Would it even be able to get through a gap like that?"

"Obviously, since that feather is inside rather than out. Ravens don't exactly make great pets, so why else would the feather be here? Besides, there's blood on some of the quills. Could be an indication that he or she injured themselves coming in."

"Or going out."

Gabriel nodded. "Are any of Douglass's known associates shapechangers?"

"Not that I've discovered." Illie hesitated as Marsden's phone buzzed. He gave them an apologetic look and stepped away. Illie continued. "I'm only about halfway through the Foundation's employee files. There're several shifters listed, but none are ravens."

"Do a search through the remainder and see what you can find."

"You're not expecting a result, are you?"

Gabriel rose. "No."

"Why not?"

"Because this attack comes a little too soon after the one on us. I think someone is either covering their tracks or sending a warning. Maybe even both."

Illie raised his eyebrows. "How did you come to that conclusion?"

Gabriel told him about the message on the wall. "Penumbra is an old military project that was destroyed by fire. Given the Foundation's military links, it's quite possible that Douglass knew something about the project." Especially given her request that he and his partner investigate a break-in and her obvious disappointment—or concern—that the partner he'd turned up with was male rather than female. They'd wanted Sam there. Wanted her to do those tests. Douglass might have known why, but her death certainly ensured they'd never be able to ask her.

It was just too damn convenient.

And yet, if the military *had* killed her to prevent her from talking, why would they leave a message about Penumbra?

That just didn't make sense.

But if not the military, who else?

Sethanon?

What reason would he have to kill Douglass and stop the military from revisiting an old project?

Though if he *did* know of Sam's history, maybe he was still trying to protect her. But why would a man who possessed a ruthless and bloody determination to start a war want to protect someone like Sam? If he planned to use her abilities for his bloody cause, why wouldn't he have snatched her long before she'd come to the notice of the SIU or the military?

What was the damn connection between the two of them?

No one knew, not even Sam. Though given what she'd admitted this afternoon—that she was in telepathic contact with a man she recently met—then maybe she wasn't being as truthful as he'd presumed.

And that made it more important than ever that keep an eye on her. If Sethanon was looking out for her, then maybe his brother was right after all. Maybe she would lead them to the one criminal they'd never been able to sight let alone catch.

"So you think the military was behind the murder?" Illie asked, his voice holding a hint of skepticism.

"No, actually, I don't." He glanced past Illie as Marsden walked towards them. "Yes?"

"Seeing you SIU boys are taking over this one, I thought you might like to handle this. We've two military men outside who want to come in and view the scene."

"Talk about timing," Illie muttered.

"Let them up, Captain. I'll talk to them."

"And the first question that has to be asked," Illie commented, as they followed Marsden back into the living room, "is how they found out about the murder so quickly. Hell, even the press aren't here yet."

"Maybe they were coming here to see Douglass anyway. Why don't you see if you can find an appointment book?"

Illie's wry grin flashed. "In other words, get lost while I interview the military men."

Amusement ran though him. "Basically, yes."

"All you had to do was ask, boss." He walked away.

Gabriel shoved his hands into his pockets and waited for the two men. He had every intention of taking them into the bedroom to view the murder scene and watch their reaction, but first, he wanted to assess them.

Within a few minutes, the apartment's front door was opened and a police officer escorted the two men in. The first man was about six feet tall and broad shouldered, with a shock of silver hair that was accentuated by the dark brown of his suit. His face was flat, hard, and the red of a barely healed wound marred the left side of his face. The second man was shorter by several inches, and yet more powerful in his presence. Gabriel recognized him instantly, even though he'd only seen him once, on Sam's com-screen. General Frank Lloyd from the Hopeworth Military Base. Was he here by coincidence? Gabriel suspected the answer was no.

The crimecorder spun around in response to the two men walking in. "ID please."

"General Frank Lloyd, from Hopeworth military base."

"General Michael Blaine, also from Hopeworth."

Gabriel raised an eyebrow. "Even with the Foundation's close military ties, surely it's overkill to send two generals to investigate."

"No more than the SIU sending an Assistant Director," Lloyd said, and held out his hand. "I don't believe we've met officially."

"No, general, we haven't." He shook the man's hand. Power rose when their flesh touched, an electricity that felt oddly disturbing. "And since you specifically asked for me and my partner to investigate the break-in at the Foundation, it should come as no surprise that we're now investigating the murder of the person who ran that Foundation."

"I guess not." He paused. "General Blaine here works at Hopeworth, though not in the same area as me. His area of expertise meant he was in contact with Douglass more than I was."

Gabriel's gaze switched to the silver haired man. "How much contact?"

Blaine's expression was polite, almost disinterested, and yet there was something in the man's gray eyes that had Gabriel's hackles rising. He was facing an enemy, even if they'd only just met.

"Not socially, if that's what you're implying. We were merely business acquaintances."

"Have you talked to her in the past few days?"

"Yes."

"And did she appear distracted? Concerned by anything?"

"Not that I was aware of."

"Not even by the break-in?"

Blaine smiled. "Aside from that, no."

Gabriel switched his gaze back to Lloyd. Of the two, he seemed the more approachable—which in itself had alarms ringing simply because the general had been of very little help in the past. Except, of course, when it suited him.

"Why are you here, General? This murder hasn't even hit the headlines yet, so how did you hear about it?"

"All of those scientists and team heads involved with military projects at the Foundation have emergency-call buttons installed in their homes. As the director of the company, Douglass also had one. It was pressed at two-forty."

Ten minutes after she'd arrived home. Thirty minutes before the neighbor heard the screams and called the police. Forty minutes before her death. Given what Marsden had said about the state of the bed, did that mean Douglass pressed the buzzer and *then* seduced her attacker? Or was the seducer and the attacker two entirely different people?

"If Douglass pressed the emergency call button at two forty-five, why are you only responding now?"

"Hopeworth is a long way from St. Kilda."

"Not by helicopter." And there were military offices in the city itself. Why couldn't they have dispatched military police from one of them to investigate?

"Helicopters are not allowed to land around here, and given the sensitivity of the foundation's links with Hopeworth, we prefer to send out our own personnel." Lloyd studied him for a moment, blue eyes assessing. "Why do you suspect us of wrongdoing?"

"I'm an SIU agent and predisposed to be suspicious of everything and everyone. Especially those who have a vested interest in keeping their secrets."

Lloyd's smile was cold. "The military did not silence Kathryn Douglass, I can assure you."

Oddly enough, Gabriel believed him. "Where is the call button in this apartment?"

"In the bedroom, beside the right bedside table."

"The police found her dead in her bedroom at three twenty-one."

"Meaning the murderer savored his time with her?" Blaine

asked.

Gabriel glanced at him. There was an odd hint of amusement in the general's voice that rankled. "Given Douglass's body was torn apart, I doubt the murderer savored her death too much."

Blaine raised an eyebrow. "There are some in this world who get off on such things."

And the general was one of them. Why he was so sure, Gabriel couldn't say. Perhaps it was just the hint of hunger in the general's otherwise flat gaze.

"The police believe Douglass and her murderer had intercourse before she was murdered. They're testing for DNA."

"So it could be nothing more than rough lovemaking gone extremely wrong?" Blaine asked.

"I seriously doubt it."

Blaine's smile was unexpectedly ferocious. "Oh, so do I."

Which was an odd thing to say when he hadn't yet viewed the room in which she'd been murdered.

"May we see the scene?" Lloyd asked.

"This way." He led them into the bedroom and stepped to one side so he could see their reactions. Neither man gave much away, but the tiny hint of amusement touching Blaine's mouth was disturbing, to say the least.

"What do you make of the message, General Lloyd? How is Kathryn Douglass connected to Penumbra?"

"She's not." Lloyd's voice was flat. "As you are well aware, Penumbra is not an active project, but one that was shut down years ago."

"Forcibly shut down by fire," Gabriel amended.

Lloyd's gaze flickered towards him. "Yes."

"But if the project was destroyed and Kathryn Douglass had no involvement, why would the murder leave this particular message?"

"I don't know."

"Don't know, or won't tell?"

Lloyd's smile was flat. "I cannot withhold something I do not know."

Again, Gabriel believed him. "Were there any other survivors from the project that you haven't mentioned already?" He didn't have much hope of getting a direct answer, but the question had to be asked.

"Only the periphery project support," Blaine said. "People like nurses, teachers, trainers, etcetera."

"And they have all been assigned elsewhere?"

"Many have retired or died," Blaine said, and there was something very cold in his eyes as he said it. "That project was a long time ago, and it has not been reopened or repeated."

"And yet, evidence of it keeps appearing."

"Not through military means, I assure you," Lloyd said. He glanced at Blaine. "Though we should do a check of the surviving personnel. See if any had recent contact with Douglass."

"They haven't. I would have been informed," Blaine said.

Gabriel frowned. Again, there was something very strange in the way Blaine said that. "But if there has been contact?"

"We shall investigate and let you know the results." Lloyd held out his hand. "Thank you for your assistance, Stern."

Gabriel shook his hand and again felt that tingle of power. But if the general was trying to read him, then it wasn't through telepathic means. He would have felt any attempt to read his thoughts.

Blaine didn't offer his hand, just gave him a curt nod before following Lloyd from the room.

Gabriel watched them leave, unable to shake the feeling that Blaine *knew* him. Knew him and hated him.

Which meant, somewhere in the past, their paths had crossed, even if he couldn't remember it. He needed information on the man, and he needed it fast.

He glanced around as Illie came into the room. "Do a full search on General Blaine. I need to see whatever you can find."

In the meantime, he'd contact his family and see if anyone had any memory of the man. Then he'd head to Federation headquarters and see if there were any connecting files. Once all that had been done, he'd contact Sam. She needed to know that once again the Penumbra project had raised its head.

* * *

Sam repressed a yawn and wished, for the umpteenth time, that Wetherton would just shut up and go home. Night-watch duty always took several days—or rather, nights—to get used to, and she was tired as hell.

Right now, it was two in the morning and they were in a nightclub situated right in the heart of the King Street club scene. The place was packed with wildly gyrating teenagers and adults, and the music was so damn loud her body vibrated with it. The air was filled with an array of perfumes—the source of which was both male and female. When combined with the odor of sweating bodies, the result was stomach churning.

The one thing the place *didn't* have was a watcher on her. She'd spotted the man Gabriel had following her several times and had finally phoned Stephan about it. The big man had disappeared very quickly after that. As much as his presence had offered her some comfort, she'd be damned if she'd allow someone to risk their life to protect hers. Especially when that someone was the husband of a woman she liked.

She stood in a corner opposite Wetherton's table, squashed between a pole and the wall and trying not to breathe too deeply. While uncomfortable, the position allowed her to watch both Wetherton and anyone who approached his table. Not that anyone *had* for the last four hours. She sipped on a juice and wished it was coffee. She had a feeling she was going to hit a wall soon when it came to energy, and at least the caffeine would have helped fend that moment off a little longer. But the bar didn't serve the hot stuff. And as much as she wouldn't have minded a mixer with the juice, her tiredness and the fact she hadn't eaten much over the day meant it would more than likely go straight to her head.

Not a good thing when she was supposed to be protecting the minister's back.

Although *that* was most definitely not the only reason she was here. She glanced at the other man at the table. Wetherton's "meet" was a tall, thin man who didn't appear to be another politician. His brown suit was rumpled, his face haggard and unshaven, and there was nothing polished or practiced about the way he spoke. On first sighting him, she'd thought "reporter" but after watching him for the last four hours, she'd revised that to criminal. There was something very guarded about the way his gaze continually roamed the room.

There was also something oddly familiar about him, though she'd swear she'd never met nor seen him before. It wasn't even so much his looks as his "feel."

If that made any sense.

She'd managed to grab a couple of shots of him with her viaphone and, when she had the time, fully intended to do a search to see who he was. She figured the name he'd given her—Chip Braggart—was just a little too weird to be true. And she couldn't remember him listed among Wetherton's known associates. Even as tired as she was, it was doubtful she'd forget a name like that.

And why was Wetherton, a government minister, meeting with the likes of Braggart? Was he a contact from the real Wetherton's past, or was he a part of the clone's very recent past? Or was he even, perhaps, the contact between the made-man and the creator?

Very likely, she thought, studying the cold wariness in his dark eyes. This man was more than just a petty criminal. And there was something very familiar in the way he moved, the way he reacted.

She frowned, trying to chase down the intuition, but at that moment, the presence of evil crawled across her skin like foul electricity, making it hard not to react instinctively and draw her gun. She placed the glass on a nearby table and casually looked around.

For quite a few minutes she couldn't see the threat. The main dance floor was too crowded, and the table-lined edges too shadowed. Then the strobe lights pulsed, briefly hitting a group on the far side of the room and illuminating the hair of one man, making it a gleam like a beacon of molten red.

The hair color of Hopeworth's creations.

The face of the man who had tried to kill both Wetherton and her last night.

Only it couldn't be the same man, because he was dead. And although this man's features were almost identical, his nose was just a little bit sharper.

Unlike the rest of the people in his group, he was neither talking nor drinking, simply standing still as his gaze roamed the confines of the room. When his gaze neared where she stood, she ducked back into shadow, but she had an odd feeling he'd know she was there—that he would feel her presence as easily as she felt his. When she risked another look in his direction, he was gone.

Fear shot through her. The hunt was on.

She pushed away from the wall and walked across to Wetherton. "I'm sorry, Minister, but we need to leave."

Wetherton glanced up, his expression annoyed. "I'm not finished here, yet."

"Sir, I have reason to believe your life is under threat. Continue this conversation in the car if you must, but right now, we need to move."

His scowl deepened. "It would be inopportune for Mr. Braggart and I to be seen together right at this moment."

"Minister, you asked the SIU for protection. If you do not wish to follow my advice, I can only presume you do not, after all, wish such protection."

He sighed, though it was more a sound of exasperation than compliance. "If you insist—"

"And I do."

He glanced at Braggart. "We'll continue this tomorrow night, then. Make sure you bring the information I requested."

Braggart nodded, but his gaze was on her and a chill ran down her spine. There was something in his eyes that suggested he saw more, knew more, about this situation and about her than she could ever guess.

This man *knew* her. How or why she couldn't say, but she had a feeling she'd better find out, and quick.

Wetherton downed the remainder of his drink in one gulp and dug a hand into his pocket. "I'll call my chauffeur to make sure the car is waiting out front."

She scanned the immediate area, but she couldn't see the flame haired stranger. But she could feel him. His presence itched at her skin, stronger and closer than before. "Hurry," was all she said.

Wetherton made his call and rose. "Let's go"

She waved him ahead of her. She didn't have eyes in the back of her head, and with the crowded state of the nightclub, she wasn't about to leave his back unwatched. At least if she followed, she'd have a chance of seeing a threat coming from the front or either side.

Wetherton pushed his way past those in his way, seemingly oblivious to the angry retorts thrown his way. She followed, her gaze constantly on the move, watching and waiting. The foul energy of the flame haired stranger followed them. He was close—very close. And yet, no matter how hard she tried, she couldn't pick him out in the crowded confines of the dance club.

The sooner they were in the car and driving away, the better.

They exited the main room and strode up the long hallway

to the main doors. She risked yet another look behind her. Though no one else had entered the hallway after them, the doors were still swinging, as if someone had. And she could certainly still feel him. A shiver ran down her spine. If the flame haired stranger was a Hopeworth creation, who knew what other abilities he had? Invisibility might be a figment of fiction and comic books up until now, but if *she* had the capability to fade into shadow, then how much bigger a step was it to create someone who could fade into shadow *and* light?

Not much, she thought, her gaze straying to the deeper shadows to the left of the swinging doors.

Was it her imagination, or did something stir in the half lit corners?

Another shiver ran down her spine. She pressed a hand against Wetherton's back and pushed him a little.

He swore at her, but nevertheless moved faster. Two security guards opened the door for them. The cold night air swirled in, thick with the promise of rain.

She shivered again, this time with cold, and glanced around for the minister's car. It was up the street, parked in a bus zone, and was a little too close to the nearby alley and its encroaching shadows for her liking.

But the foul energy of the stranger was behind her, still in the nightclub, and the shadows ahead held no threat as yet.

It was just nerves, nothing more, that made her fear them.

She grabbed Wetherton's arm and propelled him forward even as she slipped her other hand inside her coat and wrapped her fingers around her gun. The cool feel of the metal pressed against her flesh was comforting, and some tiny part of her relaxed a little.

It shouldn't have.

Nine

They'd barely reached the car when the sensation of wrongness rolled across her skin. Not from the man who'd followed them from the club, but from the alley and the shadows. She opened the car open, thrusting Wetherton inside even as the feeling of wrongness sharpened.

Something was about to attack.

She slammed the door shut, barely avoiding the minister's feet, and swung around.

She'd expected it to be the red-haired stranger.

It wasn't.

It was the vampire Stephan had unleashed to attack Wetherton and therefore give substance to her being his bodyguard. She drew her weapon and pressed the trigger, but he moved so fast the bright beam of the laser tore through his shoulder rather than searing his brains to dust.

The sharp smell of burned flesh filled the air. He snarled, a shrill sound of anger, then he was upon her, spindly arms flying, face gaunt, and pupils mere pinpricks. A junkie in need of a fix, she thought, and wondered if in this case it was just blood he needed or actual drugs.

She ducked his first blow and let fly with one of her own. Her fist sank deep into his stomach but he didn't even grunt in response. Too far gone with lust, she thought, as he snarled, revealing elongated teeth.

A shout came from the direction of the club entrance. A call for them to stop fighting or else. She blocked another of his blows and hit the vamp over the head with her gun as hard as she could. He staggered back, shaking his head and spraying blood in the process. It splattered across her coat and face, stinging like fine acid. She ignored it and raised her weapon.

"Agent Ryan, SIU," she said, speaking loud enough that the rapidly approaching bouncers might hear. "Raise your hands and don't move, or I *will* shoot."

The vampire was obviously too far gone to hear or understand. He snarled and launched himself at her.

She pulled the trigger.

The shot hit dead center in the middle of his forehead and burned through his skull, cindering flesh and bone and brain matter along the way.

He dropped dead at her feet and didn't move. She didn't look down. She barely even dared breathe lest the smell make her lose the control she had over her stomach.

Instead, she wiped her face with the sleeve of her coat, then got out her badge and showed it to the two horrified bouncers. They stopped immediately, the aggression that had been so evident moments ago slipping away. She got her viaphone and made a call to the SIU.

"Agent Sam Ryan, badge number 1934," she said, when Christine came on line, "Clean up team needed at my current location. And please inform Director Byrne that the escaped prisoner has been dealt with."

"Clean up team three has been notified," Christine answered, her digital tones sexier than any computer generated form had a right to be, "and a message has been sent to Director Byrne."

"Thanks, Christine." She hung up and glanced at the bouncers. "You want to keep the gawkers back for me?"

They nodded and began to deal with the gathering crowd. She stepped over the body of the vamp and opened the car door. "You all right, Minister?"

He nodded, his face a little paler than normal. "How did you know that vampire was outside?"

"I didn't. He was an entirely different threat than the one I felt before." She lifted her gaze and let it roam the street. No sense of anything evil or even out of place. Not until she looked past the crowd to the nightclub's entrance, anyway. Braggart was there, watching, a hint of amusement touching his thin lips. And if the tingle running across her skin was anything to go by, the redheaded stranger was there, too, even if she couldn't see him.

Not that she could do anything about his presence right then. She didn't dare leave Wetherton alone and give chase to the unseen stranger. After all, he might be nothing more than a decoy meant to draw her away from the minister's side. And though she wanted to get out of here as much as Wetherton did, she couldn't whisk him away until the SIU had arrived and the vampire had been dealt with. Protocol had to be followed, most especially in this situation.

She met Wetherton's gaze again. "I have to give my report to the SIU team I called in, and until then, I'm afraid we'll just have to wait here."

He scowled. "Why can't I just go inside and continue my meeting? Braggart hasn't left yet, surely."

"He hasn't, no. But we're being watched, Minister, and I prefer not to take a risk right now."

"Watched?" A hint of—not fear, not panic, but something in between—flitted through his eyes. He looked around briefly, and then met her gaze again. "By whom?"

"I don't know." She briefly toyed with the idea of telling him their watcher was more than likely military, but let it go. Until she knew where, exactly, Wetherton's alliances lie, it was better not to give him too much information. For her sake, as much as his.

He grunted his displeasure, then reached forward and grabbed the car's phone. "Shut the door, please. I have a few personal calls to make."

Ungrateful bastard, she thought, as she slammed the door shut. Not even a damn thank you for saving his life. But then, he probably figured she was only doing what she was being paid to do—risking her life to save his lab-made ass.

When she glanced back at the gathered crowd, Braggart had gone. She studied the street beyond the club, but couldn't find any sign of him. Unusual for a human to move so fast in such a brief space of time—unless, of course, he was something more than human.

And she had a strange feeling Braggart was, even if she hadn't sensed him as such. Why she was so certain, she couldn't say, but maybe it was connected to the odd sensation that she knew him. Knew the "soul" of him, if not the outer layer.

Which in itself suggested a shapeshifter of some kind.

She frowned but let the thought go, simply because it was just another question for which she had no answer.

As she looked back to the club's doorway, she noticed the red-haired stranger had also slipped away. His presence was a fading tingle, getting more distant by the minute. The night felt cleaner for his disappearance.

She put her weapon away, rubbed her arms and leaned back against the car, waiting and watching.

It took ten minutes for the clean up team to arrive. Two men took care of the vamp's body, while the man in charge—an agent she didn't recognize—took statements from her, Wetherton and the driver.

As he moved on to interview other witnesses, she opened

the door and climbed into the car. "We can go now."

"About time," Wetherton muttered, glancing at the driver. "Henry, take me home."

She didn't comment on his tone or the inference that she'd delayed purposefully, simply leaned back in the seat and watched the lights flash by. Tiredness washed over her, and it was all she could do to suppress a yawn. Thankfully, King Street wasn't that far from his Collins Street apartment. Once the driver had stopped in the secure underground parking garage, she climbed out and checked to make sure there was no one about, then signaled the driver to pop the trunk. She retrieved her overnight bag and com-unit, then opened Wetherton's door. He grabbed his briefcase, climbed out and headed for the elevator.

It turned out that the minister's apartment was on the top floor with good views of the bay. The apartment's living area wasn't huge, but the ceiling to floor wall of glass made it seem otherwise. The city stretched before them, an unending sea of twinkling lights that merged gradually into the dark waters of the bay.

She dumped her bags on one of the black leather sofas, then caught Wetherton's arm as he walked past her.

"Minister, I should check all rooms first."

"This apartment building is fully secure," he said, exasperation in his voice. "No one could get in here."

"There's no such thing as a fully secure building. All security can be breached, even that of the SIU."

He grunted, but waved her on irritably. She walked to the nearest room, which turned out to be the bathroom. Nothing out of the ordinary, despite the marble tiling and gold-plated taps. The same could be said for the bedroom—though the silk clad bed had to be the biggest bed she'd ever seen. It dominated the room, leaving little space for anything else. She walked past it into the walk-in closet and dressing area, noting with a frown that the minister's suits were all top of the line. And there were enough of them that he could wear a different one every day for a month. Surely politicians didn't make *that* much. Between the apartment, the suits, the family home and the family itself, Wetherton had to be running himself dry.

Unless, of course, he had a secondary source of income no one knew about.

As she turned around to leave, her gaze fell on a grate

covering what looked like a large vent. The paint work around one edge had been scratched, as if the vent had been opened recently, or often. Frown deepening, she knelt and ran her fingers around the covering's edge. It was loose. She pried to open and carefully looked into the hole.

Darkness and air rushed up at her. She shuddered, and quickly drew back. Small places had *never* been on her list of favorites things. Especially when they were small places that seemed to drop down to unending darkness.

But why was this here? It didn't appear to be part of the air conditioning system, as it seemed to go straight down. And if it was a laundry chute, why was it here rather than in the bathroom, like most installed into serviced apartments? Why wasn't there a proper cover?

"What the hell are you doing?" Wetherton appeared in the doorway, his expression darker than usual.

She sat back on her heels and indicated the vent. "What is that used for?"

"It's a vent."

"Its cover has been pried away many times."

He shrugged. "They're in the process of placing a laundry chute in the building. Workmen have been in and out all week, fiddling with the damn thing and generally being a nuisance."

Some of those scratches were more than a week old, but still, the explanation was reasonable enough.

So why did she sense he was lying?

"It's a dangerous thing to have such an easy access point in your apartment, Minister."

He snorted. "No man could fit in the vent, let alone climb it."

"No man, but maybe a shifter."

"A bird wouldn't have the strength to shift the grate with their wings or their claws, Agent Ryan. Now, will you just get out of my bedroom so I can go to sleep?"

"Only doing my job, Minister." She shoved the cover back, taking careful note of the existing scratches, then rose. "The agent assigned for day shift will be here at seven. Do you wish me to wake you at that time if you're not already up?"

"Yes. Now get out."

She did. But she stayed near the closed door, listening. She wasn't entirely sure what she expected to hear, but there was something about Wetherton that scratched her instincts.

He was up to no good, she was sure of that. And it was something he didn't want *her* to know about.

But the soft sounds coming from the bedroom suggested he was doing nothing more than getting ready for bed. She gave up after a few minutes and walked over to the sofa where she'd left her com-unit. After sitting down, she pressed her thumb into the lock.

"Voice identification required," the unit stated.

"Sam Ryan, SIU officer, badge number 1934."

"Voice scan correct. Eye confirmation required."

She looked into the small scanner fitted into the left-hand side of the unit. A red beam swept over her eye.

"Eye scan correct." The unit clicked open.

Izzy's pink fluff form appeared onscreen. "It's a little early in the morning to be up and about, isn't it sweetie?"

"Tell me about it," she said dryly, and barely repressed a yawn. "Has Hopeworth replied to our request for ID information about the gray haired man?

Izzy's feather boa twirled. "Not a whisper, sweetie."

"Well, his name is General Blaine, and he apparently does work at Hopeworth." She paused, looking towards Wetherton's room. The soft sound of steps indicated he was still moving around. But when bedsprings squeaked, she relaxed and looked down at Izzy. "See what you can find out about him. Use all channels available."

"Oooo...freedom to search where I please. Thanks, sweetness."

She snorted softly as she retrieved her viaphone and plugged it in. "And do an identity check on this man," she said, as she transferred the image of Braggart. "His alias is Chip Braggart. Dig me up any and all information about him."

Izzy's boa twirled faster. "Darlin', I can only do so many things at once."

"Izzy, you're a computer, not a human."

"That doesn't mean I'm without limits."

She grinned. They were definitely making these things too real. "You'll live Iz. Let me know when you find anything."

She closed the screen and set the com unit to one side, then lifted her feet onto the glass and chrome coffee table. Without really meaning to, she dozed.

A soft sound woke her. She blinked, briefly noting that it was still night as she glanced sideways at the clock on the wall. Four o'clock. She'd been asleep just about an hour.

She frowned, listening to the silence, feeling guilty about sleeping on the job and wondering what the hell had woken her. Then she heard it again—a whisper-soft bump of something against metal. It came from the direction of Wetherton's room.

She rose, reaching for her weapon as she padded towards the door. After grasping the handle, she carefully inched the door open. Wetherton was a blanket covered, unmoving lump in the bed who made no noise.

She frowned and pushed the door open a little more, quickly peering around the corner. Nothing unusual here. No reason for the sound she'd heard.

Pressing her fingertips against the door, she pushed it all the way open. The room was still and dark, and Wetherton's after shave—a spicy, musky scent that was far too powerful for her liking—filled the air.

She stepped quietly into the room and looked around. Still no noise. No indication that anything was wrong.

Half wondering if the noise she'd heard was nothing more than a figment left over from stolen sleep, she took another step forward.

And realized it wasn't Wetherton in the bed, but pillows bunched together to take on the appearance of a sleeper if anyone happened to look in.

The man himself was nowhere to be seen.

She raised her gun and cautiously approached the walk-in closet, all senses alert. Another duck around the door frame revealed that Wetherton wasn't hiding in there, either.

What the hell...? She lowered her weapon and looked around the room, then up at the ceiling. No trap doors, no windows. No Wetherton.

A man his size couldn't just disappear...

Her gaze went to the vent. It was open.

"Shit." She dropped to her knees and peered into the dark hole. Fear rose, threatening to engulf her, but she ignored it the best she could and listened.

From far down came another thump and the soft squawk of a bird. Then silence.

She pulled back from the hole and sat on her heels.

Wetherton wasn't just a clone, he was a shapechanger.

But if he was so afraid for his life, why would he leave this apartment—and her protection—so abruptly? Why put himself in danger like that?

Unless, of course, he needed to report to his master and this was the only way he could do it without raising suspicion. After all, the real Wetherton was human, not changer. This Wetherton had been in a mighty hurry to get her out of the room so he could sleep.

She rose and left, closing the bedroom door behind her. Whatever his reasons, it was obvious he didn't want her to know he was gone. And it certainly played better for her if he didn't know that she knew.

After shoving her gun away, she flopped back onto the sofa and opened the com-unit again. Izzy's fuzzy face came on line instantly. "And here I was thinking you were sleeping."

"I was. Can you send an urgent email to Director Byrne? Tell him Wetherton is a changer. Tell him I need a tracer sent in with Jenna Morwood this morning, if possible."

"Request sent. Still waiting on search results."

"Ta, Iz."

She shut the com-unit down and settled back to wait. It was an hour before she heard the soft sound of movement in the bedroom. After a few seconds, the door opened and Wetherton's tousled head appeared.

"Anything wrong, Minister?" she inquired politely.

"Thought I heard something," he said, in the best just-woken-from-sleep voice she'd ever heard.

"Nothing's moving. I'm struggling to keep awake, in fact."

"Make sure that you do," he snapped, and closed the door.

Ass, she thought, and wondered how the hell she was going to get through months of this tedium.

With a sigh, she leaned back against the sofa and watched the dawn break slowly across the night-held sky. Jenna arrived just before her shift started. She was a pretty woman of Spanish descent.

After checking her ID, Sam let her in and introduced herself. Jenna smiled, the merry twinkle in her dark eyes belying the hint of steel in her handshake. "Director Ryan sent this for you," she said, handing her an interoffice envelope. "What's Wetherton like?"

Sam glanced at the still closed bedroom door. "He's a politician."

Jenna grimaced. "Says it all, doesn't it?"

"Yeah." She tore open the envelope. Inside were two small

plastic packets. Stephan wasn't taking any chances—he'd sent two tracers, one for each of them. She got one out and handed it to Jenna. "He's also an unrecorded changer. He disappeared on me last night, but he doesn't know I know. Keep an eye on him, and try to place the tracer on him without alerting him."

She nodded, pocketing the packet quickly as Wetherton came out. When his gaze fell on Jenna, his whole demeanor lightened. Sam didn't know who she felt sorrier for—Jenna for being placed on a twelve-hour watch with a lecher, or Wetherton if he actually tried to harass her.

Though personally, she wouldn't have minded seeing Jenna kick his sorry ass to kingdom come.

She made the introductions, then donned her jacket, grabbed her bag and com-unit, and got the hell out of there.

The morning sunlight was so bright when she came out of the building that she had to shade her eyes and blink against a sudden rush of tears.

That's when she saw Gabriel. She stopped briefly as surprise and something else, something close to excitement, ran through her.

He was leaning against one of the concrete columns, arms crossed and looking as tired as she felt. "What's wrong?" she asked, stopping a few feet away from him. His scent ran around her, spicy and warm, stirring a longing that she hadn't felt in a long, long time.

And it steeled her earlier resolve to pursue whatever it was between them. Whether or not she succeeded, whether or not there was ever going to be anything more than destiny between them, didn't matter. If she *didn't* do something, if she simply sat back, accepting his statement that his heart belonged to someone who was long dead, she'd regret it.

"Heard you requested information about a General Blaine." He shifted his hand, revealing a manila folder. "Thought you might like to share why over breakfast."

She raised an eyebrow. "Breakfast doesn't get you out of lunch, you know."

A wry smile touched his lips. "I guessed that. This is a business breakfast, not an apology."

That *she'd* guessed. He wouldn't be here, otherwise. "Why are you curious about my interest in Blaine?"

"Because I met him last night. Since you saw him when the Wetherton attack went down wrong, I wanted your opinion of him."

He motioned her forward, and then pressed his hand lightly against her spine to guide her toward his car. The warmth of his touch trembled across her skin. Yep, she had it bad for the damn man. But if he noticed her reaction, he didn't say anything. Didn't react in *any* seeable way himself.

"I know this sounds catty, but why does my opinion of the man matter to you?"

He slanted her a look as he opened the car's passenger door for her. "Because you have an innate skill for feeling evil in people. I want to know if you sensed it in him."

She waited until he'd climbed into the car before replying, "Yes and no."

He started the car and pulled out smoothly into the early morning traffic. Then he flicked on autodrive and programmed it to head to the address of the hotel where she'd been staying. She certainly hadn't told him she was staying there, so he'd obviously dug it out of her personnel file. If she wasn't so tired she might have felt annoyed, but right now all she felt was vague amusement.

"What does that mean?" he asked.

"It means that when Wetherton's car was attacked and I was trying to save his ass, I got no sense of evil from Blaine. And yet yesterday afternoon, as he was coming out of Wetherton's office, my skin fairly crawled at the sight of him."

Gabriel raised an eyebrow. "Do you know why he was visiting Wetherton?"

"Something to do with military funding." She shrugged.

He frowned. "What time was this?"

She shrugged again. "I didn't really look at a clock, but it had to have been after six. Why?

"Because I was called to a murder scene when you left to go up to Wetherton's office and both General Lloyd and General Blaine turned up about ten minutes later." He glanced at her. "Blaine couldn't be in two places at once. Unless, of course, one of them *wasn't* him."

"Why would someone bother impersonating Blaine? And how would the impersonator even get away with it if Lloyd wasn't also a copy?" She paused to frown. "And why were they both turning up at a murder scene?"

"Because the woman murdered was Kathryn Douglass, director of The Pegasus Foundation, which has strong military ties."

"That doesn't explain why Lloyd and Blaine would turn up."

"Many of the projects the foundation was involved in came from Hopeworth. Blaine was Douglass's military contact."

"But..." She hesitated, mulling over the little she'd heard or read about the foundation. "Don't they make big hardware, like fighter planes and stuff?"

"Yes. But they also work on smaller, more experimental weapons for Hopeworth. Illie and I were called in there a few days ago to investigate a break-in."

"Illie being your new partner?" Meaning he didn't have something against partners, just against her?

He hesitated. "Not by choice, I can assure you." His gaze met hers for a long moment, and she saw not only annoyance but a loneliness and a longing that was as deep as anything she'd ever felt.

If ever she needed encouragement to carry on with her crazy seduction plan that was it. The problem was how far should she push? And how soon? Given the situation—and her reassignment—it wasn't going to be easy, no matter what she decided.

Which meant that maybe she needed to seduce him sooner rather than later—and hit him hard and fast. Give him no time to think, just react.

She looked out the window and wondered if she could even do that. Wondered if she'd do nothing more than make a fool of herself. Lord, she hadn't even kissed the man, and here she was, thinking of full-blooded seduction. And she only had her hormones and his sister saying that he *was* interested.

While she might see loneliness and need in his eyes, it didn't actually mean that either were aimed at *her*.

"Sam?"

She jerked out of her thoughts and met his gaze. "What?"

He studied her again, his gaze shrewd, almost judgmental. "I said, so what made you order that search on Blaine the other night if you felt no evil in him?"

She hesitated, but something in the way he was looking at her suggested this was a pivotal point in their relationship. That if she lied about this, she could forget about the future and whatever plans she might hold. "Because I recognized him."

"How?"

"From my dreams."

His eyebrow rose. "And what was he doing in those dreams?"

She blew out a breath, battling a sudden reluctance to talk about it. What if the dreams were fake? What if they were nothing more than images of an overactive imagination?

What if they weren't?

If she wanted to know the truth, she had to start trusting someone with her nightly journeys. Someone other than Joe, whom she might not be able to trust.

"They were training me to use gifts I don't appear to have right now."

"Hopeworth was?"

"I can't say for sure it was Hopeworth, because the dreams never included a location. It was just a room—or rather, an arena—with the scientists in an observation room above me."

"And was it just you in the dream?"

"In the training arena? Yes." She hesitated. "But I am never alone in the dreams. Joshua is always with me."

"And is Joshua this Joe Black you mentioned earlier?"

"In all honesty, I don't know. Joe looks nothing like the boy in my dreams. His coloring is completely different, for a start."

"But he could be?"

"I guess so. Anything is possible, especially when I don't even know if the dreams are real or a figment of a warped imagination."

He considered her, hazel eyes shuttered. "Is Joe real?"

"I've already said yes to that question. Though I doubt Joe is his real name."

He shrugged, as if that in itself meant nothing. Which she guessed it didn't. Whoever Joe was, it was logical that he wouldn't give her his real name—not until he knew he could trust her. Which was an odd thought.

"Do the dreams feel real?" Gabriel asked.

"Yes." Too real, too painful, even if she didn't entirely believe them.

Or maybe that should be even if she didn't entirely *want* to believe them.

"If you are so sure, why have you never mentioned them?"

She hesitated. "Just because they feel real, doesn't mean they *are* real. For all I know, they could have been planted in my subconscious for some nefarious reason." She looked ahead as the car began to slow and saw they were nearing the hotel. She returned her gaze to his. "That's what you were thinking, isn't it?"

A smile fleetingly touched his lips. "At first, yes. But I think it's becoming increasingly obvious you're from one of the Hopeworth projects, though whether that project is Penumbra or something else is anyone's guess right now. That being the case, you've obviously slipped their noose until now. Which means you had help."

"Because a teenager could not escape the might of the military alone."

"A normal teenager, no. But you are not normal, Sam."

"If that wasn't apparent before, it sure is now." She smiled to counter the bitterness in her tone. "But even so, my memories—or lack thereof—and the fact that there has been a careful 'refinement' of my past suggests that someone, somewhere, knows who and what I am. And they have gone to great lengths to hide it."

"Yes." He paused. "Have you asked this Joe Black about it?"

"He says I will remember when I need to remember."

"Helpful."

"Yeah. And I've asked who he is, and I get the same answer."

"Then perhaps you need to find another source."

She raised her eyebrows. "You don't think I've been trying?"

"I meant another Hopeworth source. Have you ever gone back to see that woman who claimed to be your nanny in Hopeworth? The one who called you Josephine?"

"No."

"Then perhaps we should."

"What? Now?"

"Is there anything else you particularly want to do right now?"

"How about sleep?"

He looked at her for a moment, and then he laughed a little sheepishly. "Yeah, I guess you would. How about I come back later this morning?"

How about you come join me in bed? She rubbed a hand across her eyes and tried to ignore the impulse to say the words out loud. For all that she wanted this man, it wasn't the right time for a seduction. And in all honesty, her planned lunch probably wasn't the best time, either, though she had a feeling there was never going to be a "good" time.

But if she wanted to know for sure whether that something between them was more than just a side effect of genetics, of breeding, then she had better force her reluctant feet forward and at least *try,* wrong time or not.

"No. Let's do it now, then I can sleep the rest of the day."

He raised his eyebrows. "And the apology lunch?"

"Can become an apology brunch." She leaned forward and programmed the nursing home's address into the autodrive. The car shot back into traffic and drove on.

He didn't comment, just nodded. She wasn't getting much from him at the moment—not even little insights via body language, which meant he was controlling himself very tightly.

No surprise, really. He'd been doing that from the first time they'd met.

"So," she continued, "what did you actually learn about Blaine?"

"Not a great deal. Basically family and education stuff. Information all but froze when he went into the military at eighteen."

"Did he go straight into Hopeworth, then?"

"No. Records show he enlisted into the army and went through basic training. The records are listed as high security after that."

"I thought Stephan's security listing was high enough to get access to such records."

"He has access to all but Hopeworth. It is a law unto itself."

She snorted. "I'm thinking that's not exactly wise."

He grimaced. "The military would argue that given the sensitive nature of much of their research, it is a necessity."

"So, if Stephan has access to all but Hopeworth, why haven't you got the rest of it?"

"Because Stephan is currently home with Lyssa and his new son."

"Lyssa's had her kid? Hey, send her and Stephan my congrats. What did they name him?"

"Devyn Charles Oswald Stern."

She blinked. "That's one hell of a moniker for a little kid to carry."

He grinned. "He's the first grandson, so he was destined

to carry the first name of both grandfathers. It's something of a tradition."

"And a nice one. The past is never forgotten that way." There was sudden sympathy in his expression and she knew he was thinking about her lack of a past. Given she didn't particularly want to dwell on the reasons for that right now, she rushed on before he could say anything, "She didn't have any problems, then?"

"Not as many as we expected. She's had a bad pregnancy and isn't strong—as you know, because you've met her—and it was an extremely long birth. But she's fine. Tired, but fine."

What *she* knew was that Lyssa was stronger than her family was giving her credit for. She *had* met the woman, and beneath that pale, frail build was a steel determination that was breathtaking. Anyone who could handle being kidnapped and isolated for six months and still come out of it sane could certainly cope with anything else life threw at them.

"So, has the proud uncle been to see the newest addition to the family yet?"

He hesitated, and darkness flashed through his eyes. "Not yet."

"Why not?"

"Because sometimes there are things more important than family."

"Nothing is more important than family." Says the woman who hasn't got one, she thought with resignation.

"Some things are."

And the brief glance he gave her made her pulse skip, then race. Did that glance imply what she thought it implied? Or were her overactive hormones making her read far too much into it?

"Like what?" she asked, as casually as she could.

"Like stopping a madman intent on starting a war."

Amusement and perhaps a touch of disappointment ran through her. So much for all the pulse racing, she thought wryly. "So, you still think Wetherton has connections to Sethanon?"

"Do I believe it? Yes. Do I have any proof? No. Other than the body of the real Wetherton, and the fact that Sethanon was behind the attempt to replace the Prime Minister with a clone, that is."

"And Wetherton's connections to Hopeworth?"

"Could be a means for Sethanon to keep track of what is

going on in there. Or maybe Wetherton is merely the go-between for Sethanon and his military source."

She raised her eyebrows at that. "You think Blaine is working for Sethanon?"

"It's not beyond the bounds of reason. I certainly don't think it's a coincidence that it was Blaine's image the multishifter imitating him used."

"Why?"

"Multishifters need to come in constant contact with someone to take their shape. It takes a little time for cells to reconfigure, and the longer the contact, the more exact the image."

"Really? Does it work the same for shapechangers? Or shapeshifters?"

He shook his head. "Shapechangers and shifters are born with their secondary form programmed into their cells. Multishifters have 'adaptable' cells'."

"Fascinating."

"Very."

His voice was dry and she smiled. "Maybe not to you because you grew up with it. Who actually knows what, exactly, I grew up with?" She paused, frowning a little. "You know, it seems odd to me that you all fear Sethanon, and yet you haven't been able to find out a great deal about him in the all the years you've been hunting him."

"We *do* know a lot about his organization. We just don't know much about the man himself."

"Why not? I mean, you've captured his people, interrogated them, so surely they were able to give you something more concrete."

"Only concrete in the terms of his organization, his contacts, stuff like that. No one seems to know much about the man himself."

"Don't you find that a little surprising?"

"Not really. We're talking about someone who can change his identity at a whim. It's hard to trace someone when you can't even pin down their true identity." He grimaced. "Hell, for all we know, he could be one of the contacts we have under observation. Anything is possible when your form is mutable."

She raised her eyebrows. "So, he suddenly appears on the scene sixteen years ago and starts taking pot shots at the

Federation and the SIU?"

"It's a little more than pot shots," he interrupted, his voice a little testy. "And his agenda—which he's made perfectly clear in several messages he's sent us—amounts to war."

"And yet if he intended war, why hasn't he just started it? Why warn you at *all*?"

"Because he enjoys an audience." Gabriel shrugged. "And he probably enjoys watching us run around trying to find and stop him."

"And it's hard to stop someone when you have no idea who and what they are."

"Exactly."

She considered him, thinking about what she'd said, what he'd said, and drawing conclusions that she really didn't like. Like the fact that Sethanon's appearance seemed to coincide with hers. True, it *was* probably little more than a coincidence, especially given the appearance of other Hopeworth rejects over the years, but it was still a disturbing thought. After a moment, she said, "It still doesn't make sense, you know. I mean, if he wants a war, he could have started it years ago. What is he waiting for?"

"Who knows? It could be something as simple as the fact that it takes time to build a fighting force."

Something inside her clicked, and her eyes widened. "Hopeworth."

He frowned. "What?"

"Hopeworth is the key." She reached out, grabbing his hand and wrapping her fingers around his. "*That's* what he's waiting for. Hopeworth has spent years making the perfect soldier, and from what we've seen recently, may finally be succeeding. *That's* what he's waiting for. This Sethanon of yours is planning to take over Hopeworth."

Ten

Gabriel stared at Sam for a moment, and then he said almost automatically, "He couldn't."

And yet even as he denied it, his mind raced with the possibility. It was something they'd never even contemplated. Yet, in a twisted way, it made perfect sense. If Sethanon intended to start a war against a well-armed, well-informed alliance of nonhumans like the Federation, then it would pay to get fighters that were stronger, faster, better than those nonhumans. And that's *exactly* what Hopeworth was breeding.

"He could if he's a multishifter," she said, her eyes star-bright in the darkness. "Remember, you're the one who said we had two Blaine's running around."

"Well, yeah. But that's not something that could be done over a long time."

"Why not? Stephan's been doing it for years to stay in charge of the SIU, hasn't he?"

"Hopeworth is an entirely different beast than the SIU. I doubt an imitator would go unnoticed for very long in an installation that specializes in interspecies and psi-talent development. Especially when the original is still running around."

"But if he's got people on the inside and the outside—people like Wetherton—tracking Blaine's movements, then it is totally possible."

"Only if Blaine didn't live on the base, and he does."

"But he doesn't stay on the base all the time. And who says this Sethanon of yours isn't also living on the base? You're the one who said whoever is posing as Blaine has to be in close contact to ensure a good replication."

That was true. And it was definitely an idea they would have to investigate. Though given the tight security on all Hopeworth information and records, it was going to be a damn hard undertaking. But the base itself was an entirely different proposition. They could certainly watch all the comings and goings. He shifted so that he was facing her full on, but he didn't shake her grip on his hand. There was something almost comforting in her touch—comforting in a way that was sexual and yet not.

In the darkness, her skin was almost as luminescent as her

eyes. With her fiery hair covered by the hood of her dark coat, she appeared almost ghostly. His grip on her hand tightened a little, and the fingers of his free hand itched with the sudden need to caress her cheek. To feel the softness of her skin. To reassure himself that she was real and here, and not already beginning to fade away into nothingness as Karl had warned.

"Why are you so positive about this?" he asked.

She hesitated and looked away. He reached out and, touched her chin, drawing her gaze back to his. When she licked her lips, he found his gaze drawn to the movement. Not good, he thought, and yet he couldn't pull his gaze away.

"How the hell can I be sure?" She hesitated again. "But I'm right. I know I'm right."

"Because you were at Hopeworth with the man who is now Sethanon?" The question came out of nowhere, and he had to wonder if it was an instinctive reaction to the pull he was feeling towards her.

And yet, at the same time, it *was* a natural question. She was obviously connected to Hopeworth, and there was definitely a connection to Sethanon somewhere along the line. Otherwise, why would the man have spent so much time over the years keeping an eye on her? Maybe even protecting her?

She gasped and jerked away from his grasp. Part of him regretted the loss of her touch. Part of him didn't. And he couldn't help noticing that despite her reaction, there was no hurt in her eyes, no surprise, which suggested she'd contemplated the question herself, however lightly.

"That's not true," she said. Even as her eyes said, *Please don't let it be true.*

"Sam, think about it. Your memories started at the age of fourteen. At that very same time, Sethanon makes his first appearance. And, coincidently, just before either event, a project named Penumbra was destroyed by a fire to the point that there were absolutely no records left. There wasn't even enough DNA left to identify who, exactly, died in that fire. Normal fires don't burn to that degree. Not without help."

She was staring at him, eyes wide and somewhat distant, like she was seeing things he couldn't even begin to guess at. He wondered what she was remembering, wished that she'd tell him. But he'd done very little in recent months to encourage trust, and for the first time he regretted it. Truly regretted it.

"Fire is not my element."

The words were said softly, almost automatically. He frowned. "Were they Joe's?"

She blinked, and life came flooding back into her eyes. "Joe was never at Hopeworth. At least, the man I know now as Joe wasn't. Joshua was."

"What if Joe is a shapeshifter? He could have been there as someone else."

"He's a shapechanger. You can't be both shifter and changer, can you?"

"In normal situations, no." You could be a multishifter and, on rare occasions, even a multichanger, but he'd never heard of a multishifter-changer.

But then, up until Rose Pierce began killing off Hopeworth rejectees, he'd never heard of a male-female shifter, either.

"Hopeworth isn't developing the normal," she said.

"No, they're not." He hesitated. "Your dreams haven't made any connections between Joe and this Joshua? Was Joshua one of the instructors?"

"No, and no." Her sudden smile held very little warmth. "If I believe the nanny, Joshua is actually my twin brother."

He raised an eyebrow. "A test tube twin or the real thing?"

She shrugged. "Considering I have no idea about the manner of my birth, I can't really comment about the test tube thing. And Mary never said either way. Nor did I think to ask."

"But what do your instincts say?"

"My instincts and my dreams make me believe that Mary is telling the truth—that he's my brother. My *real* brother. The other half of me." She hesitated. "But since I still don't know whether my dreams can be trusted, I wouldn't rely on them as the truth just yet."

"But what if they *are* the truth?"

She stared at him for a moment and then looked away again. But not before he'd seen the sheen of tears in her eyes. "I don't want them to be the truth. I don't want to be just another product from some mad scientist's production line."

He gently forced her to look at him again. "Whether you are or not doesn't matter, Sam. The scientists may have given you life, but they haven't made you what you are."

"And just what am I?" she said, and for the first time there was a hint of desperation in her voice. "Am I a military weapon gone wrong, or one that is merely waiting for the right trigger?"

"What you are," he said softly, "is a warm, bright woman

with a past that is undefined. But military creation or not, they are *not* the sum of your making. You have a mind and a soul that are all your own, and they are not evil. You could never be evil."

Her gaze searched his. "Are you sure of that? Truly sure? Because if my dreams are to be believed, I did some pretty horrible things in that place."

Maybe it was a trick of the night, or maybe the car had somehow shrunk, because suddenly her face seemed nearer to his, her lips nearer still. The urge to close the gap between them, to caress her mouth with his own, rose with a vengeance from somewhere deep inside. Suddenly he was drowning in the desire to kiss her and fighting for control.

"We all do what we must to survive," he said softly and gently brushed several strands of hair away from her warm cheek. She trembled slightly under the caress, but her gaze didn't leave his. And there was a challenging light in her eyes, as if she were daring him to acknowledge what was happening. Daring him to do what he wanted to do.

He didn't. Just said, "In your case, I doubt you would have done anything that you were not forced to do."

"I'm not so sure about that."

"I am."

And with that, he gave up the fight and kissed her.

He kissed her slowly, passionately, like he had all the time in the world and this kiss was not their first, but rather one of many. And it felt good. So good. As her smell entwined him, filling his every breath with the richness of vanilla and cinnamon, he groaned and deepened the kiss, wanting, needing, to taste every inch of her delicious mouth. As desire fled south, she answered in kind, her hands sliding up his chest and around his neck, until she was holding him as if she never meant to let him go. It made him hunger to taste her more fully, to skim his tongue across her warm pale skin, exploring and savoring every bit of her.

God, this kiss felt so right, so scarily right, unlike anything he'd ever experienced before. Even with Andrea. And *that* shook him. Andrea had been his soul mate. He'd been *so* certain of it back then. That being the case, he shouldn't be feeling the completeness he was feeling with this kiss, this woman. No matter how deep the attraction.

And yet he was.

So, had he been wrong so long ago, or was *this* connection, this rightness, something altogether different? Perhaps connected to the storm bond and the shadow walker genes that ran in her blood and apparently in his?

He didn't know.

But one thing was certain. Now that he'd experienced it, he *had* to explore it. He had no option. He was a shapechanger and part of that heritage was the fierce desire to find his mate— that one woman who was his other half, his destiny, his soul mate. This kiss had woken that part of him, and the hunter *had* to explore it. Especially after all these years of being convinced that his soul mate was dead and buried.

And while now was not the time for such thoughts or such explorations, the fact was, he could no longer ignore what was between them, could no longer push her away.

But could he breach the fences he'd spent so long creating?

He pulled back from her just enough to allow some breathing room between them.

"I'm sorry—"

She placed a hand on his lips, stopping the rest of his words. "Don't apologize for something I've wanted you to do for a long time now."

He wasn't apologizing for the kiss, despite his reservations and uncertainty, but rather his timing—which pretty much stunk—and his treatment of her over the past few months. One kiss *shouldn't* have changed anything, yet it had. But really, what was the point of explaining that? She probably wouldn't believe him anyway. Hell, *he* was finding it hard to believe. "Then I won't."

She smiled. "Good."

He glanced at the road ahead and saw, with surprise, that they were almost at Greensborough. The nursing home where Mary Elliott was being looked after was only five minutes or so away. Time sure flew when you were kissing your partner. Or rather, ex-partner. "I think we need to talk."

"I agree, but not here or now. Later, over brunch."

He nodded and retreated to his side of the car. But her scent still seemed to surround him, filling his every breath, forcing him to fight desire. "So, tell me about this Mary. How did you find her in the first place?"

A ghost of a smile touched her lips. She was obviously well aware he was trying to distract himself. "Joe gave me a pin with two figures on it—an abstract man and woman, standing side by side, one dark, one light. He said that by seeking its image I'd find our murderer. He also said that I'd find the first stepping stone to my past."

"So the pin led you to Mary Elliott?"

She nodded. "And to the truth about Rose Pierce."

"Which begs the question, how did he know?"

She sighed. "Maybe he *is* military. He walked military, if that makes sense."

"So, in reality, he could be Blaine?"

"In reality, no. He's a changer, as I said. A crow. And he can't be one of Hopeworth's products because he has black hair. Lloyd said all Hopeworth's creations have red hair, and that's certainly proven the case, even among the rejects."

All true. And yet, why did this Joe know so much? And how had he formed such an intimate connection with her? If he wasn't a Hopeworth product, he had to be at least a part of Hopeworth—and a part of the project that Sam had come from. A project that had been almost totally erased.

"Psychic connections such as the one you appear to have with Joe just don't happen between strangers. Despite the myths, such strong connections take time, and effort and—" He hesitated and then added softly, "Intimacy."

"Joe and I have never been lovers."

"I never said that you were. But he could be someone who was close to you in that place. Someone you leaned on for strength."

She shook her head. "There was only Joshua. In the dreams, it was always him and me against the rest."

Yet, she had said she didn't know if the dreams could be trusted as the truth. What if someone *had* altered them, perhaps not so much the content but appearances? What if her twin wasn't who she thought he was?

That would certainly make the man who seemed to know too much about her more of an option as the brother.

But why would he continue to keep his identity a secret if he was in mental contact with her now? What was he waiting for?

Since that was a question neither he nor Sam could answer, he switched topics.

"How trustworthy do you think the nurse's information is going to be when it comes to you, given Hopeworth's past habit of nullifying certain sections of their former employees' memories?"

She shrugged. "Her memories of the project *have* been restricted. I asked her the name of the project she worked on, and she said it hurts if she tries to remember."

"And yet she could talk freely about you and Joshua? You didn't think that odd?"

"No." She hesitated. "But Mary said we were all little more than numbers, so maybe that's why she could talk about us."

He frowned. "What?"

She grimaced. "Just something Mary mentioned last time. She said she wished the military would give us names instead of numbers, because she couldn't keep up with all the different names we kept coming up with for ourselves."

"So, the military might have restricted her from mentioning specific numbers, but because she knew you by particular names, she's been able to short-circuit the restrictions?"

"Possibly."

"Which means, she might also know what other aliases your brother went by?"

Her eyebrows rose. "I hadn't thought of asking that, but yeah, she might. Worth a try, anyway."

It certainly was. Hell, *anything* that gave them *any* information about her so called "brother" was a good thing, because he didn't trust her sudden revelation. Didn't like the fact that she'd been talking to someone for so many years, and yet had no clue as to that person's real identity. Hell, how could they be sure it *wasn't* Sethanon himself? It wasn't beyond the realm of possibility, especially given Sethanon's apparent interest in her over the years.

The car slid to a stop outside a large brick residence that had the air of a secure hospital rather than someplace homey and warm. Bars lined the front windows, and sturdy, locked gates guarded the pathways that led to the back of the building. There was lots of landscaping evident beyond the gates, but it did little to blunt the initial impression of a prison-like environment.

"This it?" He glanced back at Sam.

She nodded. "Hopefully, Mary's doing a little better now than when I visited her the last time. Otherwise, we won't be talking to her for long."

"How ill is she?" He climbed out of the car. The early morning sunshine was bright, despite the bitter wind, so he put on his sun glasses. And in the brief shift between brightness and shade, he thought he saw something move in the thick shrubbery beyond the gates.

He frowned, lowering the sunglasses a little and squinting against the sunlight as he studied the path along the right side of the building. Nothing more than bushes moving to the tune of the breeze.

And yet...something had moved. Something *other* than plant life swaying back and forth. Something that had darted back into the shadows with inhuman speed, and yet had been human in shape.

Frown deepening, he walked around the car, waiting until his back was to the building before he said, "Can you feel anything out of place?"

She gave him a sharp glance and looked at the building. "No." She hesitated, frowning a little. "Yes. There's a faint feeling of evil coming from the right of the building."

The right of the building was where he'd seen the shadow move. "What do you mean by faint?"

"It's not a solid sensation. It's wispier, like I'm feeling something ghostlike rather than human." She shrugged and glanced at him. "Why? What did you see?"

"I'm not sure." He stared at the side of the building for a little longer, but didn't see any further movement. And yet the sense that something was out of place remained. "I think something is about to go down. You want to get inside and talk to Mary Elliott? I'd like to check the outside of the building first."

She nodded and strode toward the front door. He headed for the suspect sideway. Neither of them had taken more than a few steps when the screaming began.

He shared a brief glance with Sam, and then ran like hell for the gates. One huge leap and he was over them, racing for the rear of the building.

He saw a shadow leap skyward on night-dark wings as he rounded the corner.

He shifted shape and gave chase.

* * *

Sam crashed through the front door, her badge raised in one hand and her weapon held low in the other. "SIU folks, stand back."

"Officer please, there's no need—"

She ignored the woman at the reception desk and ran down the hall. How many times in the past had she been in a similar situation? Being so close to possible answers only to have them snatched away by some force of evil. Whether that force was military or Sethanon's in design didn't matter right now. What did was getting to Mary's room and making sure yet another avenue of answers wasn't shut down.

Because the screams were definitely coming from Mary.

She pounded down the hall, chased by footsteps and protests, her gaze on the main prize—the open door to Mary's room.

She slowed as she neared the room, took a deep breath, then stepped inside, weapon raised.

Only to discover the receptionist had been right. There was no need, and no threat. One of the four big windows that looked out onto the garden *was* open, but nothing more than a few inches. Maybe enough to let a bird in, but certainly not a human. The screen covering the window had tumbled to the ground, and the curtains flapped slightly in the breeze. Surely neither could be the reason behind the screams coming from thin gray haired woman standing in the middle of the room. The screen dropping *could* have frightened her, but not to this extent. There was sheer terror in the old girl's voice.

Two nurses stood on either side of her, talking to her in soft tones, obviously trying to calm her down. She'd seen at least one of the women on her last visit here, so they probably weren't causing Mary's distress, either.

She put her weapon away and stepped toward the trio. "Ladies, do you need any help?" She flashed her badge as one of the nurses looked around, then asked, "What happened?"

"Day terrors," the dark haired nurse said grimly. "Sometimes happens when the mind regresses."

Sam walked into the older woman's line of sight, blocking the window and whatever it was Mary had seen. Or thought she'd seen.

"Mary?" she said softly.

The older woman blinked, and then her gaze met Sam's. The right side of Mary's face lit up in a smile.

"Josephine!" The word was slightly slurred, but not beyond understanding. Mary's stroke had robbed the left side of her face of mobility, but thankfully had left her capable of some speech. "Oh, thank God, you're here."

She lurched forward, pulling out of the nurses' grip with surprising ease, and staggered toward her. Sam caught her, wrapping her arms around the frail body. She felt the shuddering of terror through the other woman's limbs, the steel of muscle underneath it.

Mary might be old, she might be frail, but there was a lot of strength left yet in the old girl's body.

"It's all right, Mary. I'm here; no one will get you now."

The old woman shuddered. "I saw him, you know. I wasn't imagining it. I saw him."

"Shhhh. It's okay. You're safe." She stroked Mary's back with one hand, and felt the terror begin to leave the older woman's body.

"He'll be back. Now that they know I'm here, he'll be back."

"No, he won't. My partner's out there right now, hunting him down. He'll catch him. That's what he does."

Mary pulled back a little. "I know. I was talking to him."

She frowned. "You were talking to Gabriel?"

"I don't know a Gabriel. I meant Joshua. Where is he? I want to talk to him again." Her voice was petulant, like that of a child deprived of a toy. And in many ways Mary *was* a child. Much of her mind had gone, lost in memories of the past.

But did that mean she was lost now, or had she really seen Joshua? And if it wasn't Joshua who had scared her—and her words seemed to indicate it wasn't—then who or what had?

"Maybe he'll come by later."

She glanced up at the dark haired nurse, who shook her head and said, "There were no visitors today."

So, imagination. But that didn't mean she couldn't get something useful, as long as she didn't push the old girl too far. She motioned toward the sofa. "Mary, why don't you come and sit down on the sofa?"

"Oh, all right. As long as they don't stick me, again. They're always sticking me with things."

The second nurse came back into the room with a medical trolley at that precise moment, and Sam couldn't help smiling. "You don't want to be sick when Joshua visits again, do you?" She helped the elderly woman onto the sofa and knelt down in front of her. "How about you talk to me about his visit while the nurses make sure the other man didn't hurt you."

The old woman's smile broke lose at the mention of Joshua. "He was such a bonny child. You both were."

"When was he here, Mary?"

"Today, like I said. Just before that other man appeared." She shuddered. "Never did like the look of that one. He was nasty."

"How did Joshua get here? He never checked in with the nurses."

The old woman snorted. "Well, he wouldn't, would he? He hates medical types. Far easier to fly in through an open window and avoid all the fuss."

"So he came as a bird?"

"Yeah." Mary smiled. "You both had to be electronically chipped so you didn't fly beyond the compound restrictions."

It sounded like Mary was getting her mixed up with someone else, because while she had changer genes, she certainly wasn't able to change. Though, admittedly, she'd never tried to, either.

A chill ran over her skin, and she rubbed her arms. Whoever had blocked her memories had been very thorough indeed if she could not remember something as basic as the fact that she could shapechange.

Why block it in the first place, though? She could understand why Hopeworth and everything that had happened there might have been erased, but why the total erasure? Why take away from her something as harmless as the fact she had a brother or that she could shapechange?

And how was any of this connected to the mythical Sethanon?

"How many bird forms did he have?" she asked.

"Several. You always seemed to prefer the small hawk form, but him, he liked to change. A hawk, a raven, sometimes even a pigeon. None of those could fit through the window, though. He came today as one of them annoying birds—minors, I think they call them."

Again she wondered if Mary's memories were true, or if she was getting imagination and reality mixed up. She glanced up as the nurse finished her check on the old girl.

"She's fine," the nurse said. "Just keep her calm."

Sam nodded, waiting until the two nurses had left the room before continuing her questions. "Did Joshua say why he was here, Mary?"

"He said it was all right to talk. He said they couldn't stop me anymore." Fear briefly crossed her half-frozen features. "Maybe that's why *he* came. He knew."

"He who? I need to know which one of them, Mary, so we can stop him."

"The general. It was the general."

"Blaine? Or Lloyd?" It had to be one of them. Lloyd was a gynecologist, and apparently in charge of the breeding section of Hopeworth. Blaine had been the man behind the experiments and training. Maybe even the whole Penumbra project.

But which of the Blaines had been here? The one she'd met at Wetherton's car, or the one who'd been in Wetherton's office?

And did it actually matter? Just because she hadn't felt anything "off" or evil about the first Blaine didn't mean he couldn't be either.

"It was Blaine." Mary shuddered. "We used to call him the day shadow. Always creeping about, he was, and harder to spot than a ghost at dusk."

"Did he say anything?"

"Didn't get a chance, did he? He saw Joshua and scooted out of here as fast as he could."

"So he recognized Josh?"

She smiled. "You always used to call him that when you were angry with him. It was like you couldn't get his full name out fast enough."

Her dreams had never shown anger with the man who was supposedly her brother. Only fear and longing—fear of what they were doing, of what Joshua was going to do. Longing to be free, to have what she'd never had—a family, friends. Things she still didn't have.

"Did we fight often?"

Mary shrugged. "You were as different as night and day when it came to personalities. You were always the fiery one, the one quick to judge. He was more...careful." She looked away for a minute, her gaze briefly distant. "But for all that, I always thought he was the more dangerous of the two of you. He never seemed to have limits of any kind. And he did some nasty things."

"We both did," she said softly.

Mary's gaze met hers again, and she raised a slightly

shaking hand to brush Sam's skin with dry fingertips. "In many ways, you were always the good one. What you did, you had to do."

Her words made Sam remember the pin Joe had given her. Had it been more of a clue than she realized? Had the abstract man and woman on its surface—one light, one dark— represented her and the man who was supposedly her twin?

Had Joe been trying to tell her that he not only knew who she was, but who her brother was? And did that mean he was a friend or foe? For sure, he'd warned her of trouble more than once, but that didn't mean she could trust him. Hell, for all she knew, Joe might be Blaine in disguise.

"Mary, was there anyone on the project who went by the name Joe Black?"

She frowned. "Not that I remember. But then, I didn't know everyone on the project, because I was basically confined to the nursery and housing areas. Nor did I know all the secret names you two called yourselves. Only some."

"Can you remember the other names?"

She frowned. "Not really. I only remember Josephine and Joshua because that's the names you used most often."

"What about Sethanon? Is that one of them? Or maybe the name of someone who worked there?"

"Sethanon?" Her frowned deepened. "I don't think there wasn't anyone on the project called that. It's such an odd name that surely I'd remember it. But Joshua got caught reading a book by that name, I'm sure."

A chill went through her. "Sethanon is a book title?"

"Yeah. I caught him reading it well before they did, and I warned him, I did. But he took no notice."

"So we weren't allowed to read fiction?"

"No. Only what they gave you. On technologies, weapons, stuff like that." She shrugged. "No one ever knew how he got that book. When they took it off him, he got mad." She looked away again. "Joshua would never have hurt me, I knew that, but that day I was afraid. And not just of him, but both of you."

She raised her eyebrows. "Why both of us?"

Mary's gaze came back to Sam's. "Because separately you were powerful, but together—I swear Heaven and Earth trembled in fear of your wrath that day."

She swallowed heavily, but didn't ask what had happened. Right now, she really didn't want to know. It was enough to know that she was not what she'd presumed—and that the past she'd spent most of her remembered life trying to uncover was one better left alone. And yet, now that she'd started down the path of remembering, there was no turning back. The military and their rising level of interest in her ensured that, if nothing else.

Besides, the dreams were becoming relentless. Remembering was something being forced on her, whether she wanted it or not.

"If we were so powerful, Mary, how did they ever restrain us?"

Her smile was grim. "Simply by placing special pellets under your skins, and threatening the death of one if the other did anything out of place."

She remembered the dream of her and Joshua running up a slope on a moonless night. Remembered the promise he'd made as fire danced across his fingertips that soon they would have their revenge and be free.

He'd obviously found a way to remove the pellets and fulfill that promise.

"How did you escape the fire that destroyed the project, Mary?"

"I don't know." She frowned. "There was an explosion, and heat—horrible heat—and the next thing I remember I was outside on this grassy slope." She rubbed her arms. "I think an angel saved me that day. I should have died with the rest of them. The nursery was the second place the fire hit."

"And the first?"

"The arena where they used to train you both."

Something in the way she said that scratched Sam's instincts. "The both of us? What about the others?"

"There were no others. Not in..." she hesitated, and rubbed her forehead. "It still hurts if I try to say the name. Joshua told me it wouldn't."

Sam lightly squeezed the older woman's free hand. "You don't need to say the name, Mary. I know the project." She hesitated. "So, Joshua and I were the only ones in that project?"

Mary nodded. "There were others bred. Lots of others. But none of them survived past the toddler years. No one knew why. But I reckon it was because you were twins. You had each other, and you took care of each other. The other little ones had no one but themselves."

Karl had said that walkers came as a pair. Had to, or they were lost in the very power they were destined to control. Was that the reason she and Joshua had survived when the others hadn't? Because they were twins? Yet, if Joshua was her base, why then did she appear to have a connection with Gabriel?

And if Hopeworth had studied walkers, and were intermixing walker genes with those of other races, how could they not know that walkers had to come as a pair to survive?

"So we were the only twins they bred?"

"They didn't breed you as twins. It just happened. One whole became two."

A chill went through her. *Two halves of a whole.* Joe had said that, too. Another clue she hadn't taken note of.

God, who *was* he?

And was he friend or foe? Or something else altogether?

"So, once the project was destroyed, you left?"

Mary nodded. "I went on to work for several adoption agencies."

"And the military haven't tried to contact you before now?"

Mary shook her head. "Haven't even sighted them."

That being the case, why *would* they bother to contact her now? But even as the question went through her mind, she remembered Blaine's reaction as he'd come out of Wetherton's office. Remembered his certainty that they'd met before, that she knew fully just who he was and what he did in the military.

She was the reason he'd come to see Mary.

He'd wanted to confirm his suspicions, and Mary was the one person left alive who seemed able to connect her with that red-haired child bred and raised in Hopeworth.

Mary couldn't stay here. Blaine would be back, and if there was one thing she was certain of, it was that she didn't want Blaine knowing anything more about her. Mary might be living in the past most of the time, and her memories might not all be true, but what she did remember was enough to confirm any suspicions Blaine might have. And once that happened, they would come after her full force. She'd been bred to be a weapon. It didn't matter if her abilities were buried along with her memories, they'd want her back.

Maybe that was why Joshua had come here to give Mary permission to tell all. Maybe he was trying to speed up Sam's memory so she could escape Hopeworth's clutches once again.

She glanced around as Gabriel walked into the room. "Any success?"

He shook his head. "I saw a raven fly away from the window, but by the time I shifted shape and flew after it, its lead was too great."

She raised an eyebrow. "I wouldn't have thought a raven would be faster than a hawk."

"Neither would I." He stopped beside the sofa and gave Mary a smile. "Are you all right?"

"I don't know you," Mary said, somewhat crossly. She glanced at Sam. "Do I know him?"

"This is my new partner, Mary. His name is Gabriel, and he's going to arrange a nice place for you to stay while we track down Blaine."

Gabriel raised his eyebrows, but he didn't refute the statement. "Somewhere nice and safe."

The mobile half of Mary's face lit up. "A holiday would be nice. Gets boring, this place does."

Sam patted the older woman's knee and rose. "We'll just go talk to the nurses and arrange it, then."

"Lock the damn window," Mary said. "Don't want that bastard coming back to visit me while you're gone."

Sam obeyed, locking the window and closing the curtains for good measure. When they were out in the hall, Gabriel asked, "What was that all about?"

"Mary was screaming because she saw Blaine." She glanced back at the room to ensure Mary wasn't moving around, and then looked back at him. "And if Blaine was visiting her, it's because he wanted to confirm his suspicions about me."

He frowned. "The nurses said she had no visitors."

"No visitors that checked in with them. That doesn't mean there weren't any."

"Or that the old girl wasn't imagining it."

She nodded, conceding the point even if she didn't believe that was the case. "What, exactly, did you see when you climbed out of the car?"

"I thought I saw something move—something that was human in shape and yet it held no substance."

"And later, when you gave chase?"

"A raven, as I said."

She blew out a breath. "A raven is one of Joshua's shapes,

apparently." But it was also one of Joe's.

Was that a mere coincidence? Or perhaps a clue that Joe and Joshua were one and the same? But how could they be, when Joshua wasn't a shapeshifter? Joe and he had entirely different body shapes. Entirely different facial structures.

"So this Joshua of yours is Blaine?"

The sudden edge in his voice surprised her, though, as usual, there was little emotion to be seen in his expression. She shook her head. "Not unless he can be in two places at the very same time. Mary was talking to Joshua when Blaine appeared. Blaine apparently recognized Josh and ran. Joshua gave chase."

"So if it was Joshua I was chasing, what happened to Blaine?"

"Who knows? But Mary called him a day shadow— apparently he could creep around without being seen."

His eyebrows rose. "Meaning he could still be here? Can you feel him?"

She extended her senses, searching, but there was no sense of the shadowy evil she'd felt earlier. Blaine—if it was indeed Blaine she'd sensed—had gone. She shook her head.

"So, the question is," Gabriel said, "why were both men here today?"

"If you believe her—and I do—then Joshua was here to tell Mary that it was okay to tell me everything. He apparently told her the military could no longer stop her."

He studied her, face unreadable. "And Blaine?"

"As I said, I think he was here to confirm his suspicions. Mary worked in the nursery. She's probably the only one left alive who has any true knowledge about me and Joshua."

"Did you ask her about Sethanon?"

She nodded. "She didn't know anyone by that name. But she did say Joshua was punished once for reading a book with that title."

"A book? He called himself after a book?"

"Well, if Sethanon is actually Joshua, then yes. But it's a bit of a long shot, isn't it?"

He shrugged. "We've never been able to find a birth record for someone with that name, so it has to be an alias. And there's no rule stating an alias can't come from a work of fiction."

"But if Joshua *is* this Sethanon of yours, then how has he managed to remain unknown? According to Mary, Joshua is a shapechanger. She's seen him take on various bird shapes, but never another human shape. I thought you said it's not possible to be both?"

His frown deepened. "Generally, it isn't. But that doesn't mean Hopeworth couldn't have made the impossible possible."

True. "But surely the military would have known about the talent. They knew about our other talents." Though not all of them, apparently, because if the dreams were to be believed, they'd always thought *she* was the fire starter. It had always been Joshua's skill rather than hers.

"I think the only people who might be able to answer these questions are Blaine or Lloyd," he said. "Both of them were involved in the Penumbra project."

"And I think neither of them will be forthcoming with *any* sort of answer."

"I agree." He hesitated. "Look, let's get the old girl moved, and then we can go talk about this some more."

She studied him for a moment, again noting the sudden edge in his voice. "About what, exactly?"

"About ravens. The one seen here, and the people you know who are ravens."

"Why do I get the sudden feeling I'm not going to like the direction of this conversation?"

"Probably because you won't." His expression was suddenly grim. "Remember when I mentioned Kathryn Douglass being murdered?" When she nodded, he said, "Well, it just so happens we found a raven feather in her apartment. I don't think it's a coincidence. I think that either your brother, or the man you've been in psychic contact with, is a murderer."

Eleven

"You think Joshua or Joe is involved in Kathryn Douglass's murder?"

Gabriel nodded. It was just too much of a coincidence that all these ravens were suddenly showing up. He knew it, and Sam knew it. She had to, because there was no surprise in her voice, no anger. No emotion at all, really, except perhaps a hint of weary resignation. As if this was just another shock in a day that had already provided several.

"But why would either of them want to murder her when she had nothing to do with the Penumbra Project?"

Gabriel shrugged. In truth, he had no answer to that question, and certainly no proof that the feather they'd found in Douglass's apartment was linked to either the man from her past or the man in her telepathic journeys. All he had was suspicion and a feeling that his guess was the correct one.

"She was in contact with both Blaine and Lloyd on an operational level. Maybe they were discussing the possibility of reopening the Penumbra project and your brother or psi buddy discovered it. Maybe that's the reason for the warning on the wall."

She studied him for a moment, then said, "You don't believe that."

No, he didn't. While it seemed a perfectly plausible explanation for the warning, it just didn't sit well with his instincts. The warning had stated, *Do not revisit Penumbra*. It had not said, *Do not revive Penumbra*. A small but vital difference. The military *couldn't* just pick up where they'd left off, because Penumbra, as a project, had been totally destroyed—not just the building and many of the personnel, but all research materials. If the military wanted to revive the project, then for all intents and purposes they'd have to start from scratch.

Unless, of course, they'd discovered that one of their test subjects had actually survived the destruction.

And that, he realized suddenly, was what the explosion at the Phoenix Foundation had been about. Those in control of Penumbra had apparently been under the impression fire was Sam's element to control. They'd intended to use her reaction at the foundation to test whether or not she was who they thought she was—and the med check afterwards would have confirmed it either way.

So, why had they gone ahead with the test when he and Illie had shown up instead?

Had Douglass been confused as to the identity or sex of the test subject? Or was there, as Illie had suggested, deeper reasons for him and Illie being given the test anyway?

And what would they have done if the two of them had died that day?

It was probably something they would never know, since Douglass was now dead. Blaine and Lloyd were not likely to be fonts of information.

He just wished he knew what they thought about that message on the wall. Neither man had given much away, and though he believed Lloyd's comment that he had no idea why that particular message had been left with Douglass's body, Blaine had made no such comment. And Gabriel had a feeling that Blaine not only knew the reason behind it, but supported it.

An odd thing to think when Blaine was supposedly the man who'd been in charge of the project.

But none of those thoughts could be said aloud. Not to Sam, anyway. She had enough to worry about. He didn't need to add the worry of a general who seemed to know entirely too much.

"What I think," he said eventually, "is that someone is still trying to protect you. Whether that person is this unseen brother of yours, or whether it's the man you're psychically connected to, is something only you can answer."

"Why would my brother—the man you've suggested could be Sethanon—want to stop Penumbra when that very project could give him the army he needs to win his war?"

"I don't know. But I don't think it's a coincidence that the feather was found." He hesitated, then added, "But I do think it's time you started asking some hard questions."

Anger flashed in her eyes, reminding him briefly of a burst of lightning. "You think I haven't been?"

"I think you've been delaying certain issues because you're afraid to uncover the truth."

That streak of lightning seemed brighter in her eyes, and this time it was accompanied by a stirring in the air that vaguely reminded him of the crackle of energy that raced through the air just before a thunderstorm.

But before he could comment on it, his viaphone rang. He retrieved it from his pocket and said impatiently, "Assistant

Director Stern."

"Hey partner, got some news you might not want to hear."

"So spit it out, Illie. I haven't the time for games right now."

"We found another body in Kathryn Douglass's apartment. It was cut into pieces and shoved into the upright freezer."

"How did the street boys manage to miss that?"

"Well, the body parts were covered by regular meat trays and weren't immediately recognizable."

"I would have thought a severed human head would be immediately recognizable."

"A human head?" Sam asked, eyebrow raised in query. He noted with interest that the electricity in the air seemed to fade away once her interest was caught elsewhere.

"Well, it *was* at the bottom of the freezer, and it was only after undoing the black plastic around the parts that we realized what we had."

"So how did you manage to be in the freezer in the first place?" Raiding the freezer when a murder seemed pretty straight forward wasn't normal practice. *If* there could be considered such a thing as normal practice for SIU officers.

"Well, rules say we have to do a thorough search of the premises, but it was curiosity that had me looking deeper into the freezer. Douglass was apparently a vegetarian, so what was a veggie doing with a freezer full of meat?"

"Have you sent the remains to the labs for analysis?"

"Yeah. Finley's checking it out as we speak. Thought you might want to be there for his initial report."

He frowned. "Why would I want to do that?"

"Because if the head was anything to go by, the dead woman is the spit of Douglass herself. Only a little younger."

Surprise rippled through him. "Did she have a sister?"

"No immediate living family. There're two cousins and an aunt now living in the United States, but that's about it."

"I'll head over to headquarters now. Anything else?"

"Not offhand. I'm still digging into her past."

"What about Blaine?"

"That's a big, fat zero. The military is not forthcoming with information, either."

No surprise there. "Continue both investigations, and let me know if you find anything." He hit the end button, put the phone back into his pocket, and met Sam's curious gaze. "They found another body at Douglass's apartment. One that seems the spit of the murdered woman."

"She was a twin?"

"According to the records, she had no immediate family."

"Which suggests that one of the dead women is either a clone or a shapeshifter. But don't shifters resume their own form when they die?"

"They do normally, but nothing in this whole mess is what it seems." Including her, he thought, and saw the same thought reflected in her eyes. He drew his car keys from his pocket and gave them to her. "Go back to the hotel and get some sleep. I'll make arrangements to get Mary transferred to a safe house and then go talk to Finley."

She took the keys from him, her fingers touching his only briefly, yet they sent an electric charge through his entire body. A charge reflected briefly in her eyes.

"And our discussion?" she said softly.

"I'll meet you at the hotel around four this afternoon and drive you to Wetherton's. We can talk on the way."

She nodded and glanced into the room, as if to reassure herself Mary was okay, and walked away. He watched her for a few seconds, then got out his phone and started making arrangements to secure the old girl.

* * *

"How's the examination coming along, Finley?" Gabriel asked, as he strode into the lab.

Finley cleared his throat and slid his thick glasses up the bridge of his nose with a gloved finger. "Well, this is certainly an interesting situation. Two identical bodies, both chopped into pieces, one a younger version of the other."

Gabriel stopped at the end of one of the tables and examined the two sets of remains. The two women would definitely have been physically identical if not for the deeper age lines around the face of one of them. "The cuts on the younger version appear to be made from a sharp instrument."   .

"It was. It appears she was strangled before she was sliced apart."

"You've done DNA testing?"

"Prelims reveal no relationship between the two. The younger Douglass was human. The older one was a shifter."

"Then why did she hold shape when she died?"

"I'm not sure." He frowned, his sharp gaze moving back to the bodies. "But there has been conjecture over the years that a very strong telepath might be able to force a shifter or changer to hold their alternate shape during death. But, of course, those sorts of tests just can't be done."

"But there have been other trials?"

He nodded. "It's certainly proven possible for a strong telepath to prevent shifting from one shape to the other. Shifting or changing may be an inherited skill, but it is still a skill that must be learned. And like any skill, control comes from the brain. Therefore, a strong telepath can feasibly stop shifting or changing even in death."

"Is there any way we can get an ID on the shifter?"

Finley shrugged. "Her DNA might give us a clue, but only if she was from one of the shifter groups involved in the DNA mapping program the government initiated a few years back. Her teeth might also provide a clue, as she's had fillings, so there must be dental records somewhere."

"I take it you've instigated searches in both areas?"

"Yep. As soon as I know anything, I'll send it to you."

Gabriel studied the table containing the torn apart remnants of humanity, and said, "There aren't many shifters who would have the strength to tear apart someone like that."

Finley sniffed. "Most cats could, but what we're dealing with here is a bear shifter. And it's one big bear, I can tell you."

Gabriel raised an eyebrow, amused by the comment. "Most bear shifters are big."

"Think brown bear, and add half the size again."

That *was* one big mother of a bear. "How can you be sure?"

"Measured the distance between the claw slashes left on the woman's back." He hesitated, then added, "Looks like he shifted while they were...um...making love. Nasty stuff."

Especially for Kathryn Douglass, he imagined. The differences between the anatomy of a human male and that of a bear would in itself have caused a lot of pain and damage. Probably even have torn her up fairly badly. "Anything else?"

Finley shook his head. "We've collected semen samples, of course. I'll do a search of both our database and the government's to see if there's match."

Gabriel nodded. Most crims these days had DNA samples taken as a matter of course, but it had taken a lot of years to implement the procedure thanks to the civil rights activists. Which meant, of course, that the database was not only constantly being updated, but also only reliable when it came to criminals caught in the last ten years.

And he very much doubted that the person behind these murders could be tracked down so easily.

"Let me know if you find anything."

Finley nodded absently. Gabriel left the lab and headed up to his office. He grabbed a cup of coffee from the autocook, even though he knew the taste wouldn't actually live up to the aroma, and sat down at his desk.

"Computer, update."

"Please state name and rank for voice verification."

He did so. The screen flicked to life and began listing all the reports and activities going on in the SIU. With Stephan's alter ego off on official leave, and Stephan himself down at their parent's compound with Lissa and his new son, control of the SIU was nominally in the hands of Harry Krane, Byrne's second in command. However, neither Stephan nor he were about to let an "outsider" take full control of the SIU, so all reports and all decisions were covertly siphoned through to him. He then channeled all the appropriate information on, and held back the more clandestine reports for when Stephan resumed his position.

He found nothing of real interest until he read the report from the bug Sam had placed in Wetherton's office. And though it was little more than the name behind one of Wetherton's many phone conversations, it sparked a whole lot of questions.

That name was *Les Mohern.*

Why would a petty crim like Les Mohern suddenly come out of hiding to contact a government minister like Wetherton? For that matter, why would he even visit someone like Kathryn Douglass? Was there a connection between the two no one knew about?

Maybe so. After all, Les and his brother worked for Kazdan. He doubted that it was a coincidence that on his brother's death, Les had gone to ground. Maybe he'd done so for a reason—like fearing for his life.

But if that was the case, why would he now surface to contact two high profile people like Douglass and Wetherton? Surely he had to know that both would be under some sort of surveillance, given their positions? Why would he risk discovery to contact either of them?

He clicked on Mohern's name and studied the background report. Bingo—an address. He finished the remainder of his coffee in one gulp and stood.

He'd discovered long ago that when instinct scratched *this* hard, it was better not to ignore it. This Les Mohern was a key. To what, he now had to discover.

* * *

Sam slept.

And, as usual, she dreamt.

But this was not a dream she'd had before. This one was new. And terrifying.

The night was filled with smoke and fire and fear. The very air burned so hot the metal walls around them were beginning to bubble and melt. And yet the heat and flames never touched her, skittering around her as she ran through the madness. Seeking safety. Seeking freedom.

Lights flickered ahead, scattering brief patches of luminescence through the smoke-filled darkness and highlighting the figure ahead. For an instant that figure seemed huge and hairy, with fearsome claws that rent and tore at those stupid enough to try and stop him. Then the lights went out again, and it was just Joshua running ahead, telling her to hurry, that this was their chance. Their only hope.

And she obeyed. Running after him hard, ignoring the many screams, even rejoicing in them.

Until she heard that one scream.

Mary.

She stopped abruptly. Ahead, Joshua also stopped, his actions reminding her briefly of a puppet jerked to stillness by its master.

He swung around. "There's no time for this, Samantha."

"She cared for us, Josh. I can't let her die for that."

"She was *paid* to care for us. It was her job, her duty. She is no better than the rest of them."

"She sang us nursery rhymes and told us stories that made us laugh. She gave us dreams of a life beyond this place. And she left the window open for us at night, giving us what freedom she could. Because of all that, I will not let her die."

"It's too late. I can't let you—"

"You can't stop me."

Before he could react, she thrust out her hand. Power flowed through her, surging from the floor—from the earth itself—up though her body and out through her fingertips, leaping the distance between them and hitting him hard. It flung him backwards, into the thickness of the fire and out of sight.

He wasn't hurt. The fire could never hurt him. It *was* him, a part of his soul, a part of his being.

But it was *his* protection that was keeping her safe from the flames, and as that protection briefly flickered, then went out, the full force of the firestorm hit. Heat flowed over her, scalding her skin, her lungs.

She closed her eyes and called to the sky and the power of the storms. Wind swept in, buffeting the flames away, bringing with it the coolness of the night, giving her air to breathe that wouldn't scorch her insides.

With the wind swirling around her, providing a buffer from the flames and the heat, she backtracked, running through the halls to the nursery area.

To discover hell itself.

Fire was a wall that ran on for as far as the eye could see—a seething, writhing mess of red, gold and white fury that crawled up the walls and across the ceilings. It was hot and hungry and very, very deadly. Surely no one could survive in the fiery doom that the nursery rooms had become.

And yet, Mary's scream rent the air, her voice high pitched and filled with pain and terror.

A trap? Maybe. Probably.

But something inside wouldn't let her walk away until she discovered the truth. The older woman had made the darkness of this place survivable in so many small ways. They owed her her life, at the very least.

A hand grabbed her arm, its touch cold and violent as it yanked her back. She knew without even looking that it wasn't Josh.

That it was Lloyd.

Fear leapt, and her heart began to race. It was instinctive, that fear, bred into her from birth itself. And yet, there were monsters far worse than Lloyd walking these halls. But neither those monsters, nor Lloyd himself, was going to stop her tonight. Not when the havoc Josh had created had finally given them the hope of freedom.

Energy crackled across her fingertips as she swung around, but she kept her fists low, out of sight. Lloyd wore a fire suit and breathing apparatus, and though the mask distorted much of his features, his fury was still evident in the glow of his eyes.

"Stop it, you little bitch." He shook her violently enough to rattle her teeth. "Stop it now, or I'll kill your brother."

She reached into the pocket of her overall and pulled out the small electronic device that would have injected the lethal poison into Josh's skin. Josh had hers safely tucked away in his pocket. She had no idea why he wanted to keep them, but she obeyed his wishes, as she usually did.

"You mean with this?" She raised the device so that he could see it.

He swore and raised his hand, as if to hit her. She gathered the energy that danced all around them and froze his blow in mid-motion. Surprise, then fear, flickered through his eyes. It felt good. So very good.

Never underestimate your enemy was a lesson drilled into them from babyhood, yet it was a lesson their controllers had never fully understood.

Or perhaps it was more a case of never fully understanding what they had created.

Either way, it had finally culminated in this moment, where she and Josh held the power, not them.

"No more," she said softly. She glanced down to where his fingers gripped her arm, and telekinetically pulled them away one by one, snapping bone each time.

Sweat broke out across Lloyd's forehead, but he didn't utter a sound. And she wanted him to say something. Wanted him to scream, as she had screamed so many times.

She stepped back from him, keeping him still and in place as she raised her hand. Lightning arced between her fingertips, small flashes of fury that lit the smoky orange air with a pure white light. "Fire is not my element. It was never was my element, but you people would never see that."

He opened his mouth, but no sound came out. Probably just as well, as she had no doubt it was just more abuse or yet another threat. She smiled coldly and unleashed the lightning. It arced around him, playing with him like a cat with a mouse, touching, leaping away, and then touching again. When it finally settled, he screamed.

She closed her eyes, breathing deep the sound. It felt good. So good. But after a second or two, she telekinetically picked him and threw him against the melting, bubbling metal wall. It melted his suit, his skin, and his screams reached a fever pitch before shutting off abruptly. He was dead before he hit the ground.

She studied his body for a second, feeling little. Not even the pleasure she'd thought she'd feel. Damn it, she'd been dreaming of this moment for as long as she'd been able to form conscious thought, and yet now that it was here, there was nothing. But now was not the time to worry about such things. She spun to face the wall of flames that was the nursery.

The firestorm had grown, but Mary still screamed. Where the hell was she? There were few places that would provide shelter from such fury, not for this length of time, anyway. She bit her lip, and half reached for the full power of the storms, and then stopped. She couldn't afford to douse the flames, not if she wanted to escape this place, and calling to the storms would do that. She might be able to call them, might be able to channel some of their power and some of their elements, but she wasn't strong enough to control their full force, because control was something she was still teaching herself. The scientists thought she was earth and sun and that Josh was wind and water. They had it half right. She was earth and wind, Josh was sun and water. She could call storms and quakes, Josh fire and floods. In the long barren years of their childhood, she'd always sat in on Josh's lessons, and him hers, each learning what they could while continuing the lie, then practicing when they were alone and beyond the watchful eyes of the scientists. Though, to some extent, their abilities *did* overlap. If she called in the storms, he could control the water, and he would do so now because he wanted everyone dead. But she was also earth and earth was the ruler of the other elements. She could stop him, but not without bringing the entire complex down and therefore destroying the one person she was trying to save.

She blew out a breath and directed some of the cold wind that swirled around her at the flames, forcing the heat and the fire away enough to form a corridor. Then she ran through.

The heat battered her, despite the swirling air. Sweat dribbled down her spine, her forehead. The smoke was fierce, a wall of darkness threatening to overwhelm her narrow corridor. She ran as fast as she could, following the screams, and praying for a miracle.

And after praying for such an occurrence all her life, it seemed someone was finally listening.

Mary was in the shower room with all the water taps turned on, so that she was surrounded by a ring of water. The heat was still enough to scald her skin and clothes, yet she was alive and awake and conscious. A miracle in itself since the outside walls of the shower rooms were a maelstrom of destruction.

Mary's expression was an odd mix of fear and hope as

she spun around. "Josephine? What is happening? What have you done?"

"We're doing what we promised we'd do. Escaping." She hesitated and held out her hand. "Come with me. I'll keep you safe."

Mary studied her for a heartbeat, and then her gaze went to the flames. "The heat alone will kill us."

"No, it won't," a voice said behind Sam.

She turned and met her brother's gaze. Saw both the fury and the understanding. "Don't try to stop me, Josh. I have to do this."

"Even at the risk of recapture?"

"Even at." She hesitated. "But Lloyd is dead."

"Lloyd will never be dead." He smiled and touched a hand to her cheek. His fingertips were tinder hot, and yet inexplicably tender. "It seems you are not the weapon that either they or I might hope you to be. Not yet, anyway." He glanced past her. "Mary, we haven't much time. Move it."

Though he was barely a teenager, Josh's voice held a depth of command not even their trainers had achieved. Mary obeyed.

He caught Mary's hand and said, "I have to do this for your own safety, so sorry in advance." Before Mary or she realized what he was doing, he'd knocked the older woman unconscious. But he didn't let her fall, catching her kinetically before glancing at Sam. "She'd have slowed us down, otherwise. You lead. I'll keep the flames at bay."

He did, but it was still a close run. He might be flame, but flames often gained a life of their own once given the freedom to run, and these flames had grown beyond the life—though maybe not the intent—of their creator.

They ran from the complex's maelstrom into the dark cold night. But it was a far from silent night—shouts, confusion and fear came from the many people who milled nearby. Some manned fire trucks, some hoses, and some whatever came to hand—like tractors scooping earth into the flames. But not one of them saw the three of them leave. Night was their ally, their only friend, and even when fire lit, it protected them from sight.

They ran up the hill and collapsed at the top, at the place where they'd spent so many nights staring at the stars and dreaming of this moment.

And, like when she'd confronted Lloyd, now that the moment was here, it didn't feel as good as it was supposed to.

She listened to the sounds filling the night, to the screams of people and the groan of a building ready to collapse, sounds that were interspersed with the harshness of their own breathing. It was Josh who broke the silence.

"You must finish it."

She closed her eyes, knowing that for those who still remained alive inside it was better to end it quickly, and yet not wanting to be the one who took their lives. "There are some who deserve death who are not in those buildings."

He nodded. "Blaine, for one."

"Yes."

"I have plans for him, never fear." His voice held the deadness that always chilled her. This was not her brother, but rather the weapon the military had bred but could never fully control.

"And those plans do not include death? After all he has done?"

His smile was bitter, and yet so cold. So very cold. "No. Not as yet."

A shiver ran down her spine. "If I do this, I want out. Totally out of it all. I don't even want to remember it."

He glanced at her, smoky blue eyes suddenly seeming blacker than the night itself. "Neither of us can escape what we are."

"Maybe not, but I want the chance to live a normal life, Josh. Even if it's just for a while."

His gaze left hers. For several minutes he didn't say anything, simply studied the confusion below them. Then he sighed. "It will be hard for both of us. We are two halves of one soul, Sammy."

She smiled at his use of her nickname. It was the only one no one knew about, just as his secret name was one only she knew about. Though it was one she used rarely. "But your desires are not mine. I can't live like this anymore. I want a life. I want to be normal."

He glanced at her, his smile almost bitter. "We will never be normal."

"Maybe. But I want to try." She hesitated. "There's something else out there for me, Josh. Something, or someone, I need to find. And I need you to give me the time to do that."

He studied her a few seconds longer, and then nodded. "Okay, destroy that place, and we'll leave."

"And Mary?"

"She'll be safe here on the hill until they find her. She won't remember seeing us. I'll wipe out her memories." He hesitated. "We'll find somewhere safe for you to go, and then I'll wipe out yours."

She touched his arm lightly. "Thank you."

His smile was grim. "You know it won't work, Sammy. Not entirely. It's human nature to seek the unknown, and in your case, that will be the past wiped out."

"But in seeking, I will also be living a different life. I need that, at least for a while."

He shook his head and waved a hand toward the boundary fence. "Then let's get away from this place."

She glanced at the burning buildings and called to the earth underneath it. Power filled her, stretched her, with a rawness that felt at once so right and yet so alien. She waited, letting it run through every pore, every cell, until it felt as if skin and bone and being had melted away and she was nothing more than that rawness. Then she finally released it. A shudder ran through the ground beneath them, gathering speed and strength. With a rolling, groaning sound, the earth below the hill split asunder and whole buildings began to disappear. When everything had been swallowed, she let the earth rest again. Another shudder ran through the ground, one that echoed through her soul. She rubbed her arms and glanced at her brother.

"Let's hope we never come back to this place."

"Let's hope you never come back. Me, I have every intention of doing so. There's still too much to be done in here yet."

"Josh—"

"You have your dreams, and I have mine. Leave it at that, Sammy."

He rose and held out his hand. She clasped it and let him lead her to freedom.

* * *

The dream came to an abrupt halt and Sam woke with a start. For several seconds she did nothing more than lay on her bed, staring up at the ceiling as her heart galloped and sweat rolled down her cheek.

Or maybe it was tears.

As her heart began to slow to a more normal rate, she let her thoughts return to the dream in an attempt to grasp all the implications.

Because, as usual, the dream had answered some questions and raised many more. For a start, how had they escaped Hopeworth itself? Sure, their section might have been destroyed by flame and earth, but that quake had been very centralized and wouldn't have—and indeed, didn't—destroy the rest of the base. Plus, there was the fact that she'd had a tracker in her side—a tracker that had been inserted at birth and had been discovered by the SIU when she was being investigated for Jack's death. Surely that would have been activated as a matter of course, even if they weren't sure who had and hadn't perished in the fires and subsequent quake.

A quake *she'd* bought to life.

God, how scary was that?

She thrust a hand through her sweaty hair and wondered if she still had that power now. If she did, then it was still locked behind the walls of forgetfulness Josh had raised. She hoped they remained there forever. No one should have a power like that.

No one.

And if it started to appear, like the storm powers were beginning to appear?

She shuddered and sat upright, hugging her knees to her chest. Worry about one thing at a time, she told herself fiercely. These were dreams, nothing more, no matter how much they felt like truths. And until she found the boy—the man—she knew as Josh, until she talked to him, there was no proof that anything she dreamed had happened.

And even then, truth might not be forthcoming. The reality was, this could all be part of a larger game, one in which she was a major, if unknowing, player. And the dreams might be nothing more than a subterfuge someone desperately wanted her to believe.

Though she didn't think so.

She rubbed her arms and glanced at the clock. It was close to four. Gabriel would be here soon, so she had better start getting ready. And anything was better than sitting here contemplating the monster she might have been.

She climbed out of bed and walked across the room to the bathroom. A long shower made her feel better in body if not in soul, and by the time she'd dried her hair and dressed, it was nearly five.

And no sign of Gabriel.

She glanced at her watch to be sure the clock was right,

then picked up the phone and dialed his cell phone number.

No answer.

She swore softly. Either he'd been sidetracked, or he'd forgotten. Or both.

She left a message, then disconnected, grabbed the keys and headed out the door. If he wanted his car back, he could damn well come and get it.

The traffic was hell, as usual, and it seemed to take forever to get from the hotel to Wetherton's. She drove into the parking lot under Wetherton's building, using her SIU identification to get through the security system. Then she parked near the elevator before catching it to Wetherton's floor.

Jenna Morwood answered on the second knock, lines of tiredness around her dark eyes. Her expression could only be described as relieved.

"Pleasant day, huh?" Sam said with a grin

"You could say that," Jenna said. "Our dear minister is lucky he still has teeth left. Touchy-feely little bastard."

"Thankfully, I don't appear to be his type. Anything untoward happen today?"

She frowned. "Not really. I thought we were being followed several times, but I couldn't spot them nor could I read any thoughts of ill-intent."

"Did he do anything unusual? Meet anyone unusual?"

"Nope. All that happened today was boring politician stuff. I'm hoping like hell this mission doesn't go on for more than a few days."

So was she. Especially now that her dreams were becoming more detailed. More graphic. She couldn't keep doing her job with any sort of efficiency if she also wasn't sleeping. "Unfortunately, the boss seems to think it'll go on for months."

"Then here's hoping he's wrong." Jenna smiled wryly. "Though he generally isn't."

"No." She glanced past Jenna as a bump came from Wetherton's bedroom. "The minister took a nap at this hour of the day?"

"Yeah, the poor man was so exhausted doing all that ministerial sitting about on his ass that he had to come home for a nap at four. He left via the vent at four fifteen."

She raised an eyebrow. "Did you manage to get the tracker on him?"

"With all his attempts to feel the merchandise? Oh yeah. He flew to an abandoned apartment complex in Rathdown

Street, stayed there for half an hour, and then he went across to a low profile men's club in Spencer Street. He actually returned about ten minutes ago."

"Did we manage to get observers at either place?"

"Not the first one, but definitely at the second."

"Who'd he meet?"

Jenna gave an unladylike snort. "The minister enjoyed several lap dances, and then disappeared into the members' only section. Where, we discovered, a more exotic range of services is offered."

"So basically, the minister had himself a hooker this afternoon?"

"Better her than me," Jenna said, amusement in her low voice. "I'll do my lot for kin and country, but I have limits. And fucking a man like Wetherton is definitely one of them."

"That's not just limits, that's called having taste."

"That too." She smiled as she leaned sideways and snagged her coat off the hook behind the door. "Luckily, the lecher is yours to deal with for the next twelve hours."

"Joy."

"Indeed." Jenna waved a good-bye and retreated quickly to the elevator. Sam closed the door and turned around to find Wetherton watching her from the bedroom doorway.

She raised an eyebrow and tried to ignore the heat of embarrassment touching her cheeks. She and Jenna had been speaking softly, so there was very little likelihood of Wetherton hearing their comments. And yet, the annoyance in his eyes suggested otherwise.

"Anything I can do for you, Minister?" she asked politely.

"Where's Jenna going?"

"Shift change, Minister. You have my delightful company once again this evening."

He looked her up and down. "We're going out again tonight. You could have worn something more appropriate."

"I'm your body guard, not your date. I'm dressed very appropriately, believe me."

He grunted—whether in agreement or not, she had no idea—then turned around and walked back into the bedroom. She waited until he came back out and asked, "Where are we going tonight, Minister?"

She actually knew, because she'd read his schedule, but it never hurt to check.

"The opera. I'm meeting a friend there."

Just as well she *had* checked. The opera certainly hadn't been listed on the schedule. "Minister, until we uncover who might be after you, maybe it would be better to skip some of your social engagements."

"No. I refuse to let the actions of an idiot unhappy with current government policy curtail what I want to do. That's only giving other idiots incentive to do the same."

"I think the men behind the attempted hits are more than just idiots with a bone to pick with the government."

"You'd be surprised, Agent Ryan. These days the government certainly collects a high caliber of idiot." He shoved his arms into his jacket. "Let's go. I cannot be late."

She opened the door, checked the corridor, and then ushered him through. "Am I permitted to ask who you might be meeting tonight?"

"Just a friend." He glanced at her as he pressed the elevator button. "A male friend."

Uh-huh. He'd heard them all right. "A trusted male friend or merely an acquaintance?"

Wetherton hesitated. "Acquaintance, but I trust him."

"Doesn't mean I have to." She got out her viaphone. "Name please."

"That's unnecess—"

"It is when your life has been threatened twice," she cut in. "Name, Minister."

"The other girl is much pleasanter," he muttered, then added, "Les Mohern."

Les Mohern? Why did that name ring alarm bells in the back of her mind? Was it simply because it wasn't on the list of known associates and friends Stephan had given her? Or something else? She repeated the name into the viaphone and ordered a search. Hopefully, something would come up before the long night was over.

Now all she had to do was hope it was a long, *unexciting* night.

But even as the thought crossed her mind, instinct suggested it was going to be anything but.

Twelve

Gabriel gripped the branch with his claws, keeping his wings spread until he'd gained his balance. Once he had, he settled his wings against his sides and looked around. Dusk was settling in, and with it, a storm. Wind shook the branches, making the leaves all around him shiver and dance, and the growing darkness held the strong aroma of rain. It was a clean, fresh fragrance that did little to erase the stench of the house below.

Les Mohern hadn't lived at the address the SIU had on file for a good two years. It appeared that even before his brother's disappearance, Les had lived the life of a gypsy, never staying too long in one place. His subsequent trail had taken some searching, but the SIU's computer system was one of the best, and eventually, it had picked up a small trail of receipts that had led him here.

Mohern's latest stopover was a dump. Literally.

Whoever it was that Mohern was scared of, they had to be pretty damn bad for him to be staying in a place like this. The stink was almost nose destroying—the sort of odor that could invade your skin and hang there. The small house that Mohern was using as a refuge was situated on the corner of the refuse center, and it had to be crawling with all sorts of bugs, mice and rats. Even he, with the soul of a hawk, shuddered at the thought of staying there. Sharing his bed with cockroaches and rats was not his idea of a good time.

He studied the nearest windows carefully, but could spot no movement. And though darkness was moving in, there was no light. He walked along the tree branch, looking into other windows, but the result was the same—no immediate sign or sound of human life.

He spread his wings and took to the air again. With dusk fading into night, his brown and gold coloring was unlikely to be spotted. Though in truth, a hawk soaring over a refuse station was unlikely to cause alarm. Places like this were a Mecca for hunters of all varieties—winged or not.

He drifted on a current, studying the mounds of rubbish, seeing smaller spurts of movement that spoke of rats and other vermin, but little else of interest.

Until he reached the far edge of the dump and saw two men forcing a third man onto his knees. A fourth man watched these proceedings, a gun held at the ready by his left side.

It was, he thought, oddly silent. Though the man he presumed was Mohern struggled, he wasn't screaming. Maybe he figured there was no point. Out here, only the rats would hear.

As the fourth man raised his weapon and the captive's struggling became more violent, Gabriel swooped downwards, spreading his talons and screaming as he did so. The harsh call echoed loudly across the windswept silence.

The stranger with the gun glanced up. His eyes widened and reflected fear a second before Gabriel slashed him across his face and neck.

Blood spurted, spraying his feathers, its sweet aroma taunting his hawk senses. The stranger dropped the weapon, his hands going to the stream pulsing from his neck. Gabriel wheeled around, saw one of the men holding Mohern dive for the dropped gun. Gabriel dove and slashed with a talon, but the man ducked, grabbing the weapon and letting off a shot in one smooth movement. Gabriel flung himself sideways, felt the burn of the bullet's passage past his tail feathers. He squawked as if hit and dropped behind a mound of rubbish. There he shifted shape and, in human form, freed his weapon and carefully edged to the far end of the stinking mound. The man with the gun hadn't moved, his weapon held at the ready as he eyed the mound behind which Gabriel hid. The other man stood behind the still kneeling Mohern. There was no gun in evidence, though Gabriel had no doubt he would have one somewhere. Thugs like these rarely went anywhere without them. He fired off two quick shots that took both men out, then waited for several seconds, trying to ignore the stinking reek of rubbish as he listened to the night, seeking any sound that might mean these three men had not been alone.

But the only sounds to be heard were the pleas for help from the man whose throat he'd slashed, and Mohern's rapid breathing as he struggled to free his hands from their restraints. Not an easy thing when the restraints were wire and his hands were behind his back.

Gabriel stood up and got out his viaphone to call in a cleanup team as he walked across to the injured man. He did a quick search for ID and other weapons, and he found and secured both. Then he administered what medical help he could, using strips torn from his shirt to bandage the wound, after which, he cuffed him. Even a man in danger of bleeding to death could be dangerous if the situation was desperate enough, and the look in *this* man's eyes suggested if he was able to finish what he'd been sent here to do, he would.

He checked the other two men to ensure they were both dead, collecting their weapons in the process, then walked over to Mohern and stripped off the tape covering his mouth.

Relief was evident on Mohern's gaunt features, but his blue eyes were wary, distrustful. "Whoever you are, thanks."

"You may retract that once you see this."

Gabriel showed him his badge, and Mohern grimaced. "Typical of my luck lately. Still, being caught by a cop is better than being dead."

Gabriel put his badge away, but not the gun. He didn't trust Mohern any more than he trusted the men who'd intended to kill the man. "Why were they going to execute you?"

"Because I know too much." Mohern looked past him for a second. "Because the man they work for knows what we...I...saw."

Gabriel undid the wire restraining Mohern's hands, motioned him to rise, and then quickly patted him down. No weapons, no ID. Not that the latter was surprising since he was about to be killed. "Then tell me what you saw, and I might be able to protect you."

Mohern snorted. "Yeah, I've heard that song before. It wasn't true back then and I doubt it's true now."

"Is that because your brother told Jack Kazdan, and as a result, he was killed?"

Mohern's eyes narrowed. "Now why would you say something like that?"

"Because Kazdan was a cop, and your brother was supposedly his street ear."

"Even if that was true, why would you suspect one of your own of killing my brother? Don't you all stick together, regardless of the crime?"

"I'm not one of Jack's lot. I'm SIU. Big difference. And Jack might have held a badge, but he was still a crim. I know that, and you know that. So tell me what bit of news cost Frank his life."

Mohern studied him for several seconds longer, then said, "I want a new ID."

"That would very much depend on what it is you saw."

"I saw a murder. And I saw the murderer."

"A murder isn't big enough news to warrant the provision of a new ID."

"What if the person murdered was someone who had serious military connections? What if she actually died months ago, not just yesterday? And what if the murderer wore one face coming in, and another going out?" He paused and then added, "What if one of those faces was the face of the man who paid us to kidnap Wetherton?"

Fuck. Was Mohern saying what he thought he was saying? He hoped so—if only because it was about time they had some damn luck. "Is that why you contacted Douglass last week? Why you called Wetherton and ask for a meet this evening?"

Mohern's gaze widened. "How did you know that?"

"Because part of the SIU's duties is to randomly monitor government officials." Which was the truth, as far as it went.

Mohern grimaced. "Well, shit. My luck is really out this week, isn't it?"

"Not really. If we hadn't been monitoring, you'd now be a feast for the rats and stray dogs." He studied the man for a moment, letting the words sink in, before adding, "So why contact either of them?"

"Because I thought one might help me with a new ID in exchange for my continued silence. As you can see, my efforts at hiding were becoming less and less successful."

"And why would you think either of them would be willing to consider a deal like that?"

"Well, she wasn't, was she?" He sniffed. "But neither of them are the real deal, are they? And Wetherton can't afford to have that sort of information out, can he?"

"How do you know he's not the real thing?"

"Because the real Wetherton was killed and replaced months ago, wasn't he?"

This was getting better and better. "So who placed the clone? Jack?"

Mohern shook his head. "He indirectly gave us the job, though. Said he knew someone who was looking for a couple of hands for a snatch and ransom job. Said it paid well." He shrugged. "He gave us a number, and we called it and got our instructions. Of course, turned out the ransom part was a lie."

Why would someone like Sethanon—and they were almost ninety-nine percent sure it was the elusive Sethanon behind

Wetherton's replacement—be using two off-the-street thugs for a job as important as snatching a government minister? Unless, of course, he wanted no traceable connection if the job went sour. "Can you remember the phone number?"

"Won't do you any good if I could. It was a public phone box. I checked at the time."

Damn. *Not* that he expected anything less. Sethanon was too canny to be caught by something as careless as a traceable phone number. "So, you kidnapped Wetherton, as directed. Were you also involved in the murder?"

"No. But Frank saw the copy standing over the real version after we delivered him."

"Did anyone know Frank saw this?"

"No. And we were being well paid, so silence comes as part of the package."

"This delivery…Was it to an abandoned apartment building on Rathdown Street?"

It was a loaded question in many respects, and Mohern answered it blithely. "Yeah. How'd you find him?"

"We know because we've been tracking the minister's whereabouts for some time. I guess you didn't find the tracer when you tried to dump the body, did you?"

"So that's how you were able to escape." He stopped, as if suddenly realizing what he was admitting, and then shrugged. "Jack was really pissed off about you getting away that day."

"Why?"

"Because he got his ass kicked by the big man."

So it was Sethanon who'd wanted him beaten but alive that day. Interesting. As was the fact they'd been heading up the Dandenongs. Surely that would mean their enemy had a compound up on that mountain somewhere, and yet the many searches since had provided little in the way of anything suspicious. "How'd you get paid for that job?"

"Cash."

"Who were the other two men there?"

Mohern shrugged again. "They were there to deliver the cash and collect the body. When you were spotted, we were asked to help stop you."

"Who asked? The two men, or someone else?"

"Voice on the phone. He said it would take more than two to stop you." He paused. "You broke Frank's nose, you know."

"Frank was lucky I didn't break his damn neck." Not that

it would have mattered. Frank died not long after, probably killed by the man they'd both trusted.

"So, if you didn't see this man at either event, why are you so sure that he's behind both Wetherton's kidnapping and Douglass's murder?"

"Because we've got ears. The voice of the man who gave us the job was the same voice in the murdered chick's apartment."

No wonder Sethanon wanted this man dead—Mohern could identify him by voice and had seen at least two of his identities. As the sound of a footstep carried on the wind, he glanced around and saw agent Briggs and three other SIU officers—one of them a medic—making their way through the muck. He pointed to his still-alive captive, and then returned his attention to Mohern. "Are you sure about all this?"

Mohern nodded. "When her murder was reported in the newspaper, I knew she had to be another copy, because Frank and I had been in the apartment when she was killed."

"So you didn't actually see her murder?"

"Didn't have to. We heard the screams, as well as him wrapping the bits of her up. We checked later, of course, just to see." He sniffed. "She was a pretty thing."

A pretty thing who happened to be in the way of Sethanon's plans. "So how were you able to get into a secure building, and how come you weren't caught?"

He grinned. "Mate of ours was the night watch. He gave us the codes for a share of the profits. We only took little things, things that were valuable but weren't likely to be immediately missed. It's quite a profitable scam in a building like that." He stopped, as if suddenly remembering he was talking to a man who was basically a cop. He cleared his throat and shrugged. "As to how we escaped detection, I think it came down to luck. Our mate called us when Douglass entered the building, so we had time to hide. No one expected us to be there, so no one bothered checking for intruders."

"So how did you see the murderer moving about?"

"We were hiding in the guest bathroom. I saw him through the crack between the door and the frame."

"Give me his descriptions."

Mohern did. Gabriel wasn't surprised to discover that the identity used to gain entrance to the apartment matched the description of one General Blaine. But it was nasty to discover that the second identity was that of a scruffy man with brown hair so thick and scraggly that his face couldn't be seen, giving him the appearance of someone more bear than human. Only he was a bear who walked with military precision.

That was almost the exact description Sam had given of the man she knew as Joe.

The man she seemed to place so much trust in, the man who seemed to hold so many answers about her past, was not only a murderer, but he might very well be the man they'd been hunting for so many years. The man who had vowed to subjugate or destroy the human race.

Sethanon.

* * *

Sam crossed her arms and leaned back against the wall. The flock-patterned wallpaper scratched at her back, even through her sweater. Impossible, she knew, given the thickness of her sweater, and yet still her skin itched. Maybe it was just uneasiness. The growing sense that something was very, very wrong.

She frowned and scanned the old theater's foyer for the umpteenth time. The only ones standing out here were the usher, the pacing Wetherton and herself. Everyone else had gone inside to watch the show. And the usher didn't appear threatening—he was just a gray-haired old guy wearing a crisp blue suit and a bored expression.

There wasn't even a tingle along the psychic lines—no crawling knowledge that something was here that shouldn't be here.

And yet something was.

Or rather, some*one* was.

She could smell him. His scent was sharp, almost acidic, and though she couldn't immediately put a name or a face to the scent, recognition hummed through her.

And then it hit her.

Duncan King. The redheaded, green-eyed man who'd accompanied General Lloyd to their meet at Han's restaurant a few months ago.

At the time, she'd thought him to be nothing more than a psychic "drain," a leach who tried to suck all that he could from her mind via a seemingly harmless handshake.

But he was obviously a whole lot more. He could do invisible, for a start.

His scent was coming from the right—the same area where the bored usher stood, but more towards the corridor that led to the men's room.

There was no one actually standing there, of course. Even her psychic senses weren't coming to the party, which was odd.

Or maybe it wasn't.

When she and King had shaken hands in the restaurant, she'd not only felt the leaching sensation, but a power that was similar, and yet different, to the kind of energy that she felt in storms—one that was a little more "earthy" in feel than the ethereal energy of the storms, and yet not the same as the energy she'd drawn from the earth during her dream.

Who was to say that he hadn't been trying to use that energy to somehow make him immune to her senses? Maybe she wasn't even supposed to remember King's presence, let alone see him.

So why was he skulking around this foyer? Who was he here for?

Wetherton? Her? Or someone else altogether?

Either way, her best option right now was a cautious retreat. Better safe than sorry when confronted by someone more than human—someone who didn't *need* a weapon to be dangerous. Her dreams, and her experiences with Hopeworth of late, had taught her that much, at least.

She pushed away from the wall and approached Wetherton. "Minister, I think your date has stood you up."

He scowled and glanced at his watch. "It's a business meeting, not a date. And I have no doubt he'll be here—the matter was important."

"He's over half an hour—" Her phone rang, stopping her mid-sentence. She grimaced and took it from her pocket, stepping away from Wetherton but making sure she kept within viable protecting distance just in case the scent that was King moved or attacked.

"Agent Ryan speaking."

"Sam? Gabriel."

Like she wouldn't recognize his voice? She shook her head. The man obviously had no idea just how attracted she was to him, despite their little encounter in the car. "Would this be the Gabriel who was supposed to meet me at five to pick up his car?"

He paused. "Yeah. Sorry about that."

"Say that with a little more sincerity and I might actually believe you." She decided it was better *not* to be a bitch—as much as she might want to—and said, "What came up?"

"Les Mohern."

As he said the name, the memory kicked into place. "Mohern? Wasn't he one of the names in Jack's book?"

Wetherton swung around at the mention of Mohern's name, his scowl deepening. "What do you know of a man named Mohern?"

His voice was sharp, almost angry, and yet something in the set of his shoulders and the way he stood spoke of fear. She held up a hand to silence him, which didn't go down well, if the clenching and unclenching of his fists was anything to go by.

Not that she thought he intended to hit her. Wetherton didn't have *that* much courage.

"Frank Mohern was on Jack's list," Gabriel said, "Les is his brother. He apparently had a meet with your boy tonight."

"A meet he's late for."

"That's because he almost got himself killed. I saved his butt, and he's been singing his little heart out in an effort to get a deal."

"Any particular song I need to know about?"

There was another pause, then, "Most definitely. The Moherns were involved in the original Wetherton's snatch and replacement, and they also happened to witness the murder of the original Kathryn Douglass."

"So he can identify the murderer in both cases?"

"Yes."

Something in the way he said that made her stomach clench. And she knew, without him saying a word, just who Mohern had probably seen. She forced her voice to remain light, casual, as she said, "Anyone I know?"

Again he paused. "It sounds an awful like the description you gave of the man you know as Joe."

She briefly closed her eyes. Joe. The man who had saved her life. The man who answered her many questions without ever hinting at the whole picture.

The man who might well be the enemy of humankind.

Damn.

As she opened her eyes, air shimmered. She frowned,

studying the area to the right of the usher. The shimmer happened again, reminding her briefly of smoke coiling away from a small breeze. Only it wasn't smoke, wasn't just air, but a signal that King was on the move.

"Gabriel, I've gotta go. Meet me later and we'll talk."

"Sam, wait—"

She didn't, cutting him off and putting the phone back into her pocket. With King on the move, the sensation of wrongness had sharpened. And she had a bad feeling that she and Wetherton really should get the hell away from the theater and that man.

"Minister, I'm afraid your date has had a slight accident and has been taken to the hospital. If you'd like, I can take you there."

She gripped his arm as she spoke, intending to forcibly move him on, but he wrenched himself free.

"Don't be ridiculous. I have tickets for the opera and I fully intend to use them."

"I wouldn't advise—"

Before she could get the rest of the sentence out, the shimmer that was King found form. And he had a gun pointed directly at Wetherton.

"Minister, look out!" Even as she gave the warning, she freed her weapon and whipped off two quick shots. The laser's soft hiss seemed to reverberate across the silence but it connected with nothing more than air—at least until it burned through the garish flock wallpaper and then the wall behind it.

King reappeared several feet away from his original spot and fired. She threw herself sideways, hitting Wetherton and knocking him out of the way. She hit the carpeted floor with a grunt, the bright heat of King's laser skimming her side, burning through her jacket and scalding her hip. She swore again, but rolled onto her stomach and fired another shot. Again, the bullet tore through air, not flesh.

For God's sake, how was she supposed to protect Wetherton from someone who could become as insubstantial as the wind?

She couldn't. Retreat was the only option they had left. All she could hope for was that King wasn't as fast as he was invisible.

She twisted around to warn Wetherton, only to find him lying unmoving on the floor. His face was slack, his expression frozen in a mix of surprise and horror. A sharp but neat hole had been burned into the middle of his forehead. She half-imagined she could see brain matter through that hole, even though she knew logically that *that* was impossible given the distance, the position of his body, and the fact that lasers cauterized the wounds even as they created them.

At least one of her earlier questions had been answered—King was here for Wetherton. The minister had been living on borrowed time for a while now, but they'd thought the death sentence had come down from Sethanon. So why would the military want him dead? Even if they knew Wetherton was a clone, he surely wouldn't have any knowledge about Hopeworth that could be dangerous to them.

And yet Blaine had visited him. Had been in Wetherton's office for hours. Testing him, reading him, perhaps? If that *was* the case, what had they discovered that now warranted his death?

The only person who might know the answers to that question was King. And he was on the move—not towards her but rather the door. She scrambled to her feet, caught sight of the usher cowering behind one of the ornate columns near the staircase, and grabbed her badge from her pocket to show him.

"You, call the SIU. Tell them Agent Sam Ryan has a priority one situation. Tell them I need a med-team and backup straight away."

The usher nodded. She ran out the door and into the chilled night. King hadn't found form, but for some reason, the shimmer of air that surrounded and hid his form was more noticeable in the darkness lit only by street lights. "SIU, King. Stop or I'll shoot."

Passersby glanced at her, expressions becoming alarmed when they saw the weapon in her hand. Some hurried on, and others retreated. She didn't really care either way, as long as they kept out of her line of sight. She kept her gaze on King, and her finger on the trigger.

He didn't answer, didn't turn around, didn't stop.

She lowered the laser and ran after him. There were too many people out on the street to risk firing the weapon, and King was more than likely aware of that fact.

The heels of her boots hit the concrete noisily as she ran, a quick tattoo that spoke of speed and urgency, and one that at least had people scrambling to get out of her way. But however free her path was, however fast *she* was, King was faster. The further away he got, the harder it was to see or smell him.

And then he disappeared altogether.

She swore softly as she slowed, then finally stopped. With her gun raised, she scanned the immediate area. They'd run far enough from the theater district that foot traffic was sparse. This end of Victoria Street was close to Market and Elizabeth Streets, so there were still plenty of cars passing by. Their lights skimmed the sidewalks and nearby buildings, briefly illuminating the shadows. No one hid there, not even a shimmer.

She continued to turn slowly. Movement caught her eye in nearby Leicester Street. It was nothing more than a flare of orange that died as quickly as it gained life, and yet the sight of it had her up-until-now-dead psychic senses coming to life.

The enemy waited in the deeper shadows haunting that side road.

She slid her hand into her pocket and pressed the locator button on her viaphone, then slowly, carefully, eased toward the road.

The closer she got, the more her skin crawled. Then the familiar wash of heat hit, bringing with it the certainty that the enemy who waited was a shifter—a shifter whose very essence felt malevolent.

And it was a malevolence she knew.

Her steps faltered, and her hands suddenly felt clammy against the grip of the laser. Not so much because of the thick sensation of evil, not even because she'd felt this particular baseness before.

But because Blaine—the enemy that waited in the shadows—was not alone.

He was here.

The man who had saved her life at least twice.

Joe.

And she wasn't entirely sure whether he meant her good or ill. There was something almost...gloating in his aura. As if he'd waited for this moment for a very long time.

She took a shuddering breath and released it slowly. Her best option now was retreat. She'd be stupid to confront Blaine alone. There were two men ahead and the invisible King still floated about somewhere. However much she wanted answers, however much she might want to grab King for shooting

Wetherton, she wasn't a fool. She was one against three, and while she might be an enhanced human, just like them, she was the only one who *didn't* have full knowledge of her powers.

She retreated a step, but she stopped when something cold and hard pressed against her spine.

"I can't allow you to do that." King's voice was so soft that she doubted the men ahead would even hear. "Move into the side street, please. No sudden moves."

For all of a second she thought about spinning and knocking the weapon from his hand. Or maybe even twisting sharply to shoot him dead. But the latter had already proven impossible, and she had a sneaking suspicion he'd react faster than she ever could.

So she walked on, her arms by her side and the laser still secure in one hand. She doubted he'd forgotten its presence, and the fact that he let her keep it either meant he had no fear of it, or that she'd be dead long before she could ever press the trigger.

Neither thought was a pleasant one, so she concentrated instead on the road ahead, trying to pinpoint the men who still hid in the shadows.

Blaine moved out of them once she'd entered the street, stopping in the middle of the road, his expression pleased, almost amused.

"Last place I expected to find you, General," she said, stopping several feet away from him. King didn't object, and a covert glance over her shoulder uncovered why. He was no longer behind her. She scanned the immediate area, but couldn't spot him. Nor could she smell him. But then, the soft breeze could have been blowing his scent away from her. She was sure he hadn't gone far.

Still, it was odd that he was here with Blaine. She'd been under the impression that he was Lloyd's assistant and psychic eyes, not Blaine's.

"Maybe so," Blaine said, voice all oily satisfaction, "but I must say it is extremely pleasing to see you, number 849."

The number rang distant bells, and she had a sudden memory of a room filled with clear plastic cribs, each one not only possessing a wriggling, crying baby but a black card clipped to the front that carried a number and visual details. Hundreds of babies born to the cold sterility of a lab, many of whom were destined to die long before conscious thought or fear formed.

An odd mix of anger and apprehension shot through her, but she raised an eyebrow, trying for a calm she didn't feel inside. "849? Sorry, General, but I have a name, not a number."

He raised an eyebrow, his expression still one of condescending amusement. "Maybe now, but not when you were in Hopeworth, my dear."

She knew it was useless to argue. He was too certain about her. Maybe he'd uncovered hidden files in Hopeworth. Maybe that brief moment between them in Wetherton's office had given him information that he'd been able to use. Either way, it didn't matter. She was never going to admit the truth. Not to him, anyway. "I'm afraid you're barking up the wrong tree. I've never been near Hopeworth."

"Forgetfulness is not surprising, given the horrible events of that night, but you are military in birth and in design and we both know it. And I have every intention of returning you to your birthplace *and* birthright." He paused, and then said, "Tonight."

So he thought Penumbra's destruction was an accident? That she'd escaped by chance rather than design? How could he? How could anyone in the military be breeding what they were breeding and have no true idea just what their creations were really capable of?

She took a step back, and this time King didn't stop her. "Sorry, General, but I'm not who you think I am, and there is no way in hell I'm going anywhere with you." She raised the laser, letting him see it for the first time. "Move and I'll shoot."

His sudden laugh sent a chill skittering over her skin. There was nothing sane in that cold sound. "You would never hit me with the laser, child. I am faster than the wind, and lighter than shadow. You can't kill a shadow, don't you know that? Didn't your precious nanny teach you anything?"

She blew out a breath. What was the point of going on with the pretence that she didn't know what he was talking about? All he had to do was get her back to Hopeworth and the truth would be revealed. She *wasn't* a creature of natural selection, but rather finely honed lab techniques. What she was better off concentrating on now was a means to escape this man *and* Hopeworth.

"My nanny taught me lots about humanity, General, and for that I owe her more than I can ever repay." She paused.

"Why did you want Mary Elliott dead?"

"I wanted her knowledge, but the mere fact that you came to see her was enough to satisfy my uncertainties." He gave her a cold smile. "And in the end, you walked into my trap much easier than I ever dreamed possible. King, get the laser from her."

She tensed, waiting for some sound, some sensation, some feeling that King was obeying his master's orders.

But King didn't answer. Blaine frowned. "King? Did you hear me?"

"I heard." The answer came about half a dozen steps away from Blaine's left shoulder. If she squinted, she could just make out the slight shimmer of his position. But with Blaine so close, she didn't dare squint for long.

"I gave you an order, son. Obey it."

"King is not yours to command, General."

The voice came from behind Blaine, but it wasn't King's. It was Joe's.

Thirteen

Gabriel gripped Mohern's arm tightly as he rushed him through the sterile halls of the SIU. Technically he wasn't a prisoner, so he wasn't cuffed, but Gabriel had a feeling the petty thief had begun to have more than a few second thoughts about "singing like a bird" during the car ride here.

And though it was unlikely he'd get very far away in the monitored and tightly secured halls—not to mention Briggs keeping a close eye on him from behind—Mohern had escaped Sethanon's clutches for many months and therefore had to have more native cunning than what he was currently showing.

They reached one of the interview rooms and Gabriel punched in a code. Then he pressed his hand against the print pad. The machine hummed to life, a blue light sweeping his prints before the door clicked open. He waved Mohern inside then turned to Briggs as she stopped beside him. "Give him coffee and a meal and then take his statement."

"What about my new ID?" Mohern said from the center of the sparsely furnished room.

"That'll be under discussion after you sign the statement." Gabriel looked back at Briggs. "If he doesn't sign it, keep him here until he does."

"Hey, you can't do that. It's against the law."

Briggs grinned. "We're SIU. A law unto ourselves."

"Great," Mohern muttered, as he sat down.

Gabriel kept his amusement to himself. "Get him to do a photo ID of all the men present at both Wetherton's murder and Kathryn Douglass's."

Briggs nodded. Gabriel turned and headed for the elevator. His phone rang before he got there. "Assistant Director Stern," he said, as he punched the elevator's call button impatiently.

"Mitchell from Monitoring, sir. We've just received a priority call from an usher at Her Majesty's Theatre. Apparently he did so on Agent Ryan's orders."

Gabriel's gut clenched. He should have known something had happened when she'd hung up so abruptly. And yet, she had to be all right, because he would have sensed anything else. "What did the usher say?"

"That she has a priority one situation and wants a med team and backup. The man she was with has been shot. She's gone after the suspect."

Which under normal circumstances, she could have undoubtedly handled. But given just who Wetherton might have been involved with, as well as who might have wanted him dead, it was better not to take chances.

"Send two teams immediately." He hesitated. "Has she hit the locator?"

"Yes sir." Mitchell paused. "Victoria Street, near Leicester."

"Tell the teams to take control of the situation at Her Majesty's. I'll back up Agent Ryan."

"Yes sir."

The elevator door opened. Gabriel stepped inside and punched the button for the rooftop. The fastest way to get there was by flight.

And he had a growing feeling that he had better get there *damn* fast.

* * *

There was no sense of movement. One minute, the night behind Blaine was empty, and the next Joe was standing there. It was almost as if he could wear the night like a veil, shucking it off or using it as cover where necessary. Very much like she could do herself, though she had a lot less flair.

He hadn't changed that much since she'd last seen him, sitting in the chair of a sidewalk café and sipping coffee while avoiding direct answers to her questions. His appearance was still that of a street bum, his thick, overly long hair and beard disheveled and apparently unwashed. But his brown eyes were intense and somewhat sad, and he held himself like a soldier— purposeful, balanced, powerful.

A man ready to move, to fight, at a second's notice.

Blaine swung around so that he was able to see both of them. "Who the hell are you? And how the hell did you get through the cordon of my men?"

"Who am I?" Joe repeated the question, his voice apparently amused. But she knew him through her dreams, and she could almost taste the fury he wasn't showing. "I am many people, General."

"A shifter." Blaine's voice was disdainful. "I gather you were here beforehand, because there is no other way you could have gotten past my men."

"You think so?" A smile touched Joe's lips, though she couldn't say how she knew this when the forest of his beard covered his mouth. "There's a number of ways anyone with skill could have. But perhaps it is better if I show you. King, watch him."

"Yes, General." King stepped out of the shadows. In his hand was the biggest damn gun Sam had ever seen. It was similar in size to a rifle, but wider, with an oddly shaped flat end.

Blaine's eyes widened, the arrogant confidence seeming to falter. "Where the hell did you get that? You haven't the authority—"

"No, but you have, General." The voice was Joe's, but his hirsute countenance had gone, replaced by a replica of Blaine himself.

And suddenly one large piece of the puzzle fell into place.

"It was you," she said, "I pulled *you* out of Wetherton's car that night. Not the real thing." Which was why she kept getting different reactions in his presence. Her senses *knew* Joe—and obviously they saw him as no threat, no matter what form he took.

The real Blaine was a totally different story.

And right now, his eyes were narrowed and dangerous looking. She shifted, her finger tightening just a little around the laser's trigger. He might be confident that she couldn't hit him with it, but if he moved in *any* way, she'd damn well have a good try.

But she had a horrible feeling he was working up to something bigger than a laser could handle.

Tension ran through her, and her finger tightened on the laser's trigger reflexively. A soft hum ran across the momentary silence, and Blaine gave her a quick look. There was no fear, no concern. Just amusement.

"Yes, it was me," Joe answered. "Unfortunately, that was the night the military began to realize they might have a problem." He paused. "Well, that and the killing of Kathryn Douglass."

"That was a mistake," Blaine said. "Because it was our first solid indication that someone had survived the Penumbra project." He studied his double for a moment. "Who are you?"

"Guess, General. Let's see how clever you really are."

Joe's glance ran past Blaine and met hers. Something trembled deep inside. She knew that gaze, knew the fierce hardness behind it, even if the eyes were currently the wrong color. "The general thinks he's calling in the troops. He doesn't realize he's already let them go."

Blaine snorted. "My men would not be fooled so easily."

"Your men have been fooled for years, General. And to continue the ruse, you must die. King?"

"No!" Sam said.

She raised the laser and fired, without even thinking about it. She had no real desire to protect Blaine, especially since he intended to take her back to Hopeworth. But the cop in her just couldn't stand here and let a murder happen.

King fired at Blaine at the same time she fired at King. This time her laser found its target, burning a hole though King's hand and into the weapon he held. It made a sizzling, popping sort of sound, and smoke began to rise. King swore and threw it away.

The weapon exploded before it hit the road, sending shards of metal and energy skimming through the night.

Deadly, but not as deadly as the beam that had hit Blaine.

His mouth was open, as if he was screaming, but no sound came out. His body was shimmering, moving, bubbling, as if water boiled under his skin. He didn't move, just stood there, statue-like, as his skin gradually began to darken and then peel and drift away on the gentle wind, like paper held too close to a fire. And then the boiling water began to bubble out, running down his body and splashing across the roadside. Only it wasn't just water, but blood and flesh and God knows what else.

Her stomach rose and she spun away, heading for nearest curb. By the time she'd finished heaving the little bit of food she'd eaten during the day, the splashing had stopped. The only sound to be heard on the whispering wind was the distant beat of traffic.

King had gone. She couldn't say why she was so sure of that, especially when she had a hard time getting any real sense of his presence.

But Joe was here. Watching. Waiting.

She wiped a hand across her mouth, took a deep, shuddering breath and turned around. He still wore Blaine's form.

"You killed him to take his place?"

"I've been taking his place for years. It was useful, while

it lasted."

She remembered a teenager saying, in that same sort of dead voice, *I have plans for him, never fear.*

The same teenager who said he had every intention of going back to that place once he'd taken care of her, because there was still too much to be done at Hopeworth.

A chill that was soul deep ran through her. Yet she kept her thoughts to herself, saying only, "And is that why you killed Kathryn Douglass?"

His smile was gentle, amused. "She decided to play both sides of the fence. That is always an unwise decision."

"Why go back as Blaine afterwards? To gloat?"

"Partially. I also wanted to see how Lloyd took the warning." His sudden grin was fierce. "Neither he nor the military took it well."

"But that Lloyd is not the real Lloyd." She hesitated. "I killed him the night Penumbra was destroyed."

"If you remember that, then you should remember that *that* Lloyd was yet another replica. The real general donated his body for scientific purposes on his death years before, and his replication became the military's first real success."

But not their last. "And what were we, Josh? Their fourth? Tenth? Fiftieth?"

He smiled, and this time it was a smile she remembered. A smile that echoed all the way through her, bringing tears to her eyes.

He began to change, shift, his body seeming to fade into the night for several heartbeats before it regained form. Became an older version of the boy who'd haunted her dreams for so long.

Part of her was fiercely glad to see him again.

Part of her feared him, because she suddenly remembered the conversation she'd had with Gabriel in the car. Her comment that Sethanon was waiting for Hopeworth to breed him an army. His comment that Sethanon was someone she knew in Hopeworth, someone who had been involved in the project.

No, no no, she thought. *No Josh. Not her brother.*

Yet the more the thought lingered, the more it made sense.

"We were never considered a successful creation," Joe said, "More of a frustrating one. They never could control us— not totally."

He studied her for a moment, and the sadness she'd often

noted in her dreams of him was back in his eyes. Only it was deeper this time. Much deeper. Then he looked up, and his expression changed, became hard.

"I can feel you up there, Assistant Director. Please come down and join in on the discussion."

There was a flutter of wings and a soft thump. Then footsteps coming from behind her. Gabriel stopped beside her, close enough that his warmth washed over her, yet not so close that he was touching her. His gaze met hers. "You okay?"

She nodded. "Josh won't hurt me."

His gaze moved to her brother. "I wouldn't be so sure of that."

"You would be if you knew anything at all about the two of us." Josh's gaze was every bit as cold and hard as Gabriel's. "And you'd certainly not consider firing the laser you have in your hand."

Even as he said the words, Gabriel revealed the weapon. It was a laser, all right, and a lot bigger than the one she held. "I'm not firing it, just using it to place you under arrest. You willingly admitted you murdered General Blaine and the shifter impersonating Kathryn Douglass, and you more than likely murdered the real one as well."

Josh raised an eyebrow. "You were floating about up there for longer than I thought."

"I guess I was. Raise your hands or I *will* shoot."

Josh flexed his fingers. And suddenly the stirring wind seemed to be a whole lot hotter. Fear raced through her.

"Josh, no!"

The words were barely out of her mouth when a bright blue beam of light lit the darkness. Her heart seemed to lodge somewhere in her throat, and her fear intensified until it seemed her entire body shook under the force of it. It wasn't just fear for Josh, but her own safety as well.

Why, why, why?

The question rolled through her mind as the normally swift and deadly blue beam arced across the night in seemingly slow motion. Josh watched it, eyes narrowed, moving only when it seemed too late. The laser sliced through his forearm, skimming through his jacket and shirt before burning a trail along his skin.

She knew, because she felt it. Pain ripped through her, and she staggered backward, gasping in shock and dropping her laser to the ground. Sweat broke out across her forehead, but she clamped down on the scream that bubbled up her throat, so that it came out more like a hiss. She grabbed her wounded arm with her free hand, supporting it carefully.

"What the hell?" Gabriel's voice was soft, but it hinted at pain. He, too, had felt the burn of the laser, but indirectly through her. "Sam, are you okay?"

"Yes." She stared at her brother as the final pieces began to fall into place.

"Two halves of a whole," he said softly.

She closed her eyes. Took a deep breath. The pain of the laser burn was fading, but not the deeper pain that came with realization. She might not remember everything, but she knew enough.

"That's why you saved me," she said. "You cannot exist without me."

"Sam, you want to explain what's happening?" Gabriel said.

She glanced at him. The laser was still held straight and steady. He might not know what had happened, but he was still intent on capturing Josh.

Not realizing—or maybe not caring—that Josh would never, ever, allow himself to become someone's prisoner again.

Not knowing that in trying to maim or kill Josh, he'd be doing the exact same thing to her.

"You felt what I felt," she told him.

"I know that. But why the hell were you feeling what he was feeling?"

She wrapped her fingers around his arm. If he tried to fire the laser, she'd feel the movement of his muscles. Would try to stop him.

"Josh and I are twins. Two parts of a whole."

He frowned, and glanced at her quickly. "Fraternal twins. So?"

"So, we are military creations, born in a lab from sources that were not human." She hesitated, and licked her lips. "Our life forces are connected and combined. If he dies, I die."

His shock was evident in the way his muscles tensed. "That's not—"

"Just as it's not possible for you to feel when she is hurt?" Josh commented. "We are linked, the three of us, more than any of us could want."

She glanced sharply at him. "You once said that you would

let Gabriel rot in hell except for the fact I would come and rescue him. But that was a lie, wasn't it? You knew, even then, that hurting him would hurt me."

He smiled. "It wasn't a lie. Just not the entire truth."

"Many things you say aren't the entire truth, Josh."

"Would someone care to fill me in on this conversation?" Gabriel's voice was filled with frustrated anger.

And that was dangerous, given the situation.

She squeezed his arm and wished he'd lower the weapon. "Josh is Joe. They are one and the same man."

"And who is Joe?" His voice was hard. Cold. Like he'd already guessed and just needed confirmation.

Josh glanced at her. "Tell him."

She closed her eyes and took a deep breath. "Sethanon."

Gabriel's muscles moved. She threw her weight against him, knocking him sideways. The deadly blue beam shot skyward, briefly illuminating the rooftop of a nearby warehouse before disappearing from sight.

She hit the ground with a grunt, but rolled swiftly to her feet. Josh was gone, cloaked by night and moving swiftly away.

You have chosen your path, and it is not mine. His words rolled through her mind, at once soft and sorrowful and yet somehow determined. *I have given you time, as you asked that night, but I shall wait no more. It begins, Sammy. Do not try to stop me.*

I have to, Josh. This time, I have to.

Then we shall truly discover who is the stronger power.

I guess we will.

He disappeared from her mind and her senses, just as her arm was grabbed and she was swung around roughly.

"Why the hell did you do that?"

"Because you would have killed him."

"And rid the world of a monster!" He spat the words, his fury so great it was almost smothering her, making it difficult to breathe.

"And in killing him, you would have killed me." She raised her eyes to his. "Or was that a price you are willing to pay?"

For a long time, he didn't answer. She began to think he wouldn't when he released her arm and pushed her away from him, almost violently.

"He shot Andrea. That was the face of the man who shot her."

Oh God. She closed her eyes and battled the sting of tears. No wonder he'd walked into this situation armed and ready to kill.

"I didn't know—"

"Would you have cared?" he asked, savagely. "You know Sethanon is responsible for hundreds of SIU deaths across the country, and yet you protected him here tonight."

"Because—"

"Because you believe a lie," he spat. He thrust a hand through his hair. Then he made what sounded like an anguished growl and walked away without a word.

She took a deep breath and released it slowly.

The war Jack had warned her about was about to begin.

And she was stuck in the middle between a brother she couldn't support and a man who would do whatever it took to avenge the death of the women he had once loved.

A death that had been caused by her brother.

It was laughable to think that she'd once believed that when she discovered who she really was all would become right in her world.

But nothing was right. It had all just gone straight to hell. And it had taken whatever hopes she might have had about a relationship with Gabriel with it.

With everything that had happened tonight, with all that she'd remembered and discovered, it was *that* that probably hurt the most.

She blew out a breath and turned around. To discover Gabriel waiting for her at the end of the alley.

Hope ran through her.

He didn't say anything as she approached him, his expression neutral and the green-flecked hazel depths of his eyes giving little away.

She stopped in front of him. Her heart was beating a mile a minute, dread and hope combining to make her stomach churn. But she somehow kept her voice calm as she said, "I cannot help my past. I cannot change what I am. And I certainly can't let you kill him." She hesitated, and added softly, "I don't want to die, Gabriel."

He studied her for a moment longer and said, "But will you help me stop him?"

"Yes." Because she didn't want this war anymore than he did. She wanted peace. All she'd *ever* wanted was peace.

And somewhere to call home.

"That's all I can ask for, then." He held out his hand.

She placed her fingers in his, felt the strength of them wrap around hers, and for the second time in her life, she suddenly felt as if she actually belonged somewhere.

It was such a powerful feeling that tears stung her eyes again.

She'd left the ruins of the Penumbra project believing there was something out there for her. Something, or someone, she needed to find.

Against all the odds, it seemed she'd found that someone. All she had to do now was hold onto him.

Printed in the United States
142546LV00002B/18/A